tHE King of WHATEVER

Kirsten Murphy grew up in Melbourne, the youngest of four children. Inspired by *Anne of Green Gables*, she studied Arts for a semester on Prince Edward Island, Canada, and travelled extensively before returning home to Melbourne and completing her Bachelor of Arts (Professional Writing). Kirsten's first novel, *Raincheck on Timbuktu*, was published by Penguin in 2002. Kirsten then returned to study a Diploma of Education while continuing to write. *The King of Whatever* is her second novel.

Praise for *Raincheck on Timbuktu*

'Wow! What a marvellous debut novel . . . it's definitely up there with other Australian classics such as *Looking for Alibrandi.*'   *Viewpoint*

'The dialogue is a brilliant reconstruction of the eclectic concerns of the average adolescent girl . . . It is clever, irreverent . . . and very funny.'   *Magpies*

Also by Kirsten Murphy

Raincheck on Timbuktu

Kirsten Murphy

the
King of
WHATEVER

Penguin Books

PENGUIN BOOKS

Published by the Penguin Group
Penguin Group (Australia)
250 Camberwell Road
Camberwell, Victoria 3124, Australia
(a division of Pearson Australia Group Pty Ltd)
Penguin Group (USA) Inc.
375 Hudson Street, New York, New York 10014, USA
Penguin Group (Canada)
10 Alcorn Avenue, Toronto, Ontario, Canada, M4V 3B2
(a division of Pearson Penguin Canada Inc.)
Penguin Books Ltd
80 Strand, London WC2R ORL, England
Penguin Ireland
25 St Stephen's Green, Dublin 2, Ireland
(a division of Penguin Books Ltd)
Penguin Books India Pvt Ltd
11, Community Centre, Panchsheel Park, New Delhi -110 017, India
Penguin Group (NZ)
Cnr Airborne and Rosedale Roads, Albany, Auckland, New Zealand
(a division of Pearson New Zealand Ltd)
Penguin Books (South Africa) (Pty) Ltd
24 Sturdee Avenue, Rosebank, Johannesburg 2196, South Africa
Penguin Books Ltd, Registered Offices: 80 Strand, London WC2R ORL, England

First published by Penguin Group (Australia), a division of Pearson Australia Group Pty Ltd, 2005

10 9 8 7 6 5 4 3 2 1

Text and cover design by Marina Messiha © Penguin Group (Australia)
Cover photograph by GK Hart/Vikki Hart/Getty Images
Typeset in Rotis Serif by Post Pre-Press Group, Brisbane, Queensland
Printed and bound in Australia by McPherson's Printing Group, Maryborough, Victoria

National Library of Australia
Cataloguing-in-Publication data:

Murphy, Kirsten, 1977– .
    The king of whatever.

    ISBN 0 14 300137 X.

    1. Brothers and sisters – Fiction. 2. Self-esteem in
    children – Fiction. I. Title.

A823.4

Australian Government

This project has been assisted by the Commonwealth Government through the Australia Council, its arts funding and advisory body.

www.penguin.com.au

Acknowledgements

I would like to thank Christine Alesich for her continued brilliant editing and perfecting the balance of humouring and reining in.

Thanks must also go to my family and friends for their constant support and tireless facing out of my books in bookstores nationwide.

Finally, thank you to anyone who bought the book and anyone who let me 'borrow' parts of their lives without threatening legal action.

For Mum,
in lieu of rent,
and for the real Ed.

What lies behind us and what lies before us
are tiny matters compared to what lies within us.

Ralph Waldo Emerson

'We're waiting, Joe.'

'Pardon?'

'Your work, please.'

'Sorry?'

'I need your work, so I can distribute it along with every-one else's.'

'What?'

'Well, no one can dispute your grasp of synonyms.' Miss Barker prised the foolscap page from his hands. 'Thank you, Joseph.'

Joe looked across at Lawrence.

'But Miss, you said that we were swapping our work with the person beside us.'

Miss Barker's face softened. 'I did say that, didn't I? And then I changed my mind.'

'It's just, what I've written, it's a bit – personal.'

'Mr King, that was the task – to write a personal piece.'

As if temporarily possessed by the spirit of Dannii Minogue, Joe felt compelled to have another go, despite the odds against success. 'Yeah, but I'd like to write mine again. It's . . . messy and I'm not happy with it.'

'Joe, is your work encrypted so that Lawrence Barry is the only other living soul with a chance of accessing it?'

'No.'

'That is a bonus then.' Miss Barker began handing out the students' work. 'I want you all to write a carefully considered response to the person whose work you receive.' She handed Joe a page. 'A carefully considered, neat response. No encrypting.'

'So you're really going to quit?' Lawrence asked as he and Joe walked to their lockers at recess.

'I'm really going to quit. Why? Don't you think I should?'

'No, I don't. You've worked there over three years. I just don't get why.'

'Because, Lawrence, supermarket light is unflattering.'

Lawrence placed his ear in the vicinity of Joe's bottom, this obviously being the opening through which he was now talking. 'Sorry, can you repeat that?'

'Because I hate the guts out of it. Because people are stupid and can't find lettuce. Because a lady once called me "shop boy", and last week a man asked me where the waldorfs were, and because people can't grasp a concept as simple as when the light's off, the register's closing.'

2

Lawrence looked confused. 'You're seventeen and it's a part-time job. They're supposed to be shit. That's the rules. Do you think standing outside the Kmart fitting rooms, giving people coloured tags is my brother's passion? Or do you think your brother loves smelling like he's rolled around in chicken fat when he gets home from a shift at KFC?'

'Laws, I've got forty years to do a job that I despise, like my dad does. So while I can get away with it, I choose to live a final year job free. I don't see the problem.'

'I do. Money for a start. What are you going to do, pair socks again for your mum?'

'Maybe. That's nothing to be sneezed at. Mum's raised her price. It's ten cents a pair now.'

'And?'

'Well, it used to be five.'

'So did we, Joe.' Lawrence sighed. 'Doesn't have anything to do with *her* does it?'

'No.'

'So it has *everything* to do with her then. Joe, it's been, what? Two months?'

'Something like that. I dunno.'

'Let it go.'

'It's called a mourning period, Lawrence.'

It had been 53 days. Joe had a knack for remembering the finer details of his more embarrassing moments. It had happened at a Coles employee function at a theatre restaurant. At the end of the evening, after an overdose of Fanta and a Spice Girls medley, Joe had seized the opportunity to declare his feelings for his register counterpart, Claudia Hughes. His plan had been nothing short of masterful; he'd only had to do fourteen congas before he'd sidled up behind her, placing his hands on her hips. It's now or never, he remembered thinking, as four witches and a warlock took to the stage to sing 'Wannabe'. Never, as he was to learn, was sometimes a very underrated option.

He pulled Claudia out of the conga line and kissed her nose. He hadn't consciously decided to go for her nose. Like many of the blunders in his life, it had just happened that way.

'What are you doing?' she asked.

He was no expert but he didn't suppose that that was a particularly good sign.

'I like you, Claud, and I think we should go out some time.'

'You and me? Like on a date?'

'Yeah, like on a date.'

Claudia paused for a moment and then began to giggle. 'Ooh, and then maybe we could get married. Let's get married. We could come back here for our reception.'

Horribly embarrassed, Joe looked down at the floor, but the sight of Claudia's casual, yet stylish, footwear only made him more enamoured. 'Forget it. It doesn't matter,' he mumbled. 'Really, just forget I said anything.'

She looked at him more closely. 'You're serious. Oh, shit. I think the witch put something in my drink. I'm so sorry. I really thought you were joking.'

He hadn't been joking, but he *was* Joe King, and it was obvious, as far as he was concerned, that that was where all of his troubles had begun. It could have been worse. He could have been called Wayne. So as far as that went, he was grateful. But this incident had done little to dispel Joe's long-held suspicion that he was basically crap at everything, declarations of love now included. In his more positive moments he'd thought that being crap at all things known to man was really quite a talent. If you broke it down, this meant that he was crapper at everything that anyone else. The crappest, and therefore the best at being crap.

'Oi. Dickheads. Heads up.'

Joe turned around just in time to see a football flying at his face. Brad Cooper quickly followed. 'I'd say nice catch,' he said. 'But it was really more of a demonstration of the foetal position.'

Lawrence laughed.

'Maybe I would have caught it if I'd had more warning,' Joe protested.

'Yeah, maybe if I'd told you back in 2003,' Brad said.

'So have you actually spoken to Claudia since . . .'

Joe subtly motioned in the direction of Brad. 'We can talk about that later, Laws.'

Brad looked incredulous. 'Is he still going on about that chick from work?'

'No, Brad, he's not,' Joe said.

Lawrence offered a furtive nod.

'Bloody hell, Joe. She gave you the red card. Actually,

that's not right, is it? You'd have to be on the field to get carded. It's more like she left you on the bench.' Brad gazed thoughtfully towards the heavens. 'You may have possibly carried the drinks. You need to move on. *Girls* get over this shit quicker than you.'

'Aren't you always telling Joe he *is* a girl though, Brad?' Lawrence said.

'Yeah.'

'Thanks, Laws.'

'No, I'm helping, Joe. If you were a girl, you'd be over it by now, ergo you mustn't be a girl.'

Joe was touched by Lawrence's loyalty. 'That's great. There I was going by the old-fashioned male genitalia.'

'Hey. Hey Brad. I'm talking to you,' a disgruntled voice called from the end of the corridor.

Brad turned around. 'Hi, Timmy. Heads up.'

Tim ducked and stepped aside, letting the ball fly straight past him. It clipped the side of the photocopier and dropped to the floor.

'That's exactly what Joe did when I threw it to him – except you're still standing.' Brad laughed. 'And be careful with the school equipment there, Tim,' he added. 'I was going to photocopy my bum in my free after lunch.' He looked at his watch. 'What took you so long, mate? Recess is nearly over. Where have you been?'

Tim held his pencil case up with a look of unmistakable scorn. '*Someone* planted the security tags from the library books in my pencil case *and* folder *and* legal studies text book – *and* ARSE!'

Brad laughed appreciatively. 'Any leads, mate? Any idea who?'

'You are not to touch my stuff – or me – ever again. Next time you need some paper, for one of your aeroplanes, forget it. It's bad enough that you wasted my new sharpie doing Jade Pryce's faux henna tattoo last week. A sharpie which I don't recall you replacing, despite promising to.'

'The henna tat must have worked its magic, Bradley,' Lawrence said. 'Jade just started going out with Harrison Lehmann, didn't she?'

'Must be the Lynx effect,' Joe laughed.

'You don't do stuff just so a girl will go out with you. Girls can make great, valuable friends,' Brad said. 'I nearly got that out without laughing. I'd done the work and Lehmann swooped in when my back was turned, the loser.'

'Depends on your definition, really,' Joe said.

'This time you've gone too far, Brad. I'm not allowed to borrow reserve books or audiovisual equipment for a week. My name is mud in that library,' Tim continued.

'It was just a joke.' Brad finished tying the laces of his sneakers. 'Cross country. Bye guys. See you, Josephine.'

'I'd better go, too,' Tim said. 'Legal studies. A burglar injures himself in his victim's home, sues them and wins. They have to pay him for the privilege of being robbed. Astounding.'

'Yeah.' Joe had to agree.

'Did I show you my crime scene photos? Murder. A son shot his own father dead. Killed him.'

'Kind of got that from the *shot dead* part,' Lawrence

said. 'Lunchtime. You bring your murder photos, I'll bring my Queensland pics. It'll be nice.'

Joe was sure that Tim's fascination with death and crime would serve him well when he joined the police force. At school, however, it was a little bit creepy.

Lawrence suppressed a laugh. 'I love it when they check in.'

Joe was still busy being slighted. 'Brad never changes your name to make it girly. And he never points out good-looking boys that you could date.'

'He says my name's already girly enough.'

'Fair point.'

Lawrence placed a hand on Joe's shoulder. 'Seriously, don't quit Coles. You'll only have to get another job next year when you go to uni.'

'Who says I'm going to uni?'

'Aren't you?'

'No. Maybe. I s'pose. I haven't really thought about it. And I'm sick of people like Miss Barker asking. How was her nerve this morning? Encrypting? Who even uses that word?'

'Rupert Giles.'

'Who?'

'Buffy's watcher.'

'Right. Apart from him?'

Joe's suspicion that his friend was not taking him entirely seriously was not helped by Lawrence's insistence on gnawing at the ten Burger Rings that he'd put on each of his fingers.

'You all right there?'

'They should make chicken Burger Rings,' Lawrence said.

Joe continued, undeterred. 'When Barker started this year, everyone wanted to crucify her for her surname, but I railed against it, remember that?'

'Not really.'

'Too obvious, I said. Like Mr Woods. Now I don't care. It's open slather. Woofy, Rover, Fido, Bitch – I don't care.'

Lawrence ate his pinkie ring. 'You already said that.'

'Actually, bitch might be a bit harsh.'

'You still haven't told me. What the hell did you write?'

Joe reached into his pocket and dug out a scrunched up piece of paper. 'That's most of it.'

Lawrence laughed. 'You're the most half-arsed person I know, yet you write a rough draft for everything.' He read Joe's passage. '*I want to float. To relish the weightlessness, like a soaring eagle. It begins with my feet and slowly rises up, engulfing me. My body, my instrument. Changing with the beat of music, the rhythm of life. Gliding. I want to feel electricity coursing through my veins. Yeah, electricity. I want to dance.*'

Lawrence snorted uncontrollably. 'Oh my God, Joe. And you definitely put your name on it?'

'Yeah. I needed the words.'

'Electricity?'

'It's from *Billy Elliot.*'

'A few questions but let's start with one: why did you pretend you wanted to be a dancer?'

'Do I really have to explain? It was my attempt at back-lash. The question was ridiculous. Who knows what they want to do with their life at our age?'

Lawrence pulled a piece of paper from his folder, ceremoniously clearing his throat. '*I would like to study geology, as I have always been fascinated by rocks. I hope to study in a place such as Canada, given its proximity to one of the most famous rock formations "the rockies". I also love playing the piano and classical guitar and would like to pursue both, whether it be professionally or for leisure.* Iain Watts knows.'

'He's got two things. That's just greedy. Besides, he's a cyborg so he doesn't count. Probably uses words like "encrypting" too. What did you write then, Larry Barry?'

'Just about wanting to do architecture.'

'That's it? You didn't write a joke or anything?'

'No. I think I also wrote a bit about wanting to travel.'

'You've gone all responsible and smart since you became School Captain. I don't like it.' Joe swiped a handful of Lawrence's Burger Rings.

'Hey, not too many. I'm going to try putting them on my toes at lunchtime.'

They got to their classroom and took their usual seats. People always sat in the same spot, unless a teacher did one of their biannual classroom shake-ups where they moved everyone to encourage socialising. It was just one of those weird unwritten school rules, like the canteen stocking strictly inedible food. Joe opened his folder. 'I can't believe my mum bought me foolscap paper again.

Seriously, why would you buy anything with the word fool in it? Fool's gold. Fool's paradise . . .'

'Fool's errand,' Lawrence added.

'What's that?'

'Um, it's like a wild goose chase, a waste of time.'

'Oh, so kind of like coming to PE.' Joe folded yet another piece of paper to fit more easily into his A4 folder. Being a child of cable re-runs, he cleared his throat, attempting a Mr T voice. 'I pity the fool who buys the foolscap paper. Pity the fool.'

'You know, Mr T, you might want to start thinking about some sort of plan, too.'

'What do you mean?'

Lawrence pulled out an official-looking pink form. 'Uni preferences. We got these in homeroom. You would've too, if you'd turned up. I saved you one. Brad reckons he's waiting till the next round to fill in his form. Or he's doing it online. He's got issues with the pink.'

'Brad has preferences?'

'Just the one. Outdoor education but only if he doesn't make the AFL draft.'

'There's a shock.'

'Isn't there anything you've ever wanted to do, Joe? Something you've been even a bit interested in? Like maybe when you were a kid?'

'No.'

'Nothing?'

'Well, you were there. Can you remember anything?'

'There were some definite phases: Shane Warne, James

Hird, Austen Powers, also known as your "oh, behave!" phase.'

'That was you, Laws. Lizzy Enright's mum called your mum when you asked her daughter if you made her horny, because we didn't know what it meant.'

Lawrence looked thoughtful. 'Might have been me, yeah. So wasn't there anything at all, Joe? Anything?'

'When I was twelve I wanted to be a Hun.'

'A Hun?'

'As in Atilla. But then I found out what a Hun was, so that was pretty much the end of that.'

'I can see how that could be a problem.'

'Yeah.'

'You know what he died of, don't you?'

'Who?'

'The Hun.'

Joe shook his head. 'Syphilis?'

'No. Why would you even say that?'

'It was always syphilis back then. Henry VIII – syphilis. Mary Queen of Scots – syphilis. The royal disease.'

'The royal disease was haemophilia. And Mary Queen of Scots was beheaded.'

'Oh. So what did the Hun die from?'

'A blood nose. They called the guy the scourge of God – and a blood nose killed him – on his wedding night no less.'

'Bummer. So if someone had've just punched his lights out, the whole reign of terror thing could have been avoided.'

'You're a thinker, Joe.'

Joe was intrigued. He loved Lawrence's filtered version of their history lessons. They saved him the trouble of listening in class. 'The levels of irony. I don't want to tell Ms Morrisette how to do her job – but that's a verse right there.'

'Speaking of Huns,' Lawrence said, as Mr Sturt entered the room, stopwatch and whistle in tow.

Joe smiled. 'Speaking of punching lights out . . .'

Mr Sturt had fallen out of favour with the boys ever since his infamous after-swimming change room speech, in which he'd brought to the boys' attention that they all had 'the same bits', so needn't worry about hiding them and causing delays in the changing process.

'I think I'm with Brad. I've got issues with the pink too.'

'Something tells me you'd have issues with all the colours of the rainbow.' Lawrence took the form from Joe, catching Mr Sturt's eye.

'Right, let's hit the oval, boys,' Mr Sturt said. 'Barry, King, you two can come in your own time. I wouldn't want you to cut short your after-pilates latte.'

Joe emptied the letterbox, careful not to disturb the nondescript black spider that had inhabited the left corner, free of charge, for the last four months. He was not cautious out of concern for the spider's welfare. He was just scared of it. Really scared. As a rule, Joe was suspicious of anything with more legs than him. He had inherited the phobia from his grandmother, along with her freakish knowledge of past TV game show co-hosts.

He had briefly given up his highly esteemed position as the King family letterbox checker when it had become clear that the furry squatter had set up house permanently. But this temporary abandonment of postal duty had thrown his family members into turmoil. On Joe's third consecutive non-letterbox-emptying afternoon, his dad had just stood and stared at the empty kitchen sideboard where the mail usually lived. Then he'd turned and pointed accusingly at the roster on the fridge. It was there, clear as day for all to see. The red crayon never lied.

> Anthony – clean fireplace & vacuum
> Belinda – dishwasher & bathroom
> Joe – bins, get mail & feed Benji.

There were a few fundamental problems with the roster as it stood, not least of which was that Benji the dog had been in that great kennel in the sky for some three years. In addition, Belinda had left the nest and country a year or so prior to Benji's departure, and Anthony had been categorically banned from operating the vacuum cleaner, after setting the old one on fire in his attempt to kill two chores with one appliance.

Vacuuming the fireplace hadn't in itself been a great problem, but sucking up hot embers hadn't ranked as one of Anthony's all-time smartest moves. Or so said his parents. There had been a lot of arm-folding, head-shaking and hip-holding that day. Joe had attempted to lighten the mood by placing part of the remaining vacuum cleaner on his head and doing his Wicked-Witch-of-the-West-I'm-melting-I'm-melting impression. But this had only resulted in his acquiring a half share of Anthony's punishment for what his father had labelled 'inappropriate skylarking'.

That was the day Joe had learned the value of keeping his mouth shut, and Anthony had learned why the comb-over guy on the Godfrey's vacuum cleaner ads always stuck to bowling balls for the suction test.

Joe sorted through the pile of letters, knowing that he had more chance of making the *Who Weekly* 'Beautiful People' edition than finding an envelope addressed to him. The only mail he ever received was the kind that said his life savings had reached a grand total of $9.89 and he would really be better off to stop wasting the bank's time and his own, and just close the embarrassing excuse for an account. Of course, they didn't actually say that last bit, but he'd watched enough television to know about subtext.

Today was first semester uni results day. He held the envelope addressed to Anthony and shut his eyes, imagining for just a minute how it would feel if this were his moment. His parents hurried through the front door with Anthony in tow.

'Well?'

He held out the envelope, which Anthony promptly snatched out of his hand.

'Joe. The letter opener,' Anthony said.

'You can use mine,' Joe offered, holding up his right pointer finger.

'Come on, Joseph. Help your brother. He's nervous,' Mrs King said, wringing her hands in a mixture of excitement and anxiety.

'I think it's in my den,' Mr King added.

Why could his father not call it a study like everyone else? Joe had looked up the meaning of den once and as far as he could see, the room that his father referred to as a den was not a wild beast's lair or a lurking place of thieves – or even a place where parental advice was dispensed, like Mike Brady's den. It was merely a crappy room with an antiquated computer and books written by retired sporting heroes and various titles in the *For Dummies* series.

He headed off to retrieve the letter opening apparatus. This letter opener business was vintage Anthony. It wasn't the opener that he needed, it was what it stood for. It was basically a chance to rub Joe's nose in it. His parents had given it to Anthony to congratulate him on his year-twelve results. Along with their undying love and promise to favour him over their youngest. Certainly, they hadn't actually said that in so many words, but again – subtext.

He rummaged through the desk drawer until finally he'd found it.

'Here it is, Anthony,' Joe called, pulling out the pewter opener.

But he was too late.

'Straight HDs,' Anthony yelled in what Joe could only assume was his brother's version of excitement.

Joe poked his head around the den door. There was hugging and crying and hair ruffling. You could keep your Olympic gold medals, Oscars and Nobel Peace Prizes. In the King household, there was no higher honour than a hair ruffle from Graeme King. Mr King patted his oldest son on the back and shook his head in awe. 'Well done, Anth. We were going to tell you at dinner but now is as good a time as any. Your mother and I are paying for your New Zealand trip. Airfare, accommodation, the lot.'

'Wow. Thanks, Dad.'

The nerve of his brother, to not even offer a token protest.

'You deserve it, Dr King.'

Dr King. Joe didn't know whether he could handle any more of his father's 'pass the salt – stat!' jokes. He could just imagine his brother on one of those medical TV dramas like his parent's favourite, *Medic Alert*. He'd be the new cocksure intern who blows into town and challenges the establishment with his unorthodox, yet effective methods. He'd get the feisty head nurse offside and step on the chief surgeon's toes, until he met his match in the form of a gutsy, sage-like senior Doctor character, played by special guest star Robin Williams, in his first return to serial TV since *Mork and Mindy*.

Mrs King opened the door Joe was lurking behind and blinded him with the flash of the camera. Great. His fears that his despair may not be captured on film for all to look back on in years to come had thankfully now been allayed.

'Got you. Come and have a drink, love. Your sister's on the phone and Aunty Gwen's here.'

Aunty Gwen was not, in fact, his real aunt, she was an old friend of his mum's. Joe wondered which sadist had thought of the idea of making up relatives. As if people didn't have enough real ones they wanted to put on the market. And where were the boundaries? You could make up a cousin or an aunt, but people had called his Uncle Barry crazy when he'd made up a wife. Joe's first impulse was to lock himself in his father's den, hoping that he'd been wrong about the wild beasts, and that one would appear any moment from the shadows and swallow him whole. But instead he went to join the festivities, heading out to the kitchen.

'Finish pouring the drinks, will you, love?' Mrs King asked.

As he poured, he heard his father ask his usual three questions of Belinda on the phone. 'How are you?/How's work?/Any news?' Then he nodded his head a lot and smiled, an irony which seemed lost on the rest of Joe's family members. Pretty soon it was time for the usual sign-off. 'Well, I'll get the mother. Take care now. Bye, love.'

Joe headed into the lounge room and handed Anthony a drink. 'So it's meant to be, then. You know exactly what you're doing with at least the next five years of your life. What's that like?'

'Hey?'

'Congratulations.'

'Thanks.'

His congratulations may have sounded about as genuine as a boy-band ballad, but at least he'd done the right thing.

Mr King gave Joe a hair ruffle. But it wasn't the kind of ruffle that counted. It was an obligatory ruffle, the kind that his father gave when he knew his demands were bordering on unreasonable.

'And what are you going to do with your life then?' Aunty Gwen had found him.

'Yeah, Joe. What are you going to do?' Anthony asked.

Joe looked around the room. It was only going to get worse. Humiliation had settled in for the evening, boots by the fire, cognac in hand. And, at that moment, he wished he was Tom Sawyer. Joe had read very few books in his life, which was perhaps the reason this one had stuck in his mind. It was only egocentricity and chicken-pox that had kept him turning the pages till the very end. Joe'd always liked to think that there was a bit of Tom in him – the lovable scamp that made good. But Joe's favourite line in the story came after another one of Tom's many wily schemes had been exposed. The reader knew that Tom was about to be in for a very public humiliation, but the author had kindly written: *Let us draw the curtain of charity over the rest of the scene.* Joe wished that someone would do the same for him.

3

Rituals. The Jewish teen-
ager had the bar mitzvah. Native Indians and Australian
Aborigines took part in initiation ceremonies involv-
ing hunting. In some Amish communities, the teenager
was given a year to live among western culture, so as to
make an informed lifestyle choice. In January, Joe's rite
of passage had also come. It had been time for him to
take his first steps as a man. Without warning, in his
eighteenth year, his parents had withdrawn the ride
to school and thrown him onto the mercy of public
transport. A ritual that was in turn to spawn its own
ritual, one common across all colours and creeds:
tardiness.

8:22 a.m. As Joe rounded the corner of the street he
could see his bus approaching. He was still some distance
away from his bus stop. He weighed up his options.

Number one involved running for the bus, even though experience had proven that he had less chance of catching it than a Jerry Springer guest had of being accepted at Mensa.

Number two was all about giving up and catching the next bus, which would get him to school about ten minutes late.

And number three, the most appealing of his choices, required killing approximately fifteen minutes till it was safe to go home and watch *Good Morning Australia* with a nice cup of Milo. Though, from memory, he'd done that last Friday.

He wouldn't have minded being late so much if it hadn't required subjecting himself to another one of Mr Woods' sarcastic tirades. A tirade which would almost definitely feature the words 'well, you're consistent King, I'll give you that', as well as a possible mock apology about school getting in the way of Joe's beauty sleep and/or social life, if Woods was on a roll.

Joe was running out of excuses, so he decided it was last resort time. He'd have to pick up the pace. He employed his usual motivational technique of pretending to run from ill-defined bad men with questionable accents like in a *Lethal Weapon* movie.

A minute or so into his sprint, he realised why top sporting heroes were not endorsing Clarke's wide-step school shoes as the ultimate in athletic footwear. But just as he was about to wave the white flag and head home for nine spoons of chocolate malt drink and the comic delights of Bert Newton, the traffic lights ahead turned red, causing the bus to come to a sudden halt.

Joe could see the next bus stop. He had a chance, if he just pushed beyond the comfort zone that Mr Sturt had spent so much time talking about over the years, and visualised the goal. As he pounded along the pavement, he saw that the light had turned green, but he noticed that there was an old woman with a shopping jeep and a lady with a pram at the stop. They had the potential to buy him valuable seconds. He ran, arriving just as the doors closed behind the jeep lady. He tapped on the door, madly signalling to the driver. He could see the driver was considering whether to pretend he had not seen a frantic, slightly uncoordinated schoolboy tapping on the window of his vehicle. Joe clasped his hands together in a begging gesture he'd perfected requesting his mother not put *A Current Affair* on the television.

Just as he was about to abort operation Ventura once and for all, the doors opened, the driver giving him a friendly 'come on then'. Joe grinned, panting like a Great Dane and thanked the man profusely. He fumbled around in his school bag to pay his fare and then set about finding a seat.

The problem with catching a bus after running like an absolute moron was, of course, that you had to then ride in the said bus for another twenty minutes, typecast by fellow passengers in the role of the running moron.

'This seat's taken,' a Chihuahua-like girl barked as Joe attempted to sit down.

And clearly she had been right. He had failed to notice her schoolbag sprawled out comfortably on the seat next to her.

'Sorry, this is saved. My friend's getting on at the next stop,' another girl said. Were you really allowed to save seats if you were older than eight or nine?

'Come sit here, love,' an old lady said. He knew that voice. He'd fallen into that trap before, but right now, he had no other option. So he sat next to June Rosenthall, retired nurse, mother of four, grandmother to three (one of whom was illegitimate), ready to hear some more about the ills of the Prime Minister and the invasive nature of a colonoscopy.

Next time he was going home to watch Bert.

Joe reached his classroom just as Tim had launched into reading another thrilling instalment of the daily bulletin. As Joe hesitated outside the door he had a sudden thought. Maybe everyone would be so enthralled by Tim's run-down of the events of the school day that they wouldn't even notice him sneaking in. It wasn't the thought of a brain surgeon, but Joe was hardly likely to think about cranial nerves or anaesthetic or gauze, or whatever it was that brain surgeons thought about.

'Late?'

Joe jumped in fright. He turned around to see Grace Kelly: Tim's twin sister and leader of the Hillview College Student Teacher Council, rather than the deceased

Hollywood starlet and royal. Joe had been a member of her organisation for about five minutes when he was in year seven, before his sense of coolness had fully developed. It was one of those things that you did when you were twelve, like joining the choir. Then in your twentieth rehearsal of Simon and Garfunkle's 'Bridge Over Troubled Water', you wised up, and later denied ever having had any connection at all.

Joe felt guilty every time he saw Grace and made a habit of avoiding her whenever possible. This was made more difficult by the fact that Grace was in most of his classes this year.

He noticed that Grace was holding her trademark clipboard and ice-cream container full of change. 'Oh. Ripper.' He reached into his pocket and pulled out a five-dollar note.

Grace smiled. 'You want to make a donation?'

'What? No, I need change for the vending machine. It'll save me going to the library. You know how they get about giving change, unless it's for their exorbitantly overpriced photocopying.'

Grace handed him some change. 'So no donation?'

'I tell you what, you break that last dollar for me again and you can keep twenty cents.'

She gave him his eighty cents and a facial expression that indicated she was not exactly impressed.

'All right. Make it forty.' He looked into the classroom. Mr Woods was sitting at his desk, legs crossed, scratching at his beard. Joe was sick of the sight of the man. He was somehow everywhere all the time, lurking. You forgot about him for five minutes, and then he'd reappear, right in your face, like Big Brother.

Grace subtly cleared her throat. 'Are you going in? Because I need to talk to your class.'

'You guys got another raising ... money ... thingy, have you?'

'A fundraiser? Yes. We've got a couple. We're meeting three times a week at the moment.'

'Jeeze, you'd want to be getting paid, wouldn't you?' He stepped back from the door. 'You can go in first, if you like.'

Brad appeared at that moment, soccer boots in hand. 'No, Joe, ladies first, off you go, love.' Brad headed in, Mr Woods giving him a friendly nod.

'What's his excuse?' Grace asked.

'Hypocrisy. Sport. Sturt keeps him late at training sometimes. Woods and Sturt are bum chums.'

'Maybe you need to take up some sport.'

'I actually play a bit of Ultimate Frisbee and I was team champion when I played nucomb.'

'Nucomb?'

'You know? Like volleyball, but you can catch the ball.' He regarded her blank expression. 'It was impressive when I was twelve.'

She smiled. 'He will see you, you know.'

'Who?'

'Mr Woods. I won't be able to block you, if that's what you're thinking, Joe.'

She'd read his mind. 'Thanks, but I think I'm a bit more mature than that.' He studied her slight frame. She could have probably blocked him if she'd had a bit more meat on her bones. 'So no invisibility cloak in that ice-cream container?'

'It's at home with my Nimbus 2000.' Grace opened the door. Joe noticed Tim giving her a smile. It seemed a sort of rule that the only females to ever smile at Tim were members of his immediate family.

'Sorry I'm late, sir.'

'Ah, the familiar mantra of Mr King. Hope we didn't disturb your beauty sleep.'

'Since you ask, sir, I didn't get my full ten hours.'

'Well, let's have it.'

'Pardon, sir?'

'What happened this time?'

'Maybe Grace would like to give us her message first?'

Grace put her ice-cream container down. 'No, I can wait.'

'Oh. Good. Thanks.'

Mr Woods shifted forward in his seat. 'I can't wait, Joseph. So?'

'Um . . . it wasn't entirely my fault. The public transport system is a debacle, sir. We're paying more and getting less.'

'Yes, you enlightened us all of this not four days ago, Mr King, in your gripping tale of a commute gone wrong.'

Joe noticed Mr Woods reaching for a detention slip. He also caught sight of a picture of Kevin Costner that had been pasted on one of those collages they did every week to waste time in personal development. 'Kevin Costner,' he said, in desperation.

'Yes?'

'OK. The thing is, I went to see the new Kevin Costner film last night . . . for educational purposes.'

'Really?'

'Yes. I'm a big fan of his work. Are you familiar yourself, Mr Woods? You look like a *Waterworld* man.'

'I saw *Field of Dreams*.'

'Great film, as was this one. What I didn't realise however, was that as well as starring in it, Kevin had directed it.'

Joe noticed a look of disbelief creep over Tim's and Grace's faces and amusement over Lawrence's. Brad, meanwhile, had decided to use the opportunity to change out of his soccer gear back into his school uniform, much to the delight of a few female admirers.

Mr Woods had started to clean his glasses. In Joe's limited experience with sight-impaired people, he'd found that they didn't generally attend to their optical wear when they were enthralled by a story. 'Your point being?'

'Costner's quite notorious for getting – a bit carried away. Don't get me wrong, the man's an auteur, but it has been noted by critics and moviegoers alike, that he has some trouble . . . cutting the cord. Let's just say there was many a superfluous scene.'

'Superfluous?'

'Would you believe, Mr Woods, that it was a 9:15 p.m. session, and it only finished just before the second bell this morning? Understandably, it left me very little time to get to school.'

'Would you believe, Mr King, that you're on detention tomorrow afternoon?'

'Yes, I surely would.'

In their English lesson that morning, Miss Barker handed out the responses to her students' personal pieces. Lawrence's was pretty straightforward. Lisa Gibbs had got his work and she'd written something about her uncle being a well-known architect and her top five cities to visit in the world. Joe had forgotten to write his response because he'd lost the piece he was supposed to respond to before he'd actually read it. But sure enough, he received a response to his work, which turned out to be anonymous and somewhat confusing.

'I don't need to ask you to write a new piece for me, do I, Joe?' Miss Barker said.

'Miss Barker, in fairness I did warn . . .'

'I want it ASAP.'

'ASAP? Someone thinks they're a doctor,' Joe said after Miss Barker left the classroom to do some photocopying.

'Isn't that STAT?'

'Whatever, Lawrence. Don't teachers get free lessons to do photocopying?' Joe asked.

'She's probably too busy flirting with Mr Sturt. I've heard rumours.'

'Don't go any further. I need the iota of respect I still have for Barker if I'm going to have a chance of learning anything.'

Lawrence leaned over Joe's shoulder. 'So what does yours say?'

'I don't know.'

'What?'

Joe read out a couple of lines. '*Take your passion and make it happen. It just comes alive, you can dance right through your life. What a feeling!* And it goes on.'

Lawrence began to laugh. 'You know what that's from?'

'Not really.'

'It's the song from that shit film your sister always used to watch – *Flashdance*. Who wrote it?'

'The film?'

'The response?'

'Oh. Doesn't say.'

'The master becomes the apprentice.'

'I wouldn't go that far, Larry Barry.'

'Pretty funny though.'

'What's funny?' Brad asked, poking his head around their classroom door. 'Where's your teacher?'

'She went to the office,' Lawrence said. 'Do you ever have class?'

Brad perched on a table. 'I've got a free. No one good's around. I put a few more of those book security tags in Tim's pencil case, but both seminar rooms were booked, so there's nothing else happening in the library. It's so . . .'

'Quiet?' Lawrence asked.

Brad had pioneered a scam in year eleven where he'd book a seminar room in the library during his free periods. The librarians had a practice of taping SBS and channel two each night in case students or teachers required information from any of their news programs. Brad would ask for the SBS tape under the guise of wanting to watch the world news. He'd then fast-forward to the movie and get his rocks off. It was among his more disturbing habits.

'So what were you girls laughing about?'

Joe closed his folder in protest. It hadn't yielded the level of bang he was hoping for. Perhaps it had something to do with the foolscap. 'Listen, Brad. I'm getting sick of this. I am clearly not a girl. Got it? NOT A GIRL.'

Brad smirked. 'Not a girl, but not yet a woman, hey, Joey?'

At lunchtime, the boys sat in their usual position on the quadrangle, soaking up the last of the sun they would get for the next few months.

'What?'

'If I was dying and the only thing that would save me was a kidney transplant, would you give me one?'

'A transplant?'

Joe was growing impatient at Lawrence's determination to make fun of his hypothetical. 'A kidney, Lawrence.'

'One of mine?'

'Yes.'

'Are we a match?'

'Yes.'

'Do you know what the odds of that are?' Tim said, unable to resist.

'In my hypothetical we match.'

'Well, yeah. Sure I would, Joe,' Lawrence said.

'You paused. You wouldn't.'

'Are we a match, Joe? Because I'd give you one?'

'Thanks, Tim.'

Tim had a sudden thought. 'Mind you, that might limit my chances of getting into the force.'

'Reneging on the kidney. Bloody lovely.'

'Sorry.'

'I'd give you one of mine,' Brad said.

'Well, thank you.'

'Can never resist a damsel in distress.'

'I wouldn't give *you* one,' Tim said to Brad, still angry at his most recent library stunt. 'Not at least until you were on the critical list.'

Lawrence blew on his pizza. 'Why do you want to know this, Joe?'

'I don't know. I suppose I like the idea of retiring of an evening, with the knowledge that my friends would give me a life-saving kidney – or wouldn't, as the case may be.'

'I said I would.'

'You paused.'

'For like a second. It *is* one of my major organs.'

'You've got another one,' Brad mocked.

'Fine then. You can have it, seriously.'

Joe laughed. 'I don't think I want it anymore.'

'Hey, I know a story about a transplant. This guy in Europe goes out one night and unbeknownst to him, someone drugs his drink . . .'

'Tim, if he wakes up in a bath full of ice, we've heard it,' Joe said.

'Never mind.'

There were still a few students getting about in stubbies or summer dresses, unable to surrender the fantasy of summer. One girl still had the baby oil out to tan her legs, but the heat was over until the end of the year and it was well and truly time to break out the pants and tunics.

'So we're all still in for the bet this year?' Lawrence said, pointing at his shorts.

'No way,' Tim said. 'I'm not getting a detention again.'

Joe was hoping that Lawrence had forgotten about their annual tradition of wearing shorts until they were forced not to by their teachers. 'I don't know, Laws. I might want to have kids one day. I don't want to freeze all my . . . you know . . . boys.'

'Kramer, the cold's good for them. It's the warm that's the problem,' Lawrence said, throwing the remains of his pocket pizza into the bin. 'I'm going to need a better reason than concern over future fertility, Joe.'

'I'm in,' Brad said, tossing a football.

Joe smiled. 'There's my reason.'

'Isn't that your sister, Tim?' Lawrence asked.

Brad temporarily abandoned his football. 'Hottie Grace? Where?'

'Relax, Bradley. It's not Grace,' Joe said, troubled by Brad's newfound interest in Tim's twin. 'And I'm pretty sure she dropped the hottie part a while back.'

Tim's younger sister approached the boys. 'Here.' She handed Tim the contents of her lunchbox. 'You may as well eat this. I'll just chuck it out.'

Joe couldn't fault the spread Mrs Kelly had put together.

Tim's sister walked away, surrounded by comforting, concerned girlfriends.

Tim sighed. 'She won't eat anything.'

Joe looked closer. 'Is she crying?'

'You noticed. She's been crying for three days. Her deb partner got glandular fever. She can't find anyone else. I offered, but she said that would be too sad.'

'She's got a point,' Brad said, taking a specky over Tim's head.

Tim watched his sister in the distance. 'Yeah.'

'So do you reckon you could get her to bring her lunch to us tomorrow as well?'

'Joe.' Lawrence laughed.

'I'm kidding. How long till the deb, Timmy?'

'About five weeks.'

'Has she got the dress?'

'She keeps putting it on.'

Joe took a bite of a lamington. 'I'll do it if she wants.'

'You?' Tim said, choking on his sister's juice box.

'If you'd trust me near your sister. I've done two debs

34

before. I don't mind telling you I'm a bit of a natural. I was told so by a Tony Bartuccio dancer.'

'A what? We couldn't ask you to do that. There are all these practices and not much time.'

'Exactly, Tim. It's not much time. It'll be over before I know it.'

'You don't have to.'

'I know. There's no problem, really.'

'There might be one problem.' Brad put his football down, adopting a serious tone. 'She wears the dress, Joe – not you. Do you think you can handle that for a night?'

'Hilarious, Brad.'

Tim handed Joe a gladwrapped mint slice. 'If you're absolutely sure.'

'I am. So it's settled. Fear not, your sister will come out, Tim.'

'Hey?'

'She'll make her deb.'

'Thanks, but we still have to convince her.'

'Leave it to me. And don't worry, she'll be in very good hands. Safe as houses.'

'I appreciate it.'

'What's her name again?'

4

When he got home that afternoon, Joe headed straight into the kitchen, quickly finding himself in an all too familiar position – in front of the open refrigerator. He stood, staring at the fridge's contents as if the white-good was the Oracle at Delphi that Lawrence had told him about, the thing that held all the secrets to life.

'It hasn't changed,' Mrs King said, shutting the fridge door.

'What?'

'All the food in the fridge. It's the same stuff that you so eloquently declared 'shithouse' not twenty-four hours ago.'

'Yeah, well, I'm hungry. S'nothing to eat around here.' Joe scowled, having a definite flashback to a similar moment when he was six years old.

'Have a muesli bar.'

'I hate muesli bars.'

'You used to love them.'

'Everyone loved them in 1992.'

'Have a banana,' Mrs King said in between squirts of *Mr Muscle*.

'They look like the bananas from home economics. I hate them when they're squishy. Mum, why are you cleaning? Isn't Mrs Stevens coming tomorrow?'

'Yes, she is. I don't want her seeing this mess.'

'Mum, she's the cleaner.'

This was true. She was the cleaner. But Mrs Stevens also happened to live only a street away from the Kings and because of this, Mrs King was paranoid about having her good name sullied in the neighbourhood. For Joe's mother, cleanliness was next to godliness, or so said the cross-stitch sampler which hung on the kitchen wall.

'Do you know where my suit is? Looks like I'm doing my deb – again.'

'Another one?'

'Yep.'

'Who with?'

'Tim's sister – Alice.'

'The fundraiser girl?'

'No. That's Grace.'

'Oh. Well, do you really have that sort of time? Have you read all your books for English now?'

'Yeah.' He'd read most of one, *The Great Gatsby*, for the very mature reason that it was the thinnest. He'd read the back of another of his texts, but got put off after the four words *The year was 1789* . . . The only thing worse than historical fiction in Joe's incredibly short book, was historical television and film. Anything that called for the donning of a beard or corset and copious drinking of tea was to be avoided.

'All of them?'

'No. But it's under control. As long as I know one pretty well, I'll be fine. I've already watched the video of another one of them, too.'

Mrs King did her famous furrowed-brow. 'You're supposed to *read* them, Joe.'

'I thought it might provide a helpful basis for comparison and . . . I don't know.' He wasn't even convincing himself. 'Have you read *The Great Gatsby*, Mum?'

'No, I don't think I have. But I did see the film years ago.'

'There's a film?'

'Not as far as you're concerned. Come on, it must have something going for it. It's considered a contemporary classic.'

'Mum, the main guy in it just keeps on . . .'

'Gatsby?'

'Yeah, that's him, I think. He calls everyone old sport. It's driving me mad.'

'Finish reading them. English is important.'

He'd gone through his whole school life hearing statements like that: English was vital, Maths multiplied your choices. But it had all been kind of abstract. He hadn't thought that the time would actually come where this stuff would pay off. He'd always felt a bit removed from the practicalities of life, like it would all just somehow work itself out. And a big part of him still hoped that it would.

'What do you think I should do when I leave school?'

Mrs King grabbed her son's cheeks. 'Whatever you want, darling.'

'Thanks, Mum, but seriously, did I ever used to talk about wanting to be anything when I was younger?'

'At one stage you wanted to be a Hun for some reason.'

'Nothing else?'

'A fireman, I think.'

'Really?' He did have a sort of fondness for fire. He began imagining himself sliding down a pole to attend an emergency. Did they still have poles?

'Actually, that might have been Anthony. So when's this deb?'

'Pretty soon. Alice's partner got glandular.'

'That's unfortunate. You're a sucker, Joe. That's why I love you.'

'Thanks.'

'Are you coming to look at dogs?'

'Dogs?'

'Yeah. We're going to the shelter to have a look when your father gets home. Your brother really wants one. It's time we had another dog, don't you think?'

'Would I have to feed it?'

'No, it'd be Anthony's dog. He'll look after it.'

'I'm not really interested. I think I'll stay home.'

'Go on, Joe, it will be fun.'

'Fun? There might be what – twenty dogs there? Of which we may or may not take one, leaving the remaining nineteen to certain death. As a sucker, I think it best that I stay here.'

'Come with us, please, Joe.'

'Sorry, Mum, but there's no way.'

'You can drive if you want.'

'Joe. Red. Joe, the light's red. Brake,' Graeme King yelled.

'It's fine, Dad. I know.' The one good thing about going anywhere with his dad was that Mr King had started letting Joe drive, keen for him to get practice whenever possible. Joe suspected that his father had been shamed into action by the Transport Accident Commission ads.

'Next time slow down a bit earlier, all right?'

'OK. So is 200 metres enough?'

They pulled into the animal shelter car park and Mr King instructed Joe where to leave the car. As they headed towards the building, Joe looked back and surveyed his parking, noticing that a courtesy buggy would not have been out of place. 'Dad, I could have parked a bit closer.'

'No, this is fine. We don't need to complicate matters at this stage. You're doing very well, Joe.'

'Thanks.' He felt a smile spread across his face. He lapped up his father's praise, partly because he saw how much it annoyed his brother and partly because it occurred with about the same frequency as a visit from Halley's comet.

'I'll move it closer, Dad. It'll be easier if we end up finding a dog,' Anthony said.

'Good one, Anth,' Graeme said, tossing him the keys.

Joe felt the smile fade from his face.

'A maximum $500 penalty if you get caught leaving your dog's mess,' Graeme said, not convinced of the merits of pet ownership. 'Walking the streets with steaming hot turds in your pocket.'

'Graeme!'

Joe raised his hands in protest. 'Don't look at me, I'm not walking it.'

They walked through the doors to reception where they were greeted by a vet nurse.

'We'd like a dog,' Mrs King announced.

'Lovely. So it's your first day of looking, then?' The vet nurse asked.

'Yeah, that's right.'

'OK, well, it's highly doubtful that you will find a dog today. What we generally tell people is it's a good idea to come in and have a look first off. Ideally, you should come with a few ideas about the sort of breed you're after, age, size – that sort of thing. Do you know what sort of breed?'

'Something small and white,' Graeme said.

'Yes, smaller would be better. Quiet would be good, too. Something that won't trample on my garden or eat the washing,' Mrs King said.

'All right. Lovely. That's a good starting point. As I say, you're most welcome to go out to the kennels and have a look around. And I'll give you a list of other shelters you might like to try. Finding the right dog can be a long process, but definitely worthwhile in the long run.'

Within minutes, the boys' parents had their eye on a Jack Russell cross. Anthony hadn't decided on anything, while Joe had decided on a Coke from the vending machine, the promise of caffeine and sugar making it not an entirely wasted trip. He sat down against the cyclone fence, certain that he was perched in some sort of dog waste. After surveying all of the dogs on offer, Anthony joined his brother. 'Give us a sip?'

'No. Can't be too careful. Remember the SARS?'

'Just give us it.'

Joe handed over the can. 'Where are Mum and Dad?'

'Dunno.'

'They're probably off adopting a cat.'

'They're asking someone about that dog in the first pen.'

'So, you do know then.'

'That was some pretty good driving, Joe.'

Joe was suspicious. 'Thanks?'

'Yeah, judging by the frequency with which Mum held the Jesus bar, I'd say you'll get your licence within your first three tries for sure.'

Short of a cutting comeback, Joe went for the standard. 'Whatever.'

'You should have some professional lessons to get the parallel park down though. Dad's crap at that.'

This was the problem, or one of the problems with Anthony. It was like having live TV for a brother. Joe was never quite sure of what was going to happen next. 'Yeah, I thought of that.'

'Course, ultimately, it's the toilets of the future that I feel sorry for.'

'What?'

'The toilets. The ones that will be riding around in the back of a truck, driven by you.'

'Anthony, I'm going to go with another "what?"'

'Why do you reckon Dad's letting you drive everywhere? It only took me six weeks to learn but I s'pose some of us are just born to drive. Comes naturally.'

'What the hell are you saying?'

'Uncle Barry told Dad you'd need your licence to work with him.'

'Dad said this?'

'Yeah, hasn't he said anything to you? Whoops. Obviously not,' Anthony said in response to Joe's blank face. 'I don't think it's meant to be a secret or anything. Barry told Dad he'd give you a plumbing apprenticeship.'

'When?'

'Next year, when else?'

'No, I mean when did he say this?'

'I dunno. How long did you really think you were going to be able to fart-arse about for, Joe? Someone has to think about your future.'

It sounded exactly like something their dad would say.

Anthony walked back across to the pens. 'What do you reckon about this dog?'

Joe didn't care about any dog. Suddenly, the Coke wasn't going down so well.

Oblivious, Anthony still wanted his brother's input. 'Well? He looks good, doesn't he?'

Joe looked over at the dog. It looked like a blue heeler, but bigger. He hadn't noticed it when he'd walked past its cage. While all the other dogs were doing their best to attract attention, this dog was sitting silently at the back of its cage. Joe walked over to it. It crept up to the fence and licked Joe's hand. Anthony looked at it more closely. 'Man, what happened to its tail? I don't know if I want a weird-arsed dog without a tail.'

Joe opened the dog's cage and crouched beside it. The dog pushed its weight into Joe's legs, snuggling like a cat. 'It has got a tail. You can't see it because it's scared.' He looked at the dog. It stared back at him with the saddest, most pathetic expression he'd ever seen. So this was where the phrase 'puppy dog eyes' came from. But Joe was determined to remain the objective, reasonable person he'd always been, not falling prey to this dog's charms. He looked into the dog's eyes a second time. It suddenly occurred to him that this poor dog had no idea what was going to happen to him and had no power over it. Joe knew exactly how he felt. They were soul mates. They had to take him home. 'This is the dog, Anthony. We have to buy him.'

'I don't know. That kelpie was pretty cool.'

'The kelpie's a puppy. It says this dog's three or four.

It'll be harder to find him a home. We could be his last chance.'

'Settle down, Joe.'

'But if you want the kelpie, get the kelpie.' Joe surveyed the property. 'Where do you think the gas chamber is then?'

'Whatever. We'll get him. I'll tell Mum and Dad.'

Twenty minutes later, the Kings were lined up at the pet adoption counter, with the newest member of the King family cowering at their feet. Mr and Mrs King weren't entirely convinced it was the right choice, but it was Anthony's dog after all, so they'd conceded.

'Oh, you found one, then?' the vet nurse said with a mixture of politeness and alarm. 'Lovely. He looks like he's got Heeler in him. They're a very active breed.'

'That won't be a worry. Anthony's a bit of a runner,' Mrs King smiled.

'He's quite a reserved dog, that one. He'll probably always be a bit that way,' the lady said.

'Yes, the man downstairs was telling us,' Mr King said. 'So will he have to be . . .' he looked around uneasily.

'Neutered?' Mrs King added.

'No, he already has been, actually. So he's ready to go home right away. '

The dog seemed a tad reluctant to get in the car. He retreated underneath the vehicle cowering for a good ten minutes, refusing to budge. Joe and Anthony crawled under their parents' old Pajero, working their way through a plethora of overpriced pet treats bought from the shelter in an effort to entice the dog out. Mr and Mrs King stood around, rather uneasily, attempting to assure passers-by that the dog was in very good hands, and was outgoing, not ingoing because of their abuse.

'Come on then, Joe. You do the driving,' Mr King said after they finally got the dog in the car.

'No, I'd rather not, Dad. I'm tired.'

Now that the dog was sorted, Joe found himself thinking about his conversation with Anthony. What troubled him most, apart from the delight that Anthony had taken in revealing it, was that his father seemed to have decided what Joe could – and therefore couldn't – do, before he'd even had a chance to think about it himself. But he'd probably had chances, lots of chances. He just hadn't used any of them. It seemed that if you didn't make plans for yourself, somebody else would make them for you. There wasn't much he could do right now, but he wasn't going to do anything that might enable his father's plan to unfold.

'You're all right,' Mr King said, impatiently. 'Come on.'

'No. I'm not sure I'm interested in learning any more.'

'What are you carrying on about?'

'There's far too much pollution in the world already. And I'm thinking of moving to Amsterdam, anyway. They ride bikes there.'

'What? In the last hour you've decided to move to Amsterdam?'

'No, I've always wanted to see Anne Frank's house.'

Mrs King was momentarily intrigued. 'Oh, was that Amsterdam? I always think it's Poland.'

'No, the Netherlands.'

'Enough of this rubbish,' Mr King ordered. 'Get driving. You need experience in all conditions.'

'Fatigue kills, Dad. OK, I didn't want to admit it, but I had a drink just before. Scotch. With rocks.'

'He had a Coke,' Anthony said.

Mr King reached into his pocket. 'Take the bloody keys and drive.'

They got into the car and headed off, Joe once again at the helm. Anthony nursed the dog awkwardly in his lap. Joe glared at his brother in the rearview mirror. 'Careful. You don't know where he's been.'

'Leave the poor dog alone, Joe.' Mrs King said.

'I was talking to the poor dog.'

Sometimes Joe just wanted to run away; to move to London like his sister had done. Somewhere where he knew no one and no one knew him. Somewhere there were no parents. It was a wonder that his father didn't burst with pride every time he looked at Anthony. Joe had concluded long ago that as the youngest son he was the leveller. He was basically there to keep his father grounded: the disappointment, or for want of a better phrase, average Joe, who provided balance. If nothing Joe did was ever going to be as good as Anthony, and there-fore enough to impress his father, could he also conclude that he didn't have to try? He liked that idea for both its simplicity and achievability.

'Keep going, Joe,' Mr King said, once they'd reached the main road. 'What are you slowing down for?'

'I'm trying to change lanes.'

'You don't slow down. You know that. You'd better hurry. You'll miss the turn-off.' Then, almost without taking a breath, Mr King continued. 'You know I think I'll build a new kennel. Benji loved his old one. It'd be easy to knock one up. I've got some old bits of wood lying about in the shed, just going to waste. Yeah, a dog needs a kennel.'

If Joe remembered correctly, Benji had treated his kennel like a holiday house, only using it occasionally and renting it out to the cats of the neighbourhood in the off-season. In a moment of anger one Sunday afternoon, Graeme had ended up putting the kennel out on the nature strip for the junk collection, as a protest against their dog's ingratitude. He had been sure that the kennel would be snapped up by some passer-by, but a few days had passed and no one had so much as touched it. The scumbags of the neighbourhood had taken the King's rusty bicycles, old vacuum cleaner and borer-filled furniture, but the kennel had stayed there, destined to be removed only by the council collection men. Joe had ended up getting Lawrence to help him load it into a wheelbarrow, and dump it a few blocks away, to spare his father's feelings. Mr King had been very excited to think that someone had finally appreciated his design and hard labour.

'I wouldn't worry about a kennel, Dad.' Joe put his right indicator on, briefly looking over his left shoulder, before moving into the right lane.

'Joe!' Mr King shouted. 'Stop, Joe! Watch out for the white . . .'

He didn't remember much after that, except the sound of an almighty crash and a blur of pointing and shouting. He'd swerved into a guy who had been right in his blind spot. He'd done his head check, but in his confusion, he'd checked over the wrong shoulder.

'Is everyone all right?' Joe heard himself ask.

'Way to calm the dog, Joe,' Anthony said.

They got out to survey the damage.

'It's not that bad, darling,' Mrs King said.

'It's not that good, either.' Anthony headed back to the car where the dog sat shivering on the back seat. 'Maybe you'll get your licence on your fourth go. Fifth tops.'

'I'll pay the excess, Dad. I'll pay whatever it costs,' Joe said, later that night.

He had a strategy. When he was a kid, he'd found a couple of dollars belonging to his mother and after he'd returned the money to her she'd told him to keep it – for his honesty. He'd set about proving his honesty for the remainder of his childhood and managed to make out like a bandit. If he offered to pay for the repairs, he reasoned, his dad was bound to let him off under the old honesty system.

'Good lad,' said Mr King approvingly. 'We'll organise a payment plan.'

'Oh.' Or maybe not.

'What is the excess, Graeme?' Mrs King asked.

'Eight hundred dollars for an unlicensed nominated driver if you're comprehensively insured.'

'That's not so bad.'

'Yeah, if you're comprehensively insured.'

'And we're not? Oh, Graeme. What does that mean?' Mrs King asked. 'What will it mean for Joe?'

'It means for the next ten years Coles New World owns my soul, Mum.'

Anthony appeared, stirring his cup of coffee.

'Cheer your little brother up, will you love?' Mrs King said.

'OK. Joe. How about a bit of *Crash Bandicoot*? Sorry, you'd probably be a bit sick of that, wouldn't you, mate? I'd better check on the dog's whiplash.'

Joe grabbed his denim jacket from the hallstand. 'I'm going to Lawrence's.'

'Not too late, Joe,' Mrs King called. 'It's a school night.'

Joe walked around the corner to Lawrence's place, keen to take advantage of his friend's temporarily parent-free house. And he really wanted to see a friendly face right about now. He walked up the crazy paving path and knocked on the back door. But there was no answer. After waiting a few minutes, he walked around to the front entrance that was ordinarily reserved for hawkers and church representatives. He knocked again, but there was still no response. Maybe Lawrence and Chris had gone out for some brotherly bonding. Joe tried the door and found it open. He walked down the hall and poked his head around the door of the Barrys' family room. 'Hello?'

'Joe!' Lawrence said, untangling himself from a girl.

Joe turned to leave. 'Sorry, Laws. The door was open. I didn't know . . .' Then he caught sight of the girl. She bore a striking resemblance to Claudia. Quite possibly because she was Claudia.

Lawrence leapt up from the couch. 'I'm so sorry, Joe. We wanted to tell you.'

Joe looked from Claudia to Lawrence in shock. 'Tell me what, exactly?' It seemed an unnecessary question but Joe's mind didn't seem to be working properly. 'Laws? Claudia?'

'We're together. Claudia and me.'

'Right.' Now Joe was getting mad. 'You wanted to tell me that? I'm sure that was at the forefront of your minds just now when I caught you KISSING ON THE COUCH!'

'I meant, we were going to.'

'I bet you that's exactly what Judas said to Jesus, right after Jesus caught him at Cash Converters spending all his silver.'

Lawrence looked confused. 'What?'

'Are you OK, Joe?' Claudia asked tentatively.

'Great. I had a slight stomach upset earlier on, but that seems to have cleared up a treat. How do you think I am? I think I should go now.'

'Don't, Joe. Please, just stay and we'll talk,' Claudia said placatingly.

He turned, shaking his head. He was tempted. Part of him wanted to hear their explanation. It really annoyed him when people stormed out during these moments in films. 'OK. Let's talk. Lawrence?'

Lawrence launched into his version of events. 'Just before Easter we were doing that loss prevention training at work and . . .'

'Wait a minute. This has been going on since April?'

'Just before, yeah,' Lawrence said awkwardly.

'How much just before?'

Lawrence put his hand up to his chin. 'A while.'

'How long? You're a shithouse liar, Lawrence. You're doing that thing with your chin.'

'It was more like March.'

'Right. So after I asked you out then?' Joe said to Claudia. 'That's nice. Carry on.' Joe was momentarily distracted by a DVD case sitting on the coffee table. 'What did you get?'

Lawrence was confused. 'Um . . . *About a Boy.*'

'Oh, right. Good film. Hugh at his best.' Joe had to remind himself of his anger. 'I wonder what Judas watched before he sold Jesus up the river – for the silver.'

'Well, nothing. The television wasn't invented, was it, Joe? Like Cash Converters wasn't invent –'

Joe raised his middle finger. 'Was this invented, Lawrence? I get so confused. And you're so smart.' He stuck up his middle and pointer fingers. 'Was this invented?'

Joe knew that he was being juvenile, but right now, he was beyond reasoning.

There was an uncomfortable pause, then Claudia broke the silence. 'I'm so sorry, Joe. Look, we didn't . . .'

Joe laughed. 'Ooh. I know this one. Plan for this to happen?'

'I was going to say finish the pizza. You're welcome to some if you want it.'

'What's on it? Actually, no. Forget it. I don't care. Because obviously, I'm just the . . . pineapple in this equation . . . and you two are . . . the pizza. There's just no place for me.'

Claudia looked fed up. 'Of course there's a place for you.'

'Yeah, this is all a bit weird, but we can work it out,' Lawrence added.

'Said Judas to Jesus.'

'Oh, come on, Joe. When did you become bible boy? We've been friends forever, let's just talk about this.'

'I've got nothing to say to you, Mr Iscariot. Ever since you became school captain, the power's gone to your head.'

'Great, Joe. My day's just not complete if you don't mention that.'

'Guys, please. Let's talk – properly,' Claudia said.

'Why would I want to talk?'

'Because we're friends.'

'Really? Well, I don't see myself benefiting too much from this friendship or whatever you want to call it, Lawrence. If I want backstabbing and embarrassment and . . . thoughtlessness, I've got my brother, thank you very bloody much.'

'Just give us a chance to explain properly and then you can go if you want,' Lawrence said.

'Us?' The sound of the plural pronoun made Joe's blood boil. 'Look I don't know how long you two have really been your own little . . . pizza, and I don't want to know. But you should know this – I don't want to see either of you ever again because . . .'

'That might be a bit of a problem,' Lawrence interrupted.

'Obviously that's not possible, I will see you, but I don't want to. And I want you to remember that every time you see me. I don't want to speak to you, because I know that if I do, you'll say something clever or nice, and I'll feel compelled to make the situation easier for you. And I don't want to. I don't think you deserve that.'

So Joe left, having received the distinct impression that he'd overstayed his welcome, like a television program with the parenthetic words 'the college years' in its title. Lawrence had always been his first port of call. On Christmas morning they'd compare presents, on birthdays they'd share breakfast, and every September, they'd gone on family holidays together. Lawrence was the kid Joe's Nanna described as 'the better-looking one' standing next to Joe in all the photos he possessed. They'd even chosen their school subjects together last year, or more accurately, Lawrence had chosen his subjects and Joe had copied them, but they'd still been in it together. Now obviously, things had changed.

5

The road to independent living wasn't without its hurdles. Joe knew that. But by week two, he'd come to the conclusion that the hurdles were too high and rather poorly spaced. It was time for some tough decisions to be made. It seemed that Lawrence had been granted custody of Brad, as Brad had decided Lawrence was slightly more masculine than Joe, thanks to the girlfriend stealing. Tim, however, had taken it upon himself to prove to Joe that in a crazy mixed-up world, he could depend on one thing – him.

'Astounded, Joe. I continue to be in a state of astonishment. One day you're riding high on the wave of friendship and the next – bam! It's like that show that's set in 24 hours. Look at all the stuff that happened there. What was that called?'

'24?'

'Yeah. Your life's changed forever. This exact thing also happened in New York. A man walks in on his wife and best friend and . . .'

'Someone was killed?' Joe offered.

'Cold-blooded murder, my friend. You must be right inside that murderer's head about now. I'm here for you, Joe. Rest assured, I would not pour water on L Barry if he were on fire.'

'Thanks, Tim.'

'Unless . . . maybe if it was an oil fire, in which case, water would be largely ineffectual.'

'Well, that would be fine then. I should have punched him, don't you reckon?'

'No. Violence is the language of the inarticulate.'

'Hey?'

'It would have hurt.'

'Maybe.'

'Besides, Joe, you punch him, he wins.'

'Not if he's got a bloody great fountain of blood pouring out his nose.'

Brad approached, carefully balancing a basketball in one hand and a pie in the other. 'Lawrence wanted me to give you a note.'

Tim relished the chance to act as Joe's Mercutio. 'And what say he, the prince of darkness?'

'Ha?'

Tim leaned closer towards Brad. 'What did Lawrence say? Where's the note?'

'Well, he'd run out of that scenty paper that Joe likes so much . . .'

'Brad. Come on.'

'I told him I wouldn't be delivering any note – because I have testicles. But he told me to tell you, Joe, that he didn't hold a grudge after you spilt orange juice in his PlayStation and stuffed it.'

Tim watched Joe, narrowly, awaiting his response.

'Tell Lawrence it was Coke and it was him.'

'Whatever.' Brad surveyed Joe's shorts. 'I thought you weren't in on the bet this year.'

'Things change, Brad. People change, friends change . . .'

'Sexes change. I get it, Joe,' Brad said, hoeing into his pie as he walked away.

'Where does he get all his money for the tuckshop?' Joe asked, noticing the more important details. 'Seriously. He's there every day.'

'Dunno, but he's always got gold coins though. That PlayStation thing – bullseye.' Tim smiled.

'Tim, it's not a competition.'

'I know. Sorry.'

'But we're winning.'

On day one of their split, Joe had embraced the idea of solitude, seeing it as a chance to unleash his previously untapped academic genius, spending some quality lunchtimes in the library. He'd seen those montages on the movies, where the combination of sheer determination and perseverance led the mediocre character to glory. But the montage wasn't moving so fast in real life, and there was a shocking absence of a kick-arse soundtrack and a shocking presence of Tim.

Tim was a good guy, but he was a good guy who could make a dripping tap sound by flicking his cheek, over and over again. He was a good guy with a story for every occasion and an uncle to match. He was somehow unaware that Joe didn't really want him to read out 'Dolly Doctor' or 'the prince of soap shortlist' at the top of his voice in the quiet study area of the library. And he'd obviously never heard the expression that a foolish man keeps talking, or that silence is golden.

Joe was starting to learn a thing or two about the beauty of the group dynamic. The more people you had, the less annoying the annoying people were. Maybe this was why Jesus had had so many apostles. To balance out the traitorous and annoying ones.

By their second week of lunchtimes in the library, Joe was pretty sure that the head librarian was unnerved by their continuous presence and Tim's penchant for teenage girl periodicals. 'Listen to this – some guy's walking his dog and he gets stopped and asked if he wants to be an actor. He says yes, now he's on a top-rating American show. He won a daytime Emmy. Astounding.'

'A what? Tim, do you hear yourself?'

Joe was unnerved by Tim's insistence on greeting every teacher who entered the library. 'You should say hello, too, Joe. It's not like Mr Dobson doesn't know who you are just because he's not teaching you this year.'

'That's right. Mr Dobson didn't know who I was when he *was* teaching me either.'

The initial plan was clearly not a keeper. But it wasn't bad for a first attempt. Joe may have been a novice in the planning arena, but he wasn't too much of a novice to recognise that it was time to move on to plan B, once he'd made one up. And then he saw it. Over by the library door. The ice-cream container, the clipboard, Grace Kelly. The embodiment of plan B. Hillview College Student Teacher Council. Three lunchtimes a week. He could kill the remaining two easily enough and he wasn't above resorting to hiding. 'Look alive, Tim. Let's go make a difference in the world.'

'Ultimate Frisbee?'

'No.'

Joe and Tim packed up their books and followed the yellow clipboard to the library seminar room where ten or so members of the group were gathered.

'Are you lost, Joe?' Grace asked.

'This is where the STC is meeting, right?'

'Yes. Hence my question.'

'I think you'll find I'm actually a member.'

Grace smiled. 'Really?'

'Yeah. Five years now.'

'Since you've been to a meeting?' Iain Watts asked.

Joe was not going to let a cyborg get the better of him. 'I've been on hiatus.'

'Hiatus?'

'Like Bob Geldof. When was the last time he recorded one of those charity songs?'

'Sir Bob Geldof actually does a lot of . . . never mind.'
Grace motioned to Tim who'd already found a seat up the
back. 'What about him?'

'Tim? Come on, he's your flesh and blood. Think of him
as a new recruit.'

'All right then.'

'So do I get a spotter's fee or something?'

She adjusted her cushion. 'Joe, we don't have a lot of
time to muck around here, so if you're serious about helping then great, but otherwise . . .'

'I'm all about the justice. I'm serious, Grace. We both
are, aren't we, Tim?'

'As a heart attack,' Tim couldn't wait to add. 'The
number one killer of men over the age of . . .' He suddenly
sensed Joe's preference for silence. 'We're serious.'

Joe opted for damage control. 'We love orphans
and . . . starving or sick kids. We want to help the under-
privileged. My dad did once. He worked with this guy
who had a gambling problem. He lost his job, house,
family, the lot. It was awful. Actually, I think my dad
might have been the one who had to dob him in but
still . . .'

Grace handed him a newsletter. 'OK. Fine. We're door-
knocking this weekend.'

'Brilliant,' Joe smiled. Now that he was becoming a
selfless philanthropist, motivated by nothing but concern
for others, he was going to be a much better person than
Lawrence Barry.

*

Anthony charged into the kitchen. 'Mum, have you seen what he's done?'

'What who's done? What's going on, love?'

'Joe stuck this on my car. In the middle of the windscreen.' He held out a fluorescent pink sticker that said, *I'm cheap, buy me now – $9.95.*

Joe stifled a laugh.

'I've been out there for half an hour with the eucalyptus spray.'

'I honestly didn't do it, but I would have been glad to help you remove it, Anth. Car maintenance is a very important part of my life. Especially girls' cars.' Brad had given him that one.

'Get stuffed.'

'If you cleaned up after your dog, I wouldn't have to take these drastic measures, Anthony.'

'I did clean up.'

'Newsflash. Dogs don't pooh once a fortnight. There are more turds out there than in our nation's capital.'

Mrs King pursed her lips in disapproval. 'Joe.'

'What? That's what Dad said. Is that a political reference?'

'Don't hurt your brain, Joe. You know what happened last time. You had to put it on the charger for a month.'

'Take it on the road, Anthony.'

'Joseph, stop referring to your brother's car as a girl's car.'

'Come on, Mum, it's a powder-blue beetle. It should be owned by a perky blonde girl named Tanya.'

'At least I've got a car.'

'Yes, and I get another sister.' The dog approached Joe for a pat. 'Are you ever going to name this poor animal?'

'He has a name. He's Ed,' Anthony said.

'Why?'

'Coz.'

You couldn't argue with coz. Anthony left the kitchen, armed with car wax and an interior spray.

'A girl and her car,' Joe said, while Anthony was still in earshot. Brad was really onto something with the whole emasculating quips idea. 'Has Anthony walked Ed yet, Mum?'

'He's a bit timid. I think he needs to get a bit more used to us. Maybe once he learns his name.'

'Couldn't have anything to do with Anthony being slack as the ace of spades.'

Mrs King smiled. 'It's black.'

'What's black?'

'Never mind. Are you going to be home for tea?'

'Yeah.'

'You're not tagging along to the beach with Anthony and Chris?'

Joe looked at his mother, puzzled. He wondered if she was aware of what she had just suggested? Him tagging along with Anthony was akin to Batman tagging along to dinner and a movie with The Joker, or Superman inviting Lex Luthor out for coffee and a chat. Or Robbie Williams hitting the recording studio for a duet with Liam Gallagher. It just wasn't going to happen.

He's my arch-enemy, Mum, my nemesis, Joe thought, frowning at her. I know he's your son and everything, but he's defected. I hate his guts. I wouldn't give him a kidney – or my blood. I wouldn't give him my last drop of water if we were lost in the desert. And if he was a wanted man – like for real, not just on one of those ye olde Sovereign Hill posters – I would dob him in, reward or no reward. Joe was getting quite worked up. And if he was on fire . . .

'Hey, Mum, if someone was on fire – an oil fire – would pouring water on them make it worse or just do nothing?'

'How do you mean on fire exactly? Who's on fire?'

'No one. Don't worry.'

'I've pressed some pants for you, too, so you don't have to keep wearing those shorts. It's getting a bit cold, don't you think?'

'Maybe. Thanks.'

'So you might go with your brother?'

'Yeah, I might do that,' he said. Just as he might one day join a doomsday cult.

He headed into the lounge room and discovered Chris Barry on the couch. Chris had the dubious honour of being Anthony's best friend as well as Lawrence's older brother.

'Yo yo yo, wassup, J-man?'

'Hi, Chris. Not much. You?'

'I's just hanging, keeping it real wit ma homies, gettin' jiggy, y'know what I'm sayin'?'

Joe laughed. 'Um. No. Actually, I don't.'

Chris was the living embodiment of the ills of a university arts degree: ample time for watching daytime chat shows resulting in a mastery of strange American accents.

'Word-up. Your bro and me was just conversatin' and we're jeepin', havin' ourselves a part-ay, celebratin' our little upcomin' trip to the Zealand of New. So what's the 411 – you comin' with?'

There was a long pause for a few moments as Chris looked at Joe inquiringly.

'Sorry, Chris. I thought you were going to finish that sentence. No, I think I'll stick around here.'

'Come on my man, what's wrong witchu? Don't be wiggin' or dissin' the Chrismeister. Peace out, brother.'

Joe shook his head. 'You're the whitest boy in the world. Isn't it a bit cold for the beach?'

'Your brother's crazy girlfriend has an assignment. She needs some samples or something. Besides, it's the beach, Joey. Fish 'n' chips. Coke. Get your coat.'

'OK, the car's looking slightly better. Let's go,' Anthony said, grabbing his bag.

'Joey's coming, Anth,' Chris said.

'Why?'

'Because I'm driving.'

'Yeah. Whatever,' Anthony said, in one of the most touching displays of brotherly love that Joe had ever witnessed.

'Actually Chris, I don't know if . . .'

'Larry's not coming, Joe. Let's go.'

That second, Joe's dad appeared, clutching tongs and a novelty 'Chief Chef' apron, obviously about to launch into his barbecuing ritual. A ritual that was to be avoided like street performers. With last week's barbecue still fresh in his mind, Joe chose to follow Chris and Anthony out to the car.

Their first stop was Coles, where they picked up Anthony's girlfriend, Isabelle, and her perpetually bronzed friend, Tiffany. Chris rolled his eyes when he saw Tiffany. He didn't have a whole lot of time for her since she had told several good-looking girls that he was gay, based on the conclusive evidence that Chris had never asked her out.

'Looks like Barbie's brought Skipper along,' he said.

Anthony smiled sourly. 'Yeah, well you brought disco Ken.'

Joe noticed Claudia and Lawrence sitting outside, obviously on a break from work.

Look at him, putting his deli hands all over her, Joe thought. He looked closer. Lawrence was snacking on a packet of black jelly beans. Tosser. Drawing everyone's attention to the fact that he was one of only five people in the world who liked the black ones, as if that somehow made him special.

Tiffany and Isabelle thought it would be amusing to yell out something about Claudia and Lawrence sitting in a tree. Joe did not. Claudia offered him a wave as they drove past, but Joe pretended to be absorbed in Tiffany's fascinating conversation about the ills of lycra underwear. The magical mystery tour was soon on its way.

'Hey, Joe, thanks for taking my shift on Sunday,' Isabelle said, struggling with her seatbelt.

'No worries. You know me. Need the cash.'

'Do you still have to pay your dad back?' Chris asked.

'Apparently so. Tight arse that he is.'

'Joe crashed his dad's car,' Isabelle explained to Tiffany in a tone that could just as easily have said Joe's favourite food was spaghetti bolognaise.

'No way.' Tiffany laughed. 'I did that a couple of times.'

'Joe probably will too,' Anthony said.

'Working tomorrow, Joe?' Isabelle asked.

'Yeah. You?'

'Yep. Oliver's supervising. I think he's still angry at you for your "Please, sir. I want some more" carry on last week. Did you hear he got a warning the other day?'

Joe loved it when authority figures were in trouble. 'What happened?'

'He fell asleep at the service desk, while reading an unpurchased magazine and eating an unpurchased kit-kat. The security camera caught him.'

'That's the tonic I need.'

'You didn't tell me Lawrence and Claudia were on together,' Isabelle said.

'Must have forgotten.' Joe was missing Tim about now. No one ran interference quite like him.

Joe and Chris sat on the beach, picking at the remaining chips like a couple of seagulls. Never one to waste a minute of potential carb-burning time, Tiffany had gone power-walking, while Anthony and Isabelle frolicked as if they were on a British pop song film clip.

'How many samples do you reckon she's collected, Chris?'

'Well, she's already got herself a fine specimen in your brother.'

'I would have thrown him back.'

'So Larry Barry and the Claudmeister,' Chris said, slipping it in like the fine strategist he was.

'Very smooth, Chris.'

'I try. So?'

'You saw them before. It looks like it, doesn't it? Lawrence must have said something to you? The bragger that he is. These are really good chips.'

'He did say something but he wasn't bragging,' Chris said, ignoring Joe's clever chip segue. 'He feels bad.'

Joe feigned concern. 'Oh no. Do you think I should call him or something?'

'Sarcasm noted. Totally understandable.'

'Damn right it's totally understandable. So shall ye sew and shall ye reap or ye – something. It's called karma, Chris.'

'Yeah. It had to hurt.'

'What?'

'Lawrence going out with the girl who you asked out.'

'Yeah. Nah, not really. It's fine.'

'My mistake, android boy. So it's so fine that you're never talking to them again?'

'That's the current plan.'

'You've never made a plan as long as I've known you.'

'It's my first one.'

'And an excellent one, too.'

'You're endorsing my decision to ditch your brother?'

'I would if I was you. The plan works. The beauty of the plan is you're not at fault. They're the wrong-doers. You get rid of them: shake off the dead wood. It simplifies everything.'

Joe laughed.

'What?'

'I'm sorry. I find it very difficult to take friendship advice from someone who voluntarily spends time with Anthony.'

'Fair enough. The only suggestion I would make to your plan is changing the part where you don't talk to your best friend in the world ever again.'

'Interesting.'

'So, just to clarify, that would mean that you do talk to him again.'

'I got that. But I'm all about the integrity of the plan and I think that may compromise it.'

'See, I think it adds to the plan's integrity. It makes a magnificent addition to the plan.'

'I'm not changing the plan.'

'OK. But maybe you and Laws will talk and . . .'

'Can we talk about something else now?'

'Fine. Such as?'

'I don't know. Current affairs. Literature. Cricket.'

'OK. Did you catch any of the cricket yesterday?'

'No. Australia weren't playing, so I wasn't really that interested,' Joe said.

'Yeah, me neither.'

*

It was quite late by the time Joe and Anthony got home. Anthony headed to his room to do some reading, while Joe decided on some channel surfing, before settling on a *Seinfeld* repeat. Mr King joined him. 'So I think that last panel-beater's quote's the best we'll do.'

'Right.'

'I'll give them the go-ahead tomorrow. If you're happy with it.'

'Yeah, that sounds good.'

'Anything's better than that first guy, hey?'

'That did seem a lot.'

'There's a job for you, Joe, panel beaters. Make a truck-load of cash.'

'Yeah.'

'So I'll book it in tomorrow.'

'Great.' Joe loved the way that his father insisted on saying the same thing fifteen times when he didn't even want to hear it once.

'What's this show?'

'It's *Seinfeld*. I'll put the news on.'

'You don't have to.'

Joe switched the channel. 'There you go,' he said, handing the remote control to his dad. 'Night.'

As he draped his jacket over a chair in his room, a piece of paper fell out of the pocket. He unfolded it and read the message:

Change the plan, Joey. It's wiggeda wiggeda wiggeda wacked!

6

Five small words officially began what was to be at least the next decade of Joe's life: 'Price check on register eight.' He was rapt to have graduated from produce to registers. It truly had been an illustrious career so far. He'd started off as a humble trolley boy at the age of fourteen and nine months, enjoying the autonomy that went with venturing out of the store and traversing the car park to herd the trolleys. But winter and the unthinkable damage that he was clearly doing to his back were two of the downsides of the job. When the produce position had come up, Joe had made an almost seamless transition into the world of fruit and veg. And now here he was, being trusted to talk to the customers and handle their money. Working on resisters was like a formal acknowledgment that you weren't incompetent.

Lawrence didn't possess great retail aspirations. He

had never moved from his initial position in the deli. He wasn't a particularly good retail person. He basically saw it as an interim measure, until he got his real job – the job that he would make an effort in. Joe didn't like to be petty, but he had heard that Lawrence always went over the amount requested when he measured out food for the customers in the deli. And he'd had to be reminded to wear his hairnet on more than one occasion.

It was common knowledge that the register people thought they were better than the deli and produce people, and those unsung heroes, the shelf-stackers. The register staff were seen as the beautiful people of the teen set who accordingly never dirtied their hands with real work. But Joe knew that it wasn't actually an issue of who did the dirtier or the harder work. The rivalry all came back to one thing: there were more girls on the registers. So if you worked on the registers, you worked with the girls.

'I saw you met Mrs Baxter before,' Isabelle said from the next register, during a lull.

'Everything's too heavy for that woman. What's she complaining about? She's got her jeep. And she's pretty solid looking. She carries on like she's Monty Burns.'

Isabelle laughed. 'You got off lightly. I once put her ice-cream cones in a bag with a packet of toothpaste. She insisted on calling the manager.'

'Quite rightly.'

'Haven't you got school today?' Isabelle said suddenly.

'I dropped out.'

'What?'

'Curriculum day.'

'This being the intended purpose of such days. Don't you have any work to do?'

Joe shoved a damaged packet of flour under his register. 'I try not to think about it. You've only got as much as you know about.'

'Do you want my shift next Friday then?'

'Want is a strong word, but I'll take it.'

'Cool. I've got a protest to go to.'

'Yeah, that is cool. I dabble a bit in justice myself. I'm on the committee at school.'

'Good on you, Joe. Maybe you can pass a bit of that on to your brother.'

Joe laughed. The idea that he could ever pass anything on to his brother had certainly never occurred to him or anyone else.

Joe had known Isabelle about two weeks before she'd said the seven words that every seventeen-year-old boy wants to hear from a nice attractive blonde girl: 'Can you introduce me to your brother?' To which Joe had posed the understandable question: 'Why?' But doubts aside, the introductions had been made, and for the last year it had been smooth sailing. Anthony owed Joe big-time for dropping Isabelle in his lap. And Joe had a sneaking suspicion that this was precisely the reason that he tolerated Joe's presence on select excursions with his friends.

'Hi, Joe,' Lawrence said, putting a Mars bar and a Kit-Kat on the conveyor belt.

Joe offered him the best glare he could muster.

'Aren't you going to say anything?'

'Hello. But please know that I greet you only out of respect for the Coles ideology. That's $3.00 exactly. And you hate Mars bars.'

'Well . . .' Lawrence did, but Claudia didn't.

'Oh.' His and hers chocolate bars. 'I'm surprised you didn't send Brad in to get your groceries.'

'And I'm surprised you haven't got Tim sitting on a little stool beside you, bagging the groceries.'

'Hey, Tim's loyal – to a fault.'

'Yeah, he's got plenty of those.'

'Haven't we all?'

'Joe, mate, please. Claudia feels pretty bad. We both do.'

Joe turned away and sprayed his conveyor belt, focusing all his attention on register maintenance. He'd always been particularly jealous of Lawrence's ability to use the word 'mate'. Whenever he tried it himself, he'd always come off sounding awkward, as if he were John Howard.

'So that's it? Don't Coles employees farewell their customers any more?'

'Have a good day. I'm sorry that Claudia is so beside herself, but if you or she ever want another greeting or farewell out of me, you'll have to come back here.'

'I wouldn't exactly say beside herself . . . Joe, what do you want me to do? Stop going out with her?'

'Yes.'

'Oh. Well, no. It's not my fault we like each other. The

going behind your back – wrong. But I think it's crap to say Claudia and I should not do what we want because of you.'

'Fine then.'

'It's fine? Really?'

'Said so, didn't I?'

'Good. Thanks. That's a relief.'

'Right,' Joe said with about as much expression as a plank of wood – or Mr Woods.

'Is it fine?' Lawrence asked. 'Or are you just saying that because that's what you say when someone apologises? Like in the movies, when someone is shown a photo of a dead woman, they always say, "she was beautiful". Have you ever seen a movie where someone says, "she wasn't particularly attractive, but I'm sure she was a nice person"? Is that what this is like?'

'No.'

'Well, OK then.'

'Do you know what the other reason for saying it's fine, might be?' Joe asked after a moment.

Lawrence looked hopeful. 'Because it really is fine?'

Joe shook his head. 'To get the person out of your house, or wherever, as quickly as possible. Like, you know in the movies, when a character suddenly realises that their work colleague or old friend is actually evil and out to get them? They'll say anything to get away. They'll arrange to meet them for a dinner they don't intend going to, or they'll remember an appointment they have to go to – that sort of thing? And only the clever ones say it casually enough to avoid suspicion from the evil-doer . . .'

'You think I'm evil?'

'If the horns fit. Just go, Lawrence, I really don't care.'

'But you do, don't you? And that's the problem. This is just like when I got school captain. You said you didn't care, you said you were happy for me, and I felt bad for beating you. I felt so bad I don't know that I even enjoyed winning, but do you know what I've realised? It's not my fault, Joe. I'm a good leader and you would have been a crap one. And you know it.'

'Is that right?'

'Yeah, it is. Who had to collect the notices for you from the office every morning every time you were class captain?'

'You offered. You should have told me if it was such a burden.'

'It wasn't a burden. But after a while, you just expected it, Joe. It didn't ever occur to you that it was your job.'

'You got to school earlier than I did.'

'Whatever. Look, I changed shifts to give you some space, but I'm not doing you any favours any more. I'll see you.'

'I hope not,' Joe called after him. It was pathetic, but he couldn't think of anything else. And he couldn't opt for dignified silence, in case Lawrence didn't recognise the dignified part and just thought that he was at a loss for a cutting comeback. 'Maintain the rage, Joseph,' he whispered to himself.

'Joe, a word please,' Oliver, one of the store supervisors, said. 'Just pop your light off for a moment.'

Joe switched his register light off. 'I can explain. That guy was my best friend – except we're fighting. I wouldn't normally be . . .'

'We had a secret customer come through a week back and she had some pretty unfavourable things to say about a few employees.'

'And I'd be one of those?' Oliver was one of those, too, if Joe remembered correctly.

'Yeah. Starting with not wearing your badge.'

A logical thought occurred to Joe and as this so seldom happened, he decided to risk appearing insolent. 'Then how do you know it was me?'

'She describes a self-confident, skinny, dark curly-haired boy with large blue eyes.'

'I'm slight, not skinny. And my eyes have a green hue to them. And I'm grossly under-confident, truth be told.'

'Joe, do you recall a recent incident at the cigarette kiosk in which Natalie refused service to an under-aged customer and you came to her defence?'

'Not really.'

'You were working the express lane and in between customers noticed Natalie was being verbally abused by a minor. And you stepped in. Familiar?'

'I may have said something.'

Oliver looked down at his clipboard. 'Something to the effect of, and I quote, "Enjoy your cancer, shithead"?'

Joe gave an apologetic shrug. 'I don't recall exactly.'

'Well, our secret customer does. She heard it all. I'm going to have to give you a warning. I'm all for employee loyalty and initiative, but the public see and hear all. In future, be a bit more careful, Joe.'

Oliver walked off, the keys hanging from his belt jangling at his side. Keys were a necessary part of the job, but the way that some supervisors wore them, like a badge of honour, infuriated Joe sometimes. It also didn't help that he'd seen Oliver with his head in a toilet at the Christmas party and now reportedly asleep on the surveillance video. 'This is not my life,' he chanted to himself, as he turned his register light back on.

'Hi, how are you?' he asked his next customer.

'Just put my groceries through, please.'

Isabelle and Joe exchanged looks of amusement. Joe scanned her items and the woman quickly gathered her bags and headed for the door. 'You're welcome,' Joe called after her. 'Have a fantastic day, won't you?'

He knew from experience that nothing he did was going to please this woman. Disgruntled in supermarket shopping equalled disgruntled in life. You could learn all about an individual by observing their shopping habits. Anthony was the kind of shopper who would end up doing the shopping on an empty stomach and go home with three packets of Doritos and six litres of coke. Tim was an interesting case. On the one hand, he was a list man, who would painstakingly write out his shopping list in order of aisle sequence, faithfully ticking it off as he went. But he was also a sucker for a fad. New soft drink flavours, new chocolate bars, anything with a shiny wrapper – he'd give it a go.

Brad was a simpler proposition. Shopping was chick stuff. Accordingly, it was likely that he would never venture into a supermarket in his lifetime. And then there was Lawrence: the confident shopper. He would walk the supermarket aisles chewing on unpurchased chocolate bars while flicking through trashy magazines which he had no intention of buying. He was the kind of shopper who checkout operators cancelled price checks for, believing whatever price he quoted was right.

He'd sneak extra items through express lanes and when he drove a trolley, people would part the aisles as if he were Moses. Even the wonkiest, wildest of trolleys would be perfectly tame under his control, as if he was some kind of trolley whisperer. Like everything else, it seemed that even when it came to trolleys, Lawrence just had a knack. And lately, Joe both admired and hated him for it.

It was Saturday morning, and Joe was feeling a great sense of anticlimax. So far, it hadn't been at all like he'd pictured it. 'Do I get a t-shirt?'

'What?' Grace said, midway through her explanation of the route to a couple of collectors.

'To identify us as official collectors. To make us look legit.'

'That would cost money.'

'Not if you got a sponsorship deal. There are always . . .'

'There's no t-shirt, Joe.'

'A cap?'

'No cap. Here, write out your name-tag. Tim, you can go with Iain, and Joe, you're with me. Here's the map. We do this side. You two do the other. Iain knows.'

'OK, you and me, Iain, my man,' Tim said.

Joe felt sorry for Iain already, and not just because his name was Iain.

Grace handed a bundle over to Tim. 'Here's your receipt book, pen and tin.'

'Cool. Let's raise some cash for the kids.'

Grace and Iain exchanged a worried look. 'Maybe you'd better hold on to the stuff, Iain. Tim, just remember what we talked about at the last meeting, you know, being courteous and professional,' she said in her twelve-minutes-older-twin voice.

Joe piped up again. 'Grace, Tim and I will be as professional as we can be – without t-shirts.'

'We've done pretty well,' Grace said, as she and Joe sat in the park at the end of the street, waiting for Iain and Tim to finish their last few houses.

'Apart from the woman trying to hose us and the man trying to abduct us.'

Grace laughed. 'He wasn't trying to abduct us. He was just friendly.'

'As all great abductors are. You're lucky I was there to protect you.'

She surveyed Joe's skinny frame.

'Hey, I'm wiry,' Joe protested. 'These hands – weapons of mass destruction.'

She didn't seem entirely convinced.

'Well, I'm better than Iain.'

She had to give him that one.

'That woman over there,' Joe said, pointing to a woman walking a Dalmatian.

Grace craned her neck, taking a good look at her subject. 'Accountant, but likes to maintain a bit of balance. She did a weekend mosaics course last month with her eccentric arty best friend who lives in Brunswick. Made a birdbath. Goes to the tennis every year – likes the night matches . . .' A man joined the Dalmatian lady.

'Who's that?' Joe asked. He'd never met anyone as good at this game as Grace.

'The new man. Works a floor down from her. She's not sure about the office romance, but he's nice, stable. '

'How do we know it's a date?'

'New running gear, make-up. Accessories. You don't normally whack on the lippy to walk the dog.' The couple passed Joe and Grace.

'So are you really named after Grace Kelly, like those thirteen old ladies asked?'

'Tragically, yes.'

'I'm no one to judge in the name stakes. Do you reckon your mum secretly hunted around until she found a guy with the surname Kelly, and that's why she married your dad?'

'No.'

'Right. Imagine if she'd called Tim, Ned. Or Alice, Kelly. Then she'd be Kelly Kelly.'

Grace took a bite of her apple. 'Imagine. It's very nice of you to be her partner – for the deb.'

'It's nothing.'

'It is to my sister – and Mum. Ally didn't eat for three days when she found out about her partner's glandular. In her head Mum had us selling the house to pay for Al's treatment in an eating disorder clinic in Canada . . . She saw it on *A Current Affair*,' Grace added, in response to Joe's obvious confusion.

'Well, it'd be worth it if you got to meet Ray.'

Grace smiled. 'I could have paired you with Lawrence today if you wanted.'

'He's here?'

'School captain. He kind of has to help out.'

'I didn't see him at any of the meetings.'

'You only came to two, Joe. He's been busy helping with the creative arts festival and debating. He's a nice guy, isn't he?'

'Oh, don't bother. He's got my girlfrie . . . a girlfriend.'

'I'm happy for him. That's not what I meant. Aren't you two good friends?'

'We were.'

'But?'

'What about that guy?' Joe said, as a tall man ran past.

'Too easy. So?'

'I suppose you could say we're like . . . *Savage Garden*.'

'Gay?'

'No. Broken up. Artistic differences.'

'I didn't know boys broke up.'

Joe needed to change the subject before she called his sexual preference into question again. 'So, going out tonight?'

'Yeah. You?'

'Sorting through some options, maybe you can help me. Should I stay in and alphabetise my CDs, remove a couple of stubborn stains from my carpet and attend to some homework or should I go out?'

'Go out.'

'With Tim.'

'Can I change my answer?'

'Where are you going?'

'Out to the movies.'

'Is this a solo outing?'

'You're pretty nosy, aren't you, Joe?'

'It's just a question.'

'I'm going with a boy.'

'Do I know this boy?'

'Harrison Lehmann.'

'What now?'

Grace was lost. 'Pardon?'

'I said "What now?". It's American. All the cool kids are using it.'

'It's not working for you, Joe.'

'Fine, but you should know you're going with a tool.'

'Oh really?'

'Sorry, but isn't he going out with Jade Pryce?'

'No. They went out a couple of weeks ago I think.'

'Sensible boy, allowing a mourning period. I can think of one boy who will be very upset about this development.'

'Who?'

'Bradley.'

'As in Brad?'

'He has a soft spot for hottie Grace.'

'He does not. Although he does give me some very weird looks.'

'His attempt at charm.'

'Disturbing. Do you know Harrison well?'

'Not well. We've been in a few classes together. I think he once told me my fly was undone.'

'He did?'

'Yeah, which probably means he's a really nice guy. He did me a favour. It would have been embarrassing to have gone around all day and had two – maybe three – people notice, as opposed to the twenty or thirty he yelled it out in front of.'

Grace picked up her collecting tin. 'Well, I don't really know him that well. He just asked me out and I've got this new policy where I'm embracing different opportunities so . . .'

'No, that's . . . good. Sorry. I didn't mean to bag your date – or whatever it is. You'll have fun. It'll be . . . fun. So, are you wishing that guy had kidnapped you right about now?'

'Kidnapped?' Tim's voice said excitedly. 'You know who was almost kidnapped? Victoria Beckham, aka Posh Spice. The plot foiled by Scotland Yard. It was astounding.'

'You two took your time,' Grace said.

Iain gave her a furious look. 'He's got to stop talking so much.'

'I'm bringing in the moolah, aren't I? Clocking up the pesos, socking away the yen? And I got us a ginger snap from that old lady. They were some great snaps.'

By the time they'd reached the last few houses that afternoon, Joe had had enough. They were in one of the wealthiest parts of their suburb and the people were far from forthcoming with the donations. Joe could see that Grace was becoming very discouraged. She wouldn't say anything, but he could tell. They walked up a driveway, past a pair of his and hers BMWs and a perfectly-manicured-by-someone-else garden and rang the bell. A ten-year-old boy answered, not even looking up from his Gameboy. 'Yeah?'

Joe had taken over doing the spiel because Grace's tone was about as inspiring as Robert's from *Everybody Loves Raymond*. 'Here you go,' the kid said, handing over about two dollars worth of twenty-cent pieces.

'Thanks,' Grace said, handing him a receipt.

Joe crouched down and pressed pause on the Gameboy, looking the kid in the eye. 'Now, buddy, judging from the make of your parents' cars, I think you can do a bit better than that, hey?'

'Joe.'

'It's all right, Grace.'

'They're company cars,' the kid said.

'And is this a company house? How many toilets you got in there? Three? Four?'

The kid nodded.

Joe pointed to a child on one of the charity's brochures. 'This kid doesn't have a toilet or a BMW.' He looked at the kid's skate clothes. 'Or big pants.'

'Hang on.' The kid disappeared and promptly returned with a five-dollar note.

'Much appreciated.'

They walked up the drive of the next house. 'Joe, we're not supposed to shame people into giving us money.'

'Five bucks is five bucks, Gracie. And that kid was a little . . .'

'Yeah.'

They knocked on the door of an even bigger house. They saw a woman look through the curtains and quickly close them. They waited a couple of minutes before it became clear there would be no door opening.

'We know you're home,' Joe called out. 'We can see you.'

'Let's just go.'

'We're not Mormons, we just want a few bucks.'

Joe could see that Grace was enjoying his total lack of regard for protocol. The woman opened a window and threw out a pile of change. 'Now go away.'

'That was about ten bucks' worth,' Joe said as they

headed back down the path. 'We might have got another couple of dollars if you'd let me tip her impatiens upside down.'

'Impatiens? Very impressive.' Grace linked her arm with his. 'Let's go and meet the others.'

They got back to school and tallied up all the money. It looked like Lawrence had brought in the most.

'Technically, I pooled my money with Andrew and Tracy so Grace, you and Joe probably raised the most,' he said generously. 'Well done.'

'We don't need your charity, Lawrence.' It had sounded OK in Joe's head.

'Actually, we do. That's kind of the point of today, Joe,' Grace smiled. 'Hang on, I forgot to count that twenty dollars. Iain and Tim are the winners.'

'But we're all winners,' one of the teachers had added, feeling a teacherly statement was called for.

Lawrence and the others headed off, leaving Joe with Tim and Grace. Joe could see that Tim was pretty proud of himself.

'I'm pretty proud of myself,' Tim said and set about regaling Joe with every detail of every house he had visited that day.

'I think I'd stay in and clean the carpet,' Grace whispered to Joe as her mother put the L-plates on her car. 'Are you coming, Tim?' she asked.

'I'm going to go around to the video shop. I'll walk home.'

'Your mum lets you drive her around?' Joe said.

Grace looked surprised. 'Yeah. I'm going for my licence next week.'

Tim had caught on. 'Grace Kelly. Car crash. Decapitated. Killed. Speculation her daughter was driving . . .'

'Thanks, Tim,' Grace and Joe said at the same time.

Within a few minutes everyone had dispersed. Joe sat on the front steps of the school, strategically waiting for a few mintues so that he wouldn't catch up with Lawrence who was also walking home. He'd never had to think about things so much in his life. He looked at his watch. About one and a half minutes had passed. Dog minutes. He wasn't relishing the thought of a night alone, unless he could somehow scoop out the contents of his brain and clock on as someone else, preferably normal, for the evening. 'Bugger it.' He got up and began running down the street. If he was fast enough he could still catch Tim.

7

On Monday morning, Joe had succeeded in pulling off nothing short of a miracle. He arrived at school one and a half minutes early. The last time he remembered being involved in a miraculous event of this calibre was a couple of years back, when his mother had finally understood and laughed at a 'Far Side' card without any explanation.

Lawrence was there too, still wearing shorts, with a definite air of smugness. Joe had taken to going to the toilets to heat his legs with the hand dryer whenever he got the chance. He'd never been colder or more uncomfortable. But he would not be beaten. At least, not by Lawrence.

As it turned out, Mr Woods, in his capacity as acting year-nine co-ordinator, was attending to a bunsen burner related incident, and was consequently a no-show for roll call.

Joe flipped his diary open and looked sheepishly at his timetable, knowing full well that after one semester, he probably should have committed his lessons to memory. But that was why you chose the same electives as your friends. Some called such a move foolhardy or immature, especially at senior level. But Joe called it strategic. Or at least he had.

Choosing electives based on friends' choices, rather than on things as trivial as your areas of interest or skill, meant that you always had someone to sit with and tell you when and where you had to go. You were saved from those awkward friendships of convenience, in which you somehow had to make it clear that you were not interested in friendship outside of the classroom. And in the event that you glazed over while vital information was being dispensed, you at least had the opportunity to find out about any pressing homework. Actually doing the homework was another matter. Of course, this plan hadn't taken into account the possibility of Joe falling out with his best friend and creator of the master copy of his timetable. Regrets, he'd had a few.

So, Joe had taken to carrying his diary around like the 'actors' on *Baywatch* carried around those little red plastic buoy things. His timetable indicated that he had double Biology first up, meaning that he would get his Mr Woods fix after all. Like his grandmother's gifts, Biology was neither bad nor particularly good. At the moment school was school. The cast was mediocre – the teachers particularly unconvincing and the stories and plot even worse.

Tim arrived at the classroom after delivering the class roll to the office. 'Tim, over here,' Joe said. 'So, that was a good movie the other night.'

Tim hadn't found it quite so memorable. 'What? Oh, yeah. It was OK. A bit predictable. And totally misrepresented the police force.'

'Yeah.'

'I just spoke to Mr Woods. Looks like Greg Robson's moving schools. He said you could keep being my lab partner, if you want.'

'Absolutely. That'd be great. If you don't mind.'

'As long as you do the work, Joe.'

'Of course.'

'It's just if I want to get into forensics eventually . . .'

'I know. You said. Every mark counts. I'll work hard.'

'Lawrence is coming this way,' Tim said in the loudest whisper that Joe had ever heard.

'Joe, we've got that Art presentation next week,' Lawrence said.

'Yeah, I know.' Though he hadn't, actually.

'Do you think we should get together and work out what we're going to say?'

'Probably.'

'You could come to my place if you like.'

'No. There are two halves. We already decided you're doing the first half, I'm doing the second. We can meet before school one morning next week and have a run-through.'

'OK. You don't think there might be too much overlap?'

'No, I think it will be fantastic, Lawrence.'

'Good.'

'Good.'

'And about the roster at work, are you sure you want to be doing midnight shifts? Won't you get a bit tired?'

'I'm fine. You know me. I'm a night person. It suits my circadian rhythm. Just thought I'd try it out for a bit. Relax, it has nothing to do with you or Claudia.'

'Oh. Good.'

'Good.'

Lawrence headed back to his seat. The nerve of him, using work as an excuse to talk to Joe. What else could you expect from a home wrecker?

'Do you think you two will ever bury the hatchet?' Tim asked.

'You mean the same hatchet that's in my back?'

'Isn't that a knife?'

'Don't worry, Tim. Can't you tell? Me and Lawrence are fine. We're more than fine. We're . . .'

'Good?'

'Lawrence Barry and Joseph King,' Mr Woods' voice boomed, seeming to enter the biology lab before he did. 'You have both been warned about flouting the school uniform code. The time for wearing shorts is well past.'

'Sir, I can't help it if we've had a bit of unseasonably cool weather. I find the shorts more comfortable.'

'The unseasonably cool weather you refer to, Mr King, is known to most of us as winter. The very inspiration for the invention of trousers. You two will begin wearing your school pants, or risk spending the rest of your Wednesday afternoons with me in detention.'

'Yes, sir,' Lawrence said in his repentant school captain voice.

'That's fine, sir, except my mum's taken my pants to the drycleaner so I won't be able to wear them until the day after tomorrow. I'd wear my tracksuit pants but my rugby top's got a big hole in it and . . .'

'Wear your pants when you get them. I'll be keeping an eye out.'

'Thanks for your understanding, sir.'

Joe opened his books, hoping that maybe today was a dissection day. But when it had become clear that once again there was not a dead animal in sight, Joe gave up on the novel idea of paying attention that lesson, and began counting the bricks at the front of the classroom. Joe was sure that this counting was probably a mild strain of obsessive compulsive disorder and as a result, had, from time to time, made a conscious effort to curb it. But somehow the lure of knowing exactly how many bricks comprised the front interior wall of Lab C had always won out. He had a similar compulsion to recite times tables whenever he was anxious. He often felt as though he was one big foible attached to a boy.

Satisfied with his count for the day, he slid a strategically folded piece of paper across the bench to Tim. Under Tim's guidance, Joe was having to do a bit more work than he was happy with, but it was better than the alternative of being alone. And contrary to his long-held suspicion, the work hadn't actually killed him.

Tim unfolded the note and surveyed Joe's latest thought-provoking pidgin French question:

Chere Tim, what do you think would be more interessant? Science avec Professeur Woods as the teacher ou Science with a piece of wood as teacher?

Tim scribbled down his carefully considered response and returned the letter incognito, jammed in the insects chapter of his *Science for Life* textbook. Joe retrieved the note, learning an interesting fact about bees as he did so. He read Tim's reply:

Joe, I asked you last week not to send me notes during class time. It's counter-productive, not to mention disrespectful to the teacher concerned. Just ask me later, Tim. P.S. I studied German, not French, but I believe you addressed me using the feminine form. You might want to look at that.

As Mr Woods wrapped up his post-mortem on their latest assignment, assuring his class it was legal to proofread their own words, Joe looked at his mark: B–.

'That's not bad,' Tim said.

'It's not like yours. It's not great.'

'You have to work for great.'

Tim wasn't so bad, thought Joe as he stuck his assignment in his folder. Maybe he hadn't laughed at Joe's 'birds of a feather must be very cold' joke the other day, but proverb jokes weren't necessarily everyone's bag. And anyway, Tim had other things going for him. He was extremely bright, making him an excellent candidate for a lifeline, should Joe ever be a contestant on *Who Wants to be a Millionaire?* He also had impeccable manners and was pretty good to cheat off during tests, on the rare occasions he forgot to construct a complex folder/pencil-case fortification to obscure the view of adjacent parties.

Tim also had the potential to make a watertight alibi in the event that Joe was ever falsely accused of a crime, and had that whole connection with the police force that could come in handy. And then there was the fact that he made Joe feel incredibly cool by comparison, and on a good day, less lonely. Tim was a good, loyal companion, with a pleasant temperament. And if the friendship venture failed, he would make an ideal family pet.

Joe was relieved when he opened his diary after lunch and discovered that it was time for the weekly year twelve form assembly. Miss Elliot always encouraged open, honest discussion during form assembly. Usually no one bothered taking advantage of the open forum set-up, due to the apathetic nature of the students when it came to all things administrative. But today was to be a departure from the norm. Lawrence performed his usual role of MC. Most people had a normal voice and a public speaking voice, the one that got a bit crackly or deeper when they had to speak in front of large groups of people. Lawrence sounded the same anywhere and any time he spoke. Joe found it particularly annoying.

'House athletics are next Friday. The house captains tell me there are still a lot of vacancies for the senior events. So if you're not in an event, get in one. It's about fun, not skill. And if you are in an event, get in another one. Contrary to popular belief, it is not a study day for year-twelves.'

A wave of laughter swept through the auditorium. Joe had heard at least half a dozen people talking in the last few days about how much work they were going to do on sports day.

'I know we're all stressed, but it's our last sports day. We set the bar. Let's make it a great, memorable day.'

An apathetic silence set in. 'Oh, and magazines and walkmans will be confiscated on the day. You're expected to cheer for your house.' There were cries of uproar from the Cosmo Girl set and Tim.

The house captains got up and attempted to recruit athletes for the many vacancies in their event schedules. Joe put his hand up for the 100m hurdles. 'Joe, you're already in five events. That's the maximum,' Joe's house captain said. 'Everyone could follow this boy's example.'

Miss Elliot seemed to find this notion very amusing.

'Does that mean I won't be able to do the pole vault?' Joe laughed.

The music captains got up and implored people to support the upcoming creative arts festival, while the public-speaking captains followed with their monthly lament about the declining numbers of debaters – an incredibly articulate seven-minute spiel which provided ample opportunity for a catnap. Grace waived her right to speak this week, as did the drama captains, who instead chose to perform a mime routine in a misguided effort to secure bums on seats for the aforementioned creative arts festival.

Miss Elliot later gave a cautionary word about the thieves that were lurking among them, and then alerted them to the more troubling tuckshop two dollar coin scam, in which someone was gluing five cent pieces together, colouring them with gold texta and passing them off as two dollar coins. Joe noticed Brad smiling smugly. So that was how Brad had managed all those tuckshops trips. Once the cries of outrage and admiration had settled a bit it was back to Lawrence.

'So we all agreed, after taking a vote, that we're doing quotes for the year-twelve pages of the magazine this year. We need to start collecting everyone's quotes ASAP. I know we're all busy, but we need your co-operation. Any questions?'

Iain Watts raised his hand. 'What happens if you don't want a quote?'

'We're all having one. That was the vote.'

'Yeah, but if you really don't want one . . .'

Crystal Stevens interjected. 'Like Lawrence said, we're all doing quotes. It will look stupid if some do and some don't. There'll just be a blank under your name and it won't work. It'll look all . . . urrgh.'

With logic like that, Joe thought, Crystal should have joined the dwindling debaters.

'If you don't provide us with a quote we'll just make something up and stick it under your name,' Sarah Close said, clearly another debating candidate.

Joe disliked the magazine committee. Maybe it was because they enjoyed all the privileges of leaders but had none of the responsibilities. They got to go to camp and leaders' day and were given a crappy school emblem tea-spoon at the end of the year. And all they had to do in return was make a few photo collages of themselves and their friends at the school formal. They were the worst kind of leader. It might have also had something to do with the fact that he had run for the magazine and not been elected.

'OK,' Lawrence continued. 'If there are no other questions about the magazine, get your quotes in.'

'Get your friends to help you, if it's a problem,' Crystal said. 'They know you the best.'

'I have a question,' Joe said, momentarily unsure of whether he'd said it out loud.

'Yeah?' Lawrence said.

'Do you really think it's fair to provide people with quotes when they don't want them? Is it not our choice to have or not have a quote?'

'Joe, you've already given us yours,' Crystal said.

'I'd like to withdraw it. I want a blank space under my name.'

'No,' Sarah said.

'No?'

'What exactly is the problem, Joe?'

'The problem, Lawrence, is that it's my right, and Iain's right and the right of those too afraid to speak . . .' he looked around at the mass of puzzled faces of his peers. 'Maybe not too afraid . . . more non-confrontational, to have their opinion voiced. We don't want quotes. They're exclusive and unnecessary.'

'Exclusive?' Crystal said.

'Yeah. A bunch of private jokes that maybe three people are privy to. You get lumped with a label and you carry it around for the rest of your life. Do you really think you have the right to define people who disagree with your . . . regime?' Now he was speaking for the high-school loners of the world.

'It's not a matter of defining anyone, Joe,' Lawrence said. 'Quotes are just a bit of fun. They're just like a snapshot of your life – who you were at a particular time.'

'Yeah, Joe,' Sarah said. 'What's wrong with a snapshot?'

'Maybe it's not the snapshot I have a problem with.' Joe looked directly at Lawrence. 'Maybe it's the photographer.'

Crystal leaned into the microphone. 'Oh, no. The guy who's doing the photos is really good. I can vouch for him 100 percent. He did my deb photos.'

'So the smart people who don't put in a quote will be given – what? "most likely to succeed"? And the shy person gets "quiet achiever"? And the person who makes a few jokes gets "class clown"? It's the same every year.'

'Class clown was actually your quote, wasn't it?' Sarah said.

Joe looked slightly sheepish. 'I said it was withdrawn.'

'What is it you want, Joe?' Crystal said.

The question may have come from a girl who used so much hairspray in her hair it warranted a flammability warning, but it was a good question.

'People who don't provide a quote, don't get one.'

Crystal looked confused.

'To paraphrase, no quote, no quote.'

'Miss Elliot, can you tell him to be quiet now?'

Miss Elliot took the mic, rapt with all the open discussion taking place. 'Sarah, I think perhaps Joe might have a point. How many other people might not want a quote?'

About twenty hands went up.

'OK. I think it's a fair compromise. I suggest, those who don't want a quote, don't have one. They will have their names placed under their photos and that's all.'

'Fine,' Crystal said.

'Yeah, no quotes,' Sarah said.

Iain Watts smiled at Joe, who was revelling in the fact that he'd had a point.

It had been petty and not even something that Joe had really believed in. He couldn't explain it. He'd just really needed to win something over Lawrence. To prove to people – and more importantly himself – that he could. That he was good enough. Lawrence would leave a legacy at this school. No matter what else he did, his name would go up on the school captains' board in big gold letters for future generations to disregard at will. And until today, Joe was destined to be just another unremarkable student who'd served his six years and moved on. But now, he too had made his mark on the school. It was slightly unfortunate and hugely ironic that that his mark would be in the form of the twenty or so blank spaces that were to appear under the names of various year twelve students in this year's school year book. But in an imperfect world you had to make your mark where there was an opportunity.

During last period, Joe sat in Art, his sketchbook positioned on his knees so that it appeared as though he was – sketching. Was he, he wondered, the worst art student in history? The thought of Ken Done momentarily cheered him, until he spotted Lawrence. 'Miss Matthews, would I be able to go and take some photos?'

'All the cameras are out, Joe. Concentrate on the write-up for this lesson.'

'The bet's off,' Lawrence said, sitting down beside Joe.

'What bet's that then?'

'The shorts.'

'And how do you figure that?'

'You heard Woods this morning. He banned us and Brad's giving it a miss too. So I s'pose it's a draw.'

'True. It would be a draw if were both to stop wearing shorts today. But I bought me an extra day. So technically, I win.'

'Your pants aren't at the cleaners?'

'Pressed and hanging in my cupboard. Both pairs.'

'Whatever. We never agreed on a prize anyway so it doesn't matter.'

'Sometimes winning is enough, Lawrence. Especially when it means that someone else loses – like you, for example.'

Joe picked up his sketchbook and sat down in an empty seat beside Grace at the next table. Anything to get away from Lawrence. Grace looked up inquiringly from her painting. 'Um, I was thinking movie night,' he improvised.

Grace looked confused. 'You want to go to the movies?'

'For a fundraiser. People organise them all the time.'

'What people are they?'

'Mr Cherish the Children: Patrick Rafter.'

'It could be a good idea.'

'Yeah,' Joe was liking the idea himself. 'Maybe it could be like moonlight cinema in the gym. I could hire a screen through my uncle and he'd help me get the movies too. It would cost us nothing and we could make a heap.'

'Sounds good, Joe, you can stay. And you do realise that you don't have to have a fundraising idea to talk to me.'

'I know.'

'I hope so. We did sit together in year seven. Remember – general studies? Kelly, King. You were the first person I met at high school. I knew you before my brother did.'

'That's right. We cheated on that Antarctica test.'

'Yeah, but only because you were so nice to me when my cat died – and you didn't understand the food chain.'

'Good times,' Joe smiled. 'Obviously – apart from the cat.'

'Having said that we don't have to talk about fundraising, do you think we should do something for the 40-hour famine?'

'Maybe.'

'Come on, Joe. Help me make a decision. Yes or no?'

'Definitely no. My sister reckons when she was at school the girls used to use it as a chance to kick off their eating disorders. And you know what the guys are like – they'll eat five packets of barley sugar and drink four litres of orange juice, which would kind of defeat the purpose. I'd do something else.'

'Right then. A decision. We'll raise money for that one some other way.'

'We could use my movie night for that.'

'What about Red Nose Day?'

'Yeah, do that for sure.'

'I'm thinking maybe we'll have a casual clothes day, too'

'But don't charge people for wearing their uniforms, I'm sure that's somehow illegal.'

'Probably.'

'So how did your date go the other night?'

'What?'

'Harrison?'

'We're going to talk about my date now?'

'We're friends, Grace.'

Grace looked around uneasily. 'It went pretty well, I think.'

'That's it?'

She looked around again. 'I don't want anyone to hear anything.'

'Are you in witness protection or something?'

'No. I just don't want to be one of those people who blabs every detail and analyses every single moment. I don't want anyone thinking I'm . . .'

'A girl?'

'Exactly. We're going out on Friday.'

'Another date. That's good.' He was getting really sick of that word.

'Yeah. How was the movie the other night with Tim? Did you have fun?'

'In a Christian youth group sort of way.'

'A what?'

'You know how sometimes you're hanging around with someone and you realise that you don't know them very well. But that's only after you've sworn your head off and made crass jokes – that you wouldn't even normally make. Then you try and act decent for the rest of the outing, but the damage is done. They think you're a blaspheming, bigoted potty mouth.'

'Not exactly, no.'

'Well, I don't think your brother really has a lot of time for me.'

'Yeah, he does. You've been friends for years.' She leant in close and whispered. 'There's something you should know about Tim and me. We're basically nerds. Big ones.'

'No you're not. Real nerds don't know they're nerds. That's how the world can go around. Otherwise there'd be chaos.'

'So that's what they mean about the Lord working in mysterious ways?'

'Tim's a good guy. He stuck by me. He's smart and he's focused. He knows what he wants. He's probably had his pink form filled in for a year. Maybe it'll rub off on me.'

'And what does he get from hanging out with you?'

Joe looked thoughtful. 'Well, I've been a successful friend in the past. I have some references somewhere here.' He pulled out his university preferences form.

'You should be able to reel off a list of your best qualities right now.'

'I would but . . . I don't want to sound up myself.'

'Really?'

'You do yours then.'

'I know mine. I asked you for yours, Joe.'

'Well . . . maybe I know mine too.'

'Quote-bashing being top of the list. You're not a fan of the quote?'

'Apparently not. I think I went a bit berserk this morning. I don't know who that was.'

'No, you were right. I've never liked quotes either. They're the source of so much bad in the world: essays, debates, quote-a-day calendars. They provide wisdom that no one can possibly live up to. And in a year book – very unoriginal. All in all, not a good idea.'

'I was right, wasn't I?'

'But at the same time, they're just stupid quotes. No one even really reads them.'

'Then what's the point?'

She laughed, looking at his blank form. 'You really don't know what you're doing, do you?'

'No.'

She pushed her palette aside and leant towards him. 'Wow.'

'Wow what?'

'I've never met anyone who was so unsure.'

'They're only preliminary choices. And who knows? It might come to me in a blinding flash. I could have one of those things . . . an epiphany. I've always fancied an epiphany.'

'I didn't mean that.'

He put his sketchbook down. 'Unsure of what then?'

'Everything.'

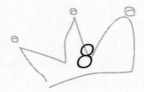

Joe was feeling good. He'd done his usual four days' training in the lead-up to sports day, the taste of those participation ribbons urging him on in the more testing moments of the previous ninety-six hours. He hoped to come home with at least one white ribbon that afternoon. He boarded the train, receiving some odd looks from passengers, as he sat with his blue spotted hair and superman t-shirt, blue being the colour of choice for his and Lawrence's particular house, Nolan. He had very little time to feel self-conscious about his appearance, with the arrival of more bright-coloured-hair folk at the next few stations. By the time the train had made its final stop, Joe's carriage was awash with colour: red-heads, blue-heads, green-heads, yellow-heads. It just wasn't sports day if the stadium didn't resemble the set of a very bad futuristic film.

Usually Joe and Lawrence passed the day together,

competing in every possible event and revving up their cheer squad in between races. This year Joe had understandably had to improvise, if improvising meant planning every second of the day to avoid uncomfortable interactions with Lawrence. This was where Grace came in. She was going to be in charge of selling drinks and snacks in the canteen. Coincidentally, it had been a lifelong dream of Joe's to sell drinks and snacks in the canteen on his final sports day. That's what he'd told Grace. She hadn't bought a word of it but she'd taken pity on him anyway. She was good like that. He liked spending time with her. It felt comfortable, effortless.

Joe got off the train and crossed the road to the sports track. He looked through the cyclone fence at the sports captains who were setting up for the day.

'Hey, Joe. Over here,' Grace called, struggling with a box of soft drink.

Joe took hold of half the box. 'Hi, Gracie.'

'Looking sharp.'

'Thanks.' He noticed that Grace was wearing her sports uniform, devoid of any extra colour.

'I don't dress up. I'm in Drysdale.'

Joe didn't follow. 'And?'

'Drysdale – yellow. It washes me out. Who can wear yellow?'

It was the first girly thing he'd ever heard her say. He hadn't really thought of her as a girl before. He'd known she had all the necessary components to make a girl, but in Joe's mind, she had just been Grace.

'So how much are we charging for the drinks?' he asked, struggling with his end of the box.

'Are you right, Joe? Because I can manage it on my own.'

'I'm fine. It was just a cramp. So how much?'

'One dollar fifty.'

'What now?'

'Joe. Seriously. "What now?" is never going to work for you.'

'A dollar fifty? Are you serious? Why don't we just give them away?'

'It's called ethics, Joseph.'

'No canteen, no other source of food. It's called . . . having them by the balls. We could make mega bucks for the kids.'

'It's not for the kids this time.'

'For the persecuted then. Simple supply and demand.'

'Is that what that means?'

'I don't know.'

'We're not helping people by screwing over other people. Cans are one fifty, not three dollars, got it?'

'How tacky is Jade Pryce?' Grace asked as Joe sat on a crate during one of his self-assigned breaks.

'Why?'

'The crop halter neck. The belly ring. The body glitter.'

'The fact that she can pull off the yellow?' Joe said. 'Jealousy's a curse, Gracie.'

'So is teenage pregnancy. Wouldn't hurt Jade to hear that.'

'Grace Kelly. Is that cattiness I detect? I thought you liked everyone.'

'I do not like everyone. I just don't have a problem with most people. Unless they're named after . . . shitty green stones.'

Joe gave a hearty laugh. This was shaping up to be among his better sports days. 'Did you check the movie night date with Miss Elliot?'

'I did. It's approved. We just have to write up a notice and she'll print it. But this one will have to be your baby, because I'm way too busy with other stuff we're doing, not to mention a little thing called homework.'

'Still with the homework, hey? When are they going to get over that? Don't worry, I'm on it. My uncle's organised for the big screen. I just have to think about the movies.'

'I can help you with that.'

Joe noticed Tim signalling him from the track. 'I have to go rake the long jump pit while Tim does his discus.'

Joe completed his first four events in spectacularly mediocre fashion. Two fourths and two second lasts. It capped off a not-so-memorable chapter of his secondary schooling. His last event was the relay. 'Change in the line-up,' Steve Porter said. 'Joe, you're running third. Lawrence is passing to you.'

'What happened to Stew?'

'Dodgy knee.'

'Shouldn't I go earlier though? You've seen me run today. I'm crap. Shouldn't I pass to Lawrence?'

'Nah, he's hurt his hammy. You'll be OK. I'm last. And Brendan's crapper than you, so that's pretty much it. You'll be right, mate.'

'Hey, Joe,' Brad said, running to his post as last runner.

'Yeah, I know. I'm in the wrong race. The girls' race is next.'

Brad smiled. 'Good luck.'

Lawrence ran up to join his team. He looked at Joe awkwardly. 'So I'm passing to you?'

'Looks like it.'

Mr Sturt instructed the teams to take their places. 'Let's go boys,' Steve said. 'The last race of our high school careers. Let's have fun.'

Joe had been in a relay for every one of his years at Hillview, each time with Lawrence. He was glad that he'd have this last one with Lawrence too, whether they were talking or not.

Steve had been right. Brendan was crapper than Joe, getting the team off to an uninspired start. Lawrence had made up for it though, despite his hurt hamstring, getting the team in front by a nose, until he'd passed the baton to Joe, who had promptly dropped it, costing them valuable seconds. But Joe had continued undeterred, running the race of his life. He'd felt it. It was the fastest he'd ever gone. Steve had very nearly gone on to win. But Brad had been too good. They'd only lost by a couple of seconds – about the amount of time it would take to pick up a dropped baton.

After their presentation, Joe headed back with Tim in tow to help Grace pack up, studying his red ribbon as he walked.

'Joe,' Lawrence said. 'That was a good race.'

Tim looked at Joe as if awaiting his signal to attack.

'At ease, Timmy.' Joe turned around to face Lawrence. 'Thanks.'

'Yeah. Well done.'

They stood awkwardly for a moment. 'Well, I'd better get going,' Lawrence said. He started to walk away.

'Hey, Lawrence,' Joe called. 'Sorry about the baton. I don't know what happened there.'

'Nah. Really, it wasn't your fault.'

'Thanks, but . . .'

'Actually, it was probably mine.'

Joe was suddenly annoyed. 'Why do you say that?'

'Well, maybe I didn't pass it properly or I might have . . .'

'You passed it perfectly, Lawrence. It was my fault.'

'Jeeze, Joe, why are you always so hard on yourself?'

'Why are you always so easy on me, Lawrence?'

'What?'

'The baton. We practised every year. We had it down. Never one drop. But this year I accidentally let it go? Maybe I subconsciously did it on purpose.'

'Don't be stupid. It happens.'

'It happens?'

'Even Olympians do it, Joe. It's an easy mistake,' Lawrence said.

'But they're all easy mistakes. Every time I stuff up you tell me not to worry because anyone could have made the same easy mistake. But it's not anyone. It's me. It's always me.'

Lawrence leant against the fence, unable to conceal his impatience. 'What are you trying to say? I don't understand.'

'I don't really either. All I know is I feel like you never expect anything from me.'

'And?'

'And you should once in a while.'

'Sorry, Joe, I still don't get it.'

'No, you don't.'

The final presentations were made, and Lawrence, in his Olympic delegate role, officially declared the sports the best ever. Tim and Joe helped Grace load the left-over fundraising food into Mr Sturt's Land Rover before heading to the train station, slightly wearied by the day's events.

Joe sat on the train, opposite Grace, watching her darting eyes as she looked out the window. He'd never noticed how people's eyes went like that before. She had very nice eyes, even when they were moving from side to side as if she were possessed. They were green with a darker outline and hazel flecks. Tim sat reading the paper, occasionally tut-tutting at peoples' disregard for the law – a pastime usually reserved for the over-sixties.

'Did you know that the singular of graffiti is graffito?'

'No, Tim. I didn't know that,' Joe said.

'Not many people do.' Tim resumed reading his newspaper.

Grace's focus switched to the inside of the carriage. 'That's Sarah Hellier,' she said, pointing. 'She's still got a box of fundraiser M&Ms.' She stood up.

'Where are you going?' Tim asked.

'To harass her.'

Joe laughed. 'You have to come down hard on those types. Do you need back-up?'

'I'll be fine.' Grace climbed over Joe and headed for her target.

'So, Joe,' Tim said, temporarily looking up from his newspaper. 'Did you want to come around to our place Saturday night, maybe watch some DVDs?'

'Yeah, why not?'

'Cool. Come for tea. Mum's putting on a spread.'

'Your mum always does, doesn't she?'

'Yeah. Did you want to choose the DVDs together?'

'If you like.'

'Because I don't really know what you've seen, so that might be better.'

'OK.'

'Grace will be there for a bit, but then she's going out so we can use her big TV.'

'Where's Grace going?'

'Out with – you know who.'

'Right. Just out of interest, what do you think of – he who must not be named?'

'Harrison? Seems nice enough. I don't think he's as bad as we thought. He's actually quite shy.'

'That's what they said about Hitler.'

'Did they?'

'Speaking of Hitler . . .'

Suddenly panic swept through the carriage as three ticket inspectors strongly resembling Gestapo agents boarded the train.

'Tickets please.'

A few passengers presented their tickets. Joe and Tim showed the lady inspector theirs, with their concession cards.

'Thanks, boys. What have you guys been up to?' she asked, obviously the designated friendly one.

'School sports day,' Joe said.

'Cool.'

'Hey, Amber,' a male inspector called.

The inspector walked over to her colleague. 'Problem?'

Joe noticed they were stopped in front of Lawrence. 'This kid has a concession ticket, no card. Says he left it at school.'

Lawrence sat uneasily, his cheeks growing redder each moment.

'So you do have a card?' The woman asked.

'Yeah. It must be in my locker. I was in a rush this morning. I've just forgotten it.'

'You must travel with a concession card at all times when you purchase a concession fare.'

'I know. I apologise.'

All heads were turned in Lawrence's direction. Joe

knew his friend hadn't actually bought a concession card, because he travelled on public transport so rarely. Mrs Barry had given him money to get one at the start of the year, but he'd spent it all on a ridiculously overpriced pair of pants. Lawrence was squirming around, as he always did when he was entering panic mode.

Grace rejoined her party. 'God, they're like the Gestapo,' she said, looking over at the inspectors.

'This is an offence punishable by a pretty hefty fine,' the man continued. 'Where did you travel today?'

Joe could sit there, taking it all in, basking in the misery. But there was just one problem: he couldn't. 'Lawrence is our school captain,' Joe said, walking over to his friend. 'He had to set up for our sports day and run in five events. He's had a lot on his mind,' Joe sat down beside him.

'School captain? Really?' Amber said.

'Yeah, he's very responsible. And he *does* have a con-cession card. We catch the bus together every day. It's a shocking photo.'

'Someone so responsible shouldn't have forgotten something so simple,' the man said.

Lawrence smiled uneasily. 'I know.'

'He knows,' Joe said. 'He's stressed. Overachievers are never too good with the practical stuff. But he's a very good school captain.'

Amber laughed. 'We'll let you off with a warning, Lawrence. Next time remember the card.'

The inspectors moved onto another carriage. Joe rejoined his friends.

'Thanks, Joe,' Lawrence said, following him down the carriage.

'Well, I have no issue with your fare evasion.'

Lawrence started to say something more but Joe stood up quickly. 'This is my stop. I'm meeting Mum at work.'

'So about six-thirty tomorrow night?' Tim said.

Joe was confused. 'What?'

'DVD night.'

'Oh, right. Actually, I think Mum said something about our relos from Adelaide coming this weekend.'

Tim smiled. 'You can call me if you like.'

'Yeah, I'm pretty sure that's what's happening. I will call if I can come though. Sorry.'

He felt bad about letting Tim down, especially with the whole fictitious South Australian relatives thing. But he just didn't feel like seeing anyone right now. Tim would understand.

When Joe and his mother got home, he emptied the letterbox and headed inside. Ed gave him one of his theatrical greetings, jumping all over him, running from room to room, picking up socks, slippers, soap – whatever he could find that he felt would impress his new owners.

'Oi. You're nicked, geezer. Orright, Joe?' Chris said from the couch in his best cockney accent, which proved the theory that sometimes the best isn't good enough.

'Hi, Chris,' Joe said, flopping into a chair. 'Why aren't you on a plane?'

'Where's your bruvver? Tell me, Joe. Where's our Anfony? Down pub? It's not grassin' if he's in trouble.'

'I've got no idea. I've just come home.'

'Can anyone verify that, then? Right, I'm going to get the toe-rag. You stay 'ere, in case it all goes pear-shaped.'

'Can do,' Joe laughed.

'You comin' tonight, Joe? Or are you hanging around here to do nowt?'

'Exactly how many episodes of *The Bill* have you watched, Chris?'

Chris smiled. 'Too bloody many. So are you coming?'

'Nah, I think I'll give it a miss. I'm stuffed. Besides, it's a bit depressing being the person who goes to the airport but never goes anywhere.'

'But I'm going to be there.'

'Yeah, I know and I'm feeling torn. Very Natalie Imbruglia, but . . . no. Television beckons. There won't be enough room in the car with all of Anthony's hair care products anyway.'

'Fair enough, Joe. You can't say I didn't offer.'

'You're right. I can say many things, Chris, but that's certainly not one of them.'

'Nice hair by the way.'

'Thanks. Sports day.'

'How'd it go?'

'Embarrassing. I won every race, was approached by a talent scout – the usual.'

'Hate it when that happens.'

'I know. I just want to have my childhood. You should ask your brother how it went.'

'Why? What happened?' They heard a strange sound coming from behind the couch. 'Shit. What's wrong with your dog? He's foaming at the mouth.'

Joe looked over the back of the couch at Ed. 'He's eating the soap again. Anthony! Come and get your dog.'

Mrs King appeared in the doorway of the living room, grabbing the soap out of Ed's mouth without blinking an eye. It had become such a common practice. 'So you didn't say whether you're coming to the airport to see your brother off?'

'If it's to make sure he goes.'

'Joe.'

'He's going for a few weeks, not a year. So I take it Dad's not going?'

'You know your father's . . . view of airports.'

Graeme King had a phobia. Airports were apparently terrorist targets.

'You'd better go and say goodbye then. We're heading off, now. Since you're not going, you can walk the dog.'

Anthony emerged from his last-minute packing. 'Ready Mum?'

'All set. Did you say goodbye to your father?'

'Yeah. I was in there for twenty minutes convincing him I wouldn't leave my bags unattended or make friends with anyone at the airport. Why did you let him watch *Brokedown Palace*?'

Joe looked up at his brother, searching for the exact right thing to say to wish him well. They may not have got along all the time, or even most of it, but Joe did love and admire his older brother on some level. He wondered what could capture the sentiment adequately? Finally he settled on a word. 'Bye.' That seemed to do the trick.

'Bye. You can have these,' Anthony said, handing Joe a half-eaten packet of Doritos. 'I don't want them.'

'See you, Joey,' Chris said, getting up from the couch.

'Bye, Chris. Have a good time.'

Joe sat, watching TV, until his father emerged from his den. 'Is this that *Seinfield*, is it, Joe?'

'*Seinfeld*, yeah.' He changed the channel to the news. 'I'd better walk Ed.'

'You can stay there, if you like.'

'It's all right. Do you know where he's hiding?'

'He saw you get the lead before. He's in the toilet.'

'Only we could get an agoraphobic dog. What else has he got? A touch of the apnoea?'

'He'll be all right. He just needs training.'

'And I wonder who's going to get that honour?'

'Do you need some help?'

'Nah, it's OK.'

When Joe arrived home after walking Ed, he saw his dad had switched back to *Seinfeld*. It appeared that his dad was beginning to like Joe's favourite TV show almost as much as Joe did. Joe didn't quite know what to do with that information. He wasn't really sure about anything right now, and he struggled to remember the last time that he had been.

Midnight supermarket shifts were surely the original source of inspiration for that famous Dickensian phrase '*it was the best of times, it was the worst of times*'. While being a register boy meant that there was potential for slackness in the later hours of the evening, Joe had learned in his four midnight shifts, that there was also a downside, namely David Ashcroft. This boy was a bit of a Dickensian himself. A nice Dickensian, but a Dickensian nonetheless.

David was one of those people who identified an area of common ground with a person and then only ever talked about that area in every conversation that he had with that person, like Joe's dad did with Uncle Phil and barbecuing. David had worked out early on that several people he had gone to primary school with had then gone on to go to high school with Joe. Therefore, his conversations with Joe tended to follow the same form:

Joe: Hi, Dave, how's it going? Catch the cricket/footy/popular American sitcom etc. last night?

David: Thomas Rudd. You know him?

Joe: Yeah, I know Tom. He's in my homeroom. Good guy.

David: Justin Grey? He goes to your school, too.

Joe missed Isabelle. She never seemed to work anymore, always off at a university protest, as if it were the 1960s.

Renishka Naidoo, the veela, was on tonight. She was among the most attractive women that Joe had ever seen in person, hence the *Harry Potter* reference. Supermarket work was just wrong for her. She should have been on a Paris catwalk or at home in her palace, ordering her groceries from Coles online, not processing other people's transactions.

Suffering from a fear of beautiful women, Joe never knew quite what to say to Renishka. On the rare instances that he had dared initiate any conversation, she had failed to get the relevance of what he'd said, saying that she'd gone to primary school in South Africa and had therefore missed out on a lot of popular culture of the Western world. So Joe would spend the remaining hours of his shifts trying to convince her that she really hadn't missed out on anything not having seen *The Muppet Show*, as he did that evening.

'Miss Piggy, animal – pure gold,' he found himself

saying. 'But Kermit was a little green joke, Renishka. Annoying voice, annoying little body. I had a frog once and he did not look anything like Kermit.'

The other bad thing about the midnight shift was the clientele of the wee small hours – the nocturnal misfits. This seemed to be the preferred shopping time of substance abusers and escaped psych ward patients. Joe was continually grateful for the presence of Frank, the store security guard.

'How was your party the other night, Frank?'

'Really good, mate.'

'So it was a real surprise? Your wife didn't pick it?'

'Nah. She didn't know what had hit her. Stayed a surprise till the end. It was great.'

'She liked the present?'

'Loved it. You were right, Joe. The blue was the best choice.'

Noticing the manager on duty approaching, Joe began cleaning his register.

'Will you be all right to help Oliver lock up, Joe? I've got a migraine. I need to go home.'

'Yeah, no worries, Rob. Feel better, mate.' No. He just couldn't pull the mate thing off. Lawrence could do the mate. Frank could do the mate. Joe could not.

'Joe, footy?' Oliver called, once Rob was clear of the store.

'What about the . . .' Joe pointed to one of the store security cameras.

'Helen's away. They won't even look at them for the next two weeks.'

'Let's go then.'

Oliver pulled out a foam football that he'd comman-
deered from the novelty aisle some weeks back. He threw
the ball to Joe, who promptly kicked it between register
eight and nine.

'Goal!' Joe cheered, starting his victory lap of the front
end of the store.

'No goal,' Oliver said.

'What?'

'I wasn't ready.'

'How old are you? Seven? Come on, you were standing
right next to me. You were ready. He was ready, wasn't
he, Renishka?'

Renishka shrugged her shoulders. 'I don't know about
this game. I went to primary school in South Africa.'

'Dave, my man? You saw. It was a goal, right?'

'Sorry, I was cashing up. Sean Bradley? Know him?'

'Yeah, Dave. All right, play on.'

As Oliver lined up to take a kick, Joe was momentarily distracted by an awfully distorted muzak song. He
just couldn't work out what it was. Michael Bolton . . .
Whitney Houston . . .

'Christ, what the hell happened?' Oliver yelled.

'What? Oh shit, ' Joe said. Scott, one of the deli boys
was coming down to the front with a blood-covered
hand. There was so much blood that it looked fake, like a
low-budget horror movie.

The colour drained from Oliver's face. 'What's happened, Scott?'

'The slicer.'

'Rob's gone home. He's the first-aid guy. I'm not doing my course till next week. Oh, I can't look,' Oliver said.

Joe dropped the football and grabbed hold of Scott, who was so quiet that he had to be in shock. 'Lie down, buddy.'

'Thanks.' Oliver gasped and sank to the floor.

'Not you, Oliver. I meant Scott. Oliver, call an ambulance. Frank, can you close the doors and go out and direct the ambulance?' Joe looked at Scott's hand. It was really bloody. He couldn't see where it was all coming from until . . . 'He's chopped off a finger . . . two fingers. Renishka, get me some bandages or tea towels, something to stop the blood. What happened, Scott?'

'Where?'

'Aisle six, Renishka. Pyjamas, shirts – anything.' Joe clamped his hands over the bleeding. 'Dave, I need you to find Scott's fingers.'

'Oh my God.'

'Dave, keep it together. Scott needs you.'

'Which ones are they?'

'What?'

'Pointer, index, thumb?'

'They'll be the ones on the floor.'

David went the same colour as Oliver. 'Shouldn't we give him some booze or something?'

'No. Come on, Dave. Get the fingers and put them in a plastic lunch bag – you know, those zip lock ones.'

'Where are they?'

'There's a display on the end-cap on aisle four. Does no one have any store knowledge? Grab a lunchbox and fill it with water and a packet of peas or something frozen. They need to go on ice.'

'Joe,' Frank called. 'This bloke just wants a litre of milk. Can I let him in?'

'No medical licence, no milk,' Joe said. 'You're going to be fine, Scotty.' Joe's hands were spasming from applying pressure. 'Oliver, can you come and help me stop the bleeding?'

'Oh, Christ. Sorry, Joe.' Oliver vomited into a waste paper bin.

'Oliver, go grab Frank. You wait for the ambulance.'

Renishka appeared with an array of bandages. The supermarket was definitely the place of choice for your emergency – hospitals aside, of course. 'Well done. Great. Frank, you're not queasy, are you? Pop your hands on there. Ta. Keep it elevated.'

'I've got them, Joe. At least, I think I have,' David called.

'Great, Dave. Get the other stuff. And . . . blow into the bag before you put the fingers in.'

Scott began wailing with the pain.

'Not long now, Scotty.'

Oliver managed to show the ambulance officers in without a further vomiting incident.

'What have we got here? A sliced hand? I said ham, not hand, mate,' one of them said. 'Scott, is it? You're going to be fine, mate.'

One of the ambulance men noticed the vomit. 'How many times has he vomited?'

'Actually, that was me,' Oliver said sheepishly.

Joe looked up and glimpsed Renishka who was flicking through a *Who Weekly*, obviously doing her bit by informing Scott of who was hot and who was not. 'Renishka, maybe you could help the man with the stretcher or something.'

'Pardon?'

'Nothing.'

'Here it is,' David said, handing the plastic-sealed, iced fingers to the second officer.

'Good going, guys. With the finger and the bandaging, excellent stuff. We might be out of a job,' the first officer said.

Oliver smiled at Joe awkwardly, well aware that the praise was in no way directed at him.

'Where will you take him?' Joe asked.

'St Vincent's. You can come if you want.'

'OK. Just so he won't be alone. Oliver, can you call his mum?'

'What?'

'Frank – red folder, service desk. Call his mum, will you?'

At the hospital, Scott went straight into surgery. His parents and sister arrived soon after. 'It could be hours, love,' Scott's mum said. 'You go home and we'll call you.'

'Thanks, Joe,' Scott's dad said, holding out his hand.

'You're welcome.'

Joe didn't go to sleep until very late. He sat in the kitchen, thinking about what had happened that night. He felt like he was in the episode of *Medic Alert* where there had been a huge train crash and all the team had had to pull double shifts, then in the end, they'd all walked across to the coffee shop to debrief. But Joe was light on confidants at the moment. Ed was a good listener, but wasn't too forthcoming with the advice.

'Can't sleep?' Mr King asked, joining Joe in the kitchen.

'Nah.'

Ed crept off his laundry bed and placed his head in Joe's lap.

'Must be the adrenaline. You've had a big night.'

'Yeah, it was.'

'Your mother waited up for a while after you called, but fatigue got the better of her.'

'That's OK.'

'How's your friend?'

'He should be all right. He's in surgery now, so I came home.'

'I said to your mum it sounded like it was lucky you were there.'

'Maybe. They would have got by.'

'If you're tired tomorrow maybe you should have a sleep in, go to school late.'

'I might.'

'They'd want to have a good look at their safety procedures, wouldn't they?'

'Who?'

'Your store. Everyone should be first-aid trained.'

'Yeah. I s'pose.'

'There won't be any more midnight shifts on a Sunday, will there?'

'No, I was just filling in for tonight.'

'Good.'

Leave it to his father to ruin a perfectly awkward conversation by pulling out the parental comments. Mr King got up and put Joe's coffee mug in the sink. 'Oh, I taped *Seinfield* for you, too. You've probably already seen it, but I just thought, you know, in case.'

'Thanks. I might put it on – see if it helps me get to sleep.'

His father lurked awkwardly in the kitchen doorway for a moment. 'It was a good one. George was sleeping under his desk at work, of all places.'

Joe smiled. 'That's one of my favourites.'

Mr King leaned over and patted Joe on the head. An unmistakable hair ruffle. 'Don't stay up too late.'

As Joe lay in bed, he had an overwhelming feeling of exhaustion and contentment. Mr King was right – Scott had been lucky that Joe was there. Had he been left to the devices of his other colleagues, he would have been plied full of alcohol, vomited on, and given his last rites from a copy of *Who Weekly*. Joe had been a star. It was like tonight had given him the tiniest glimpse of how it felt to be his brother – and he loved it.

Joe woke the next morning in a panic. It was ten a.m. He washed his face, threw his school clothes on, and sat down to a balanced breakfast. There was always time to eat.

'The hero has risen,' Mrs King said, hugging Joe from behind.

'Didn't you see your pants hanging in your wardrobe?'

Joe looked down at his shorts. 'Yeah, I thought I'd wear them tomorrow.'

'You don't have to go to school, you know. Not if you're too tired.'

He'd waited to hear those very words for the past thirteen years. But today he had to go. 'No, I've got a presentation next period. I have to be there.' He reached into his schoolbag and pulled his science folder out. 'Can you sign this, Mum?'

'What is it?'

'It's my biol assignment. Woods is making us get everything signed this term. Something about accountability.'

'B minus. That's really good, love.'

'You should have seen what Tim got. We're lab partners now.'

'I thought Lawrence was your lab partner.'

'Woods changed us around. Anyway, Tim got an A.'

'That's nice for him. But you've done well yourself.'

'Yeah.'

'You have to stop comparing yourself to everyone else, Joseph. You've always worried far too much about other people's achievements.'

'And you've always worried far too much about photographing other people's achievements.'

His mother smiled. 'Here, put this in a safe place.' She handed him his pink preferences form. 'It's been lying around here for a week, gathering toast crumbs.'

'I'd better get going.'

'There won't be trumpets, you know, darling.'

'Trumpets?'

'Someone once said that there are no trumpets when the big moments in life happen. Don't wait for divine intervention, Joe. It's as simple as making a decision and sticking to it.'

'And if it's the wrong decision?'

'You make another one. But you won't know till you try.'

'Simple as that?'

'I didn't know what I wanted to do when I was your age but I chose nursing and luckily I never looked back.'

Joe didn't like it when his mother talked about having been his age. He knew about the human life cycle and he'd seen photos, but he was still not convinced that his parents had ever been seventeen. There were some things that you just couldn't believe unless you'd been there – like Marty McFly in *Back to the Future*.

'Come on, Joe. I'll drive you.'

Joe ran down the corridor, straight into the path of Mr Woods. He wanted to find Lawrence, but right now, he'd settle for rubbing Woods' hair-filled nose in it.

'Ah, Joe.'

'Mr Woods. I know I'm late but . . .'

'But it's with good . . . no, excellent reason I hear. It's all taken care of. And I believe a "well done" is in order. You were a fine first-aid pupil. Last night was obviously evidence of that.'

'Thank you, sir.' Leave it to Woods to make the finger severing about him. Joe had forgotten that Mr Woods had been his first-aid teacher. Mr Woods walked off, looking as proud as the punch that Joe wanted to lay on him.

'Lawrence,' Joe said, spotting him at his locker, down the corridor. 'I'm sorry I didn't make it this morning, to go through our talk.'

'That's OK. Mr Woods told us all what happened.'

'He did?'

'Yeah. Who had the accident?'

'It was Scott.'

'Oh, poor Scotty. I worked with him last shift. That'll be the end of footy for this season. Is he going to be all right?'

'Yeah, looks that way. They won't know how much use he'll have of the fingers for a while.' Joe noticed that Lawrence was also still wearing shorts. He was simultaneously furious and impressed.

'Jeeze, I'll have to visit him. Well done, Joe. I don't think I took any of that first-aid stuff in.'

'You'd know more than you reckon.'

'So you just – knew what to do?'

'Sort of.'

'Were you scared?'

'Didn't have time to be. Maybe afterwards when I thought about it.'

'God, all that blood. Was there a lot?'

'Yeah.'

The bell went, signalling the beginning of the next period. Lawrence reached into his locker and pulled out a couple of sheets of paper. 'Now don't worry about the talk.' He handed Joe the paper.

'OK. What this?'

'The talk. I had a free last period, so I wrote up your bit. I figured you wouldn't have had time with last night. Your parts are highlighted in yellow.'

Joe dug around in his bag. 'I actually did write my bit. It's in here somewhere.'

'Don't worry about it.'

Joe put his bag down and waded through its contents. 'Really, I did do it.' But whether he'd done it or not, it didn't look like he had it with him. 'Maybe we could ask if we can do it tomorrow.'

'Seriously, Joe. Let's just get it out of the way. Come on, Miss Matthews is in there.'

'Yeah, OK then.' They entered the classroom.

Joe decided to do exactly what Lawrence proposed. He'd done it dozens of times, had Lawrence bail him out. And it was only the tiniest percentage of a work requirement. It barely even counted. Researching an art movement. A monkey could do the assignment. It was a waste of everyone's time.

Lawrence began with a general introduction about the meaning and genesis of the Renaissance and then it was Joe's turn to talk more specifically about some of the artists. He could see the names of the four Teenage Mutant Ninja Turtles dotted throughout his highlighted section. He'd made a joke about that in his own version of the talk. All he had to do was read Lawrence's words. Lawrence finished and looked at him expectantly.

Joe got up ready to begin. He looked down at his notes – Lawrence's notes – and went to speak but some-how couldn't.

'Joe?' Miss Matthews said.

'Miss, could we get an extension?'

'Generally not a question asked mid-talk, Joe,' Miss Matthews said.

'I know, but I've left my bit – which I did do – at

home. I know exactly where it is. It's on my desk in my bedroom.'

'Well, what have you got there?'

'It's Lawrence's work.'

'But we wrote it together, Miss. Joe's just talking about some additional stuff that he wrote – which we probably wouldn't have time to get through anyway, so he may as well just go right ahead now. Go ahead, Joe.'

'No.'

'No?'

'It's not mine, Laws.'

'I'm not sure what's going on here,' Miss Matthews said. 'Lawrence, is it both yours and Joe's work or not?'

'Yes.'

'Miss Matthews, he's making a mockery of all that the Australian Board of Studies stands for. It's not my work.'

'Joe, what's your problem?' Lawrence snapped.

'You are. Stop helping me.'

Miss Matthews stood between them. 'OK, Lawrence, let's pretend I'm a judge in a courtroom and you've taken an oath on the Bible or *Ralph* magazine – or whatever it is you boys would swear on. Is it Joe's work?'

'No.'

'Right, then. I want a presentation from each of you next lesson and you can both stay back on Friday after-noon and clean every inch of this room.'

Joe wondered what had happened to the notion of truth setting you free. 'It's not really Lawrence's fault, Miss. He was just trying to – be a friend.'

'That's touching, Joe. But your friend isn't doing you any favours.'

'What's going on?' Lawrence said, cornering Joe after class. 'I'm supposed to be working Friday afternoon.'

'I'm sorry. But I didn't want to use your work. It wasn't fair.'

'It's never bothered you before. So it's because we're fighting?'

'That's part of it.'

'But you had a legitimate reason. Last night and everything. You do things at the last minute. It's the way you work, so you didn't have a chance. If you'd just explained that to Miss Matthews, she mightn't have been too rapt, but it's understandable. You didn't need to shoot yourself in the bloody foot.'

'I wasn't going to do my work last night, because I'd already done it. And I didn't need you taking over, trying to save the day.'

'I must need glasses because it really looked like you needed some kind of help.'

'You didn't even ask me.'

'Pardon me for wanting to pass my work requirement. You don't have a brilliant track record, Joe. You have a bit of a tendency to do bugger all.'

It was true. And until recently, Joe had always been OK with it. If anything, it was somehow kind of comforting to know exactly where he fitted in the scheme of things. It was good to have a role – be it slack-arse or other. But lately he was finding that there was a problem with roles. You played one long enough, like Arnie or Jackie Chan, and you were typecast. And convincing people and yourself that you could be something else became a difficult task.

'I know. But I had done this pissy assignment. Do you think I have so little pride that I wouldn't talk to you, but I'd still assume that you'd do my work for me?'

Lawrence looked at Joe seriously. 'I don't know.'

'Great.'

'Joe, I can't believe what's going on. I don't get why you and I aren't mates any more. It doesn't make sense. I'm not saying this is going to happen, but what if I did break up with Claudia? Would we be able to get back to normal? I mean, do you hate my guts?'

'No.' Joe picked up his books. 'It's not even about that any more, Lawrence.'

'What do you mean? What else can it be about? Is this about what you said the other day about me not expecting stuff from you?'

'Maybe. I don't know. I have to go.'

'Well done on the whole saving-that-guy's-fingers thing,' Grace said, as she sidled up to Joe at lunchtime.

'Thanks. Just another day at the office really.'

'Are you OK, Joe?'

'Yeah.'

'What you did in Art was pretty interesting.'

'I s'pose it was.'

'I'm not sure why you did it, though. It was only like a quarter of a work requirement. What's with the sudden attack of conscience?'

'Hey, you've benefited very nicely from the aforementioned attack, missy.'

Grace smiled. 'I'm not complaining. I just don't get it.'

'I don't know how to explain. I mean, you have someone bail you out enough times, and you become Robert Downey Jnr. I'm just sick of being a leopard, I suppose.'

'What? Fast?'

'I meant more the spots – not being able to change.'

'Pigeonholed?

'Yeah. I'm sick of being a pigeon.'

'You could always be one of those leopards that doesn't have spots. The black ones.'

'Maybe.' Joe was suddenly a bit confused by all these animal analogies.

'Are you coming to Ally's afterparty?'

'I don't know. She hasn't really mentioned it to me. I thought maybe she'd just want her friends there – which is fine, believe me.'

Grace looked annoyed. 'Tim was supposed to invite you. He said he'd done it. Ally really wants you there.'

'I'll come if you think it'd be OK. Has Tim said anything to you?'

'About what?'

'Me?'

'Oh. I think the birthday boy's mad at you for not coming the other night.'

'I told him I probably couldn't. Besides it's not like I had a great time myself. How much fun can you have with people who hail from the city of churches? Hang on. Birthday boy? Damn. I completely forgot.'

'Yep. You missed out on some top cake.'

'Hell. I didn't even get him anything. Could I get any crapper?'

'That does seem a tall order.'

'That means it was your birthday, too.'

'That's the way it's worked for the past eighteen years, yeah.'

'I'm sorry. Happy birthday. I'll get him something good. Is there anything he needs? Something he really wants.'

Grace sighed. 'How about the same thing you do, Joe.'

Joe nodded knowingly. 'You mean a CD rack, right?'

Scott's mum called that afternoon to say that everything was looking good. Joe went straight down to the hospital with Oliver, who was keen to make up for his embarrassing performance the previous night, despite Joe's assurance that it was forgotten and would not be spoken about outside the supermarket walls. Joe was surprised at how relieved he was to see Scott. He'd really needed to see for himself that Scott was all right.

'Can you drop me off at the school?' Joe asked Oliver on the way home. 'Deb practice.'

'So, is she hot?' This of course being the only rationale for Joe partnering yet another debutante.

'She's my friend's sister.'

'Not the one whose Dad's a cop?'

'Yeah.'

'Be careful, Joey.'

'It's not like that. I'm just doing her a favour.'

'I hope so, for your sake. Otherwise, a crashed car's the least of your worries.'

'Very helpful, Oliver.'

'Thank God you did crash your dad's car though.'

'That's my first thought every morning when I wake.'

'Seriously, you wouldn't be doing half as many mids if you hadn't. Then it just would have been me. You were a champion. How did you know all that stuff?'

'I don't know. We did first aid at school. It just stuck in my head. Plus it happened on *Medic Alert* once.'

'You could be a doctor, you know.'

'I think one doctor per family is plenty. Besides, I'm lacking a few vital ingredients. Wouldn't mind riding around in the ambulances though. Fast driving and all that.'

They pulled into the carpark of the school hall. 'Thanks for the ride. See you Friday?'

'Yeah.'

'And Joe –'

'What happens in the supermarket stays in the supermarket.'

'Ta. Let's hope bugger-all happens this time. Dance well, mate.' Even Oliver could pull off the 'mate'.

Joe headed inside for his second-last deb practice.

'I can't thank you enough, Joe,' Alice said for the 476th time.

Joe smiled. 'But you can thank me too much, Alice. And that could get annoying.'

'I'm doing it again?'

'Yeah, but you're welcome. I'm glad I can help.' He swung her around.

'Beautifully done, Joe.'

'Thanks, Mrs Hopkins.'

'So you really helped save that guy?'

'Just helped him, yeah.'

'Well, you're amazing. You're saving my life, too, Joe. I'm sorry. I know that I'm doing it again, but it's true. I would have had to show my children pictures of me and my brother. How could I be any sort of example to them after that?'

'Good point. Tim would scrub up all right in a tux, though.'

'He's got a phobia,' Alice confided. 'Finds them too restrictive.'

'A phobia?'

'He hyperventilated at my aunty's wedding. We had to cut the collar off his shirt. The hire place wasn't happy.'

Joe laughed.

'You're a much better dancer than Paul – my old partner.'

'Let's not diss the guy with glandular, Ally. It's not fair to compare an amateur to the likes of me.'

She laughed. 'Grace is jealous, though. She was going to ask you to do her deb with her.'

'Me? Grace is doing her deb?'

'No. When she was going to do it two years ago.'

'Oh, right.'

'Yeah. But you were already doing it with Charlotte. There were a lot of upset girls that year.'

He wasn't quite getting it. 'Why?'

'Apparently you were a lot of people's first choice, Joe.'

'Really?' But it was all in the past. He didn't want to go over old ground now. 'So, whose exactly?'

'Susie Crane's, Brooke Wendal's . . .'

'Girls who have talked to me a total of three times in my life.'

'I think word got out you were some kind of Fred Astaire. Grace didn't talk to Charlotte for weeks after that.'

'Really?'

'Yeah. Are you catching the bus home after?'

'Yeah.' It was weird getting a glimpse of how other people had seen him at one point in time. He'd been sought after and he hadn't even known it.

'Could I come with you?'

'I'd love to catch public transport with you, Al.'

'Thanks. Grace was going to meet me and go to a movie but she ditched me for a date.'

'So, who's the date with?' Joe asked, attempting to appear aloof.

'Are you OK, Joe? Why's your eye spasming?'

Obviously there was some work to be done in the aloof department.

'Some Harrison guy. He's pretty good-looking. Do you know him?' Alice asked.

'Yeah, we're acquainted.' Joe was annoyed for the rest of rehearsal. Only because Harrison was such an idiot and it was frustrating when people you liked chose to hang around with idiots, after you'd pointed out that they were idiots. Grace'd disregarded his good advice. That was what bothered him and nothing else. He didn't go poisoning people against others merely for his own health.

'And ladies curtsy,' Mrs Hopkins said. 'Nicely done. Time for a break. Another round of applause for Joseph, my new talent.'

Joe smiled. 'Dear God, don't let ballroom dancing be my only forte.'

But there was no doubting that he was good. And he was good because he'd made sure he was, motivated by a pathological fear of looking unco. For all three of his debs, he had practised and concentrated and listened for the altruistic purpose of getting girls to notice him. As he and Alice danced the waltz in the second half of practice, it occurred to Joe that dancing was the only thing he'd ever really tried hard at. He was beginning to wonder what might happen if he ever had reason enough to try hard at something else.

'Sounds like Scott's doing well?' Mrs King said as she and Joe sat down to dinner.

'Yeah. He looked good, considering.'

'Practice went all right?'

'Yeah, no worries. We're ready. And you don't have to

come, Mum. Third time and everything. Mrs Kelly will take lots of photos.'

'Too late, Sonia's already organised it. Should be a great night.'

'It will be that.'

'You must be so tired. No one gave you a hard time about being late to school, did they?'

'No. Woods was fine.'

'I should say so. And how was Lawrence?'

'He was fine, too. Although he does deplore tardiness as a rule.'

'Joe, you know what I mean. You and he are fighting?'

'You know?'

'Anthony said something.'

'Did he?'

'Yes, because of a girl at work, he said.'

'That's how it started.'

'And how did it end?'

'It hasn't.'

'I gathered that. Why, love?'

'I don't know.'

'Well, Anth seems to think –'

'Where does Anthony find the time to compile these inside scoops?'

As usual, Ed appeared by Joe's side, excited to see him. Joe turned to him, glad of the distraction. 'I might try walking him after.'

'He's really taken with you, isn't he?'

Joe patted Ed's silky ears. 'Mum, remember when I was

in grade six and Lawrence and I got in trouble for cheating during that fractions test?'

'Yes.'

'I was copying off him. He wasn't looking at mine.'

'And?'

'Well, that's it.'

'We knew that. I also remember when you took the test over, you got a better mark than him.'

'Did I?'

'Yes. Why are you thinking about this?'

'It just popped into my head.'

'Why?'

'He's going to be an architect, you know. He'll be good at it, too. And Anthony's going to be a doctor, Belinda's a successful IT person – or whatever it is she does in England. And I'll be the next Liberace.'

Mrs King looked confused. 'A flamboyant piano player?'

'Oh. I thought he danced. Fred Astaire then.'

'You could do worse. We all have our strengths.' She draped her arms around him. Suddenly Joe felt his eyes fill with tears. Maybe it was the lack of sleep and long day, the fight with Lawrence, the sight of blood still at the forefront of his mind. Or maybe it was one of those pure moments of desperation, where you forgot the rules and just got to be a boy with his mother again. A tear ran down his cheek. He managed to fight the next traitorous drops back. 'What are mine, Mum?'

Third time, as it turned out, was the charm when it came to debs. Of all the three that Joe had been involved in, tonight had been the best. He'd danced really well and got a buzz out of how excited Alice was. She'd looked very beautiful, and was definitely one of the less wedding-cake-ornament looking girls. Mrs King had forced them to pose for more photos than the official photographer.

'Mum, that's enough. We already did the pose around the lamppost out the front.'

'Maybe just one more coming down the stairs?'

'Why don't you pull out a saxophone and a wind machine? No. That's it. Come and dance.'

After he'd danced with his mother, Joe noticed Grace sitting at her table, raking her chocolate pudding with a fork.

'You could grow a crop on that baby,' he said, holding his hand out.

'What?'

'Let's hit the floor.'

'What?'

'Cut the rug, bust a move. Dance.'

'Oh, OK'. She gave him her hand and followed him onto the floor. 'It was so nice of you to do this for Ally.'

'It's no big deal.' Joe noticed Tim for the first time that evening. 'Hey, who's Tim dancing with?'

'That's Simone. She's my friend from ballet.'

'Tim's really got the moves there.'

'That's what Simone thought.'

'What?'

'Simone, as in, his girlfriend Simone.'

'What now?'

'Are you still trying to use that phrase? For the last time, there is no possible context in which "what now?" will ever be acceptable.'

'ATD, Gracie. Agree to disagree. So how long have they been going out?'

Grace twirled. 'He didn't tell you? About a month.'

'Right.'

'I'm sure he meant to tell you. You would have met her if you came to his birthday.'

'He's still pissed off with me for that. I don't think he liked the CD rack.'

'No, he did. Who wouldn't? The thing fits 200 CDs. That's impressive.' She smiled. '195 more and it's full up.'

'Yeah.'

Alice twirled past them with her father. Joe and Grace gave them a wave.

'So who did you end up doing yours with?'

'My what?'

'Deb.'

'Oh. I didn't,' Grace said.

'Why?'

'The only decent partner was already taken.'

Joe had to stop himself from running to the microphone and shouting, 'She means me. I'm the dancing King.'

Grace stared off into the distance.

'Are you OK?' Joe asked.

'Yeah. Fine.'

Joe offered her a raised eyebrow. 'And now the truth?'

'Actually, the other night wasn't . . .'

'Joe,' a girl's voice called.

He looked around. 'Claudia. What are you . . .'

'My little brother's partnering Tess, over there.'

Suddenly Joe realised that he was standing completely still with one hand on Grace's back and the other joined with hers. He broke apart from her, immediately wishing he hadn't had to. 'Sorry, this is Grace. My . . . friend . . . Tim's sister. Twin sister actually. Twelve minutes older. I did my deb with her sister, Alice.'

Claudia smiled. 'I saw. You were great.'

'Grace and I fundraise together and we're . . . friends too. This is a smart girl, right here.'

Grace looked bemused. 'You forgot to tell her the part about me being mute.' She reached over to shake Claudia's hand. 'Hi. I'm Grace. Nice to meet you.'

'You too.' Claudia smiled.

'Claudia and I work at Coles together – with Lawrence,' Joe said.

'So, haven't seen you around much, Joe.'

'I've been busy with school and – dancing and I've done some mids.'

'I heard about Scott. Well done.'

'Thanks.'

'Lawrence and I went to see him in hospital. He looked really good, all things considered.'

'Yeah.'

'It's great to see you. Maybe we can get together and see a movie or something.'

'Maybe.' Joe hoped she wouldn't push the point. Seeing a movie or something with Lawrence and Claudia would be a little bit weird. But at the same time, a part of him hoped she would.

'Soon then, OK?'

Joe waved her goodbye and turned to Grace. 'It's all things considered, isn't it? I can't tell you how much that's always annoyed me.'

'You are a very highly strung individual, Joe. So did you two go out?' Grace asked as they watched Claudia and her family leave.

'No.'

'She seems nice.'

'Everyone seems nice when you hear them speak a total of six sentences.'

'She's not nice?'

'No. She's nice.'

'And that's a problem because?'

'It's not. Do you want to dance again?'

'No.' Grace looked thoughtful, as if she wanted to say something important. 'I'll see you back at our place?'

'Yeah.'

Joe's parents dropped him off at Tim's house for Alice's version of her deb afterparty. Mr and Mrs King always found it comforting to entrust the care of their youngest into the hands of Mr Kelly, a police officer.

'Bye darling. Have fun,' Mrs King said as he stepped out of the family Pajero.

Mr King was busy being excited at the prospect of going on to his friend's fiftieth birthday party. 'You'll probably beat us home, mate. You know what the Mitchells are like – any excuse to tie one on,' Mr King called as Joe headed up the front steps.

Joe felt himself actually flinch. Just when he thought that he'd grossly overexaggerated his father's foibles, he went and used a phrase like 'tying one on'. Mr King had learned the phrase on a Greyhound bus tour of San Francisco some twenty years ago, and was still clearly unable to surrender the idea that using it made him cool, despite his wife and children's numerous attempts to convince him otherwise.

Joe mustered up a less than inspiring attempt at a goodbye wave and rang the novelty Hawthorn Football Club doorbell that clearly set the tone for the evening. But, beggars, as the saying went . . . Joe was currently in no position to pick and choose his weekend occasions, particularly given that there were no other invitations forthcoming. That was the problem with breaking up with friends.

Tim opened the door. 'Oh, it's you, Joe.'

'Looks like it, yeah. Are you going to invite me in?'

'That's right. You have to invite vampires in, don't you?'

'Well, technically I have been in your house a number of times before, so I could walk right in . . . hang on. I'm not a vampire.'

'Righto, come in.'

Upon greeting his host and surveying the room predominantly crowded with relatives, Joe finally understood the meaning of a term that he had grappled with during his year eleven politics class. So this was what they called a non-party. Mr Kelly's next nine words then confirmed it beyond any doubt.

'Joe,' he said, leading him through to the living room. 'Come and take a swing at the piñata.'

Before Joe had time to protest, Mr Kelly had handed him a stick and fitted him with a tea towel blindfold.

Mr Kelly spun him round three times. 'OK, Joe, swing,' he said.

'Actually I don't think I . . .'

'First swing,' Mr Kelly called, operating Joe's arms for him in a puppeteer fashion.

On his first assisted swing at the piñata Joe managed to knock the papier-mâché tail off the poorly defined creature, much to the delight of the crowd of onlookers. This was to be his most successful attempt at releasing the candy, as on his second go, he only succeeded in making a clearly discernible swooshing sound, hitting nothing but air, though rather forcefully. It was his third and final attempt, however, that ensured he had the attention of every one of Tim's relatives and friends for the remainder of the evening.

'Oh, Jesus. Jesus, I'm so sorry,' Joe said, quickly offering Tim's uncle his blindfold to soak up the blood spurting from his nose.

Mrs Kelly shot Joe a look that suggested employing the use of blasphemy was not doing much for his cause. Tim's uncle, on the other hand, seized the opportunity to make a questionable Messiah joke.

'I don't know why you're apologising to Jesus. His nose isn't broken,' he said through the blood. 'Which nephew are you? Anne's boy?'

'No, I'm Joe. Alice's deb partner. I'm really sorry, Mr Kelly.'

'Oh, the dancing boy. It's fine – really.'

'Are you still bleeding? Because you should put your head forward, not back. And you should probably get some ice for the swelling.'

'Thanks, mate.'

Joe handed back the stick and got out of the living room as fast as possible. He came across Alice sitting with a group of people from the deb, playing a PlayStation game. 'Ally,' he said with relief, 'do you know where Tim or Grace are?'

'Joe, these guys know how to get onto level six. They're geniuses or is it genii? I never know.'

'And the whereabouts of your siblings?'

'Grace is around. She was outside before. Tim's over there.'

Joe looked over at Tim sitting in the corner of his lounge room talking to Simone. They were talking quietly and looking deeply into each other's eyes. The idea that Tim had things together more than Joe did was disturbing, to say the least. Part of the reason that Joe had taken Tim on, as a plumber took on an apprentice, was so that he could feel extremely cool by comparison. But Tim had gone and broken the unspoken contract.

The reason that Joe didn't know anything about Tim, including his birthday and the existence of Simone, was that he'd only ever had a handful of conversations with Tim that didn't include the words 'What do we have next?', 'What was the homework?' or 'Can I borrow a pen/pencil/paper/dollar/shoe?' (the last, in fairness, occurring only on one particular PE day). And for the first time in several months, it bothered him.

He walked over and perched on the arm of the couch. 'Tim, can I talk to you for a minute?'

'Now?'

'Yeah, if that's all right.'

Simone nodded.

Tim got up and motioned for Joe to head into the laundry. 'What's the problem?'

Joe pushed the door closed behind them. 'I wanted to say sorry about your birthday.'

'You already did.'

'Yeah, but I'm sensing you're still annoyed. I never would have missed it if I'd known. I mean, you shouldn't have had to, but if you'd said something I would have been there. You've been a really good mate lately.'

'What about your interstate relatives?'

'What? Well, I could have worked something out with Mum.'

Tim lost interest in Joe's continued lie. 'OK. We're good. Whatever.'

Where had Joe heard that before? 'Because I know birthdays are important. I get that.' Joe sensed that he needed to change his tack. 'All right, honestly, I didn't have any relatives coming. I was just feeling a bit shit and thought I'd be lousy company. But if . . .'

'I get it. You would have come if I'd done the right thing and informed you about the anniversary of my birth. It's all my fault really.'

'That's not what I mean.'

'It is, you know.' Tim pushed the fabric softener aside and sat on the washing machine. 'I don't give a crap that it was my birthday. My problem is you couldn't just come over and watch a DVD with me. There is only one day of the year where you feel that would be warranted.'

'That's not true.'

'Yeah, but it's not untrue either. This isn't a one-off. You never hang out with just me. I don't want you to come over because it's a special occasion, or because you think you owe me for my loyalty, or because you've got no better offers. I want you to come because you want to, even if you feel lousy. I want you to come *because* you feel lousy.'

'I'm sorry. I've been so caught up with trying to work out what I'm doing next year and everything with Lawrence, I've pretty much stuffed this year.'

'Yeah. Well keep this in mind while you're deciding your life's path: the world's got enough arseholes.'

'OK.'

'And you should know I've been talking to Lawrence and Brad again. Hanging out with you seemed like the right thing to do for a while, but the whole thing doesn't make sense to me any more. I'm sick of the stupid grudge.'

'Fair enough.'

He smiled. 'And I will have a gun when I'm a cop.' Tim jumped down from the washing machine. 'I know I just turned eighteen, not eight, but Joe, you really hurt my feelings.' He left, rejoining Simone.

Joe sat on a pile of ironing for a moment, deep in thought and washing-powder fumes. He knew what Grace had meant now, about what Tim had really wanted. The same thing he wanted himself: to not feel alone.

He headed out to the kitchen in search of solace.

'Are you Anne's boy?' A jolly red-faced man asked.

'No, I'm Alice's deb partner.'

'Oh, the dancer.'

'Yeah, that's right.'

He should have cut his losses and left right then. At least that way things couldn't have got any worse. But sometimes things needed to get worse before they could get better.

Joe seized the first available opportunity to subtly swipe an alcoholic-looking bottle and headed out to the darkness and solitude of the garage. He was just about to take his first swig when he heard a rustling sound coming from the vicinity of the workbench. It looked like the rats wanted a piece of the action.

'Nice drop, the Clayton's. I would have gone for the Moët myself,' a girl's voice said.

Joe looked at the label of the bottle he was cradling. True to form, he had swiped non-alcoholic wine.

'Here,' the girl said, handing him her bottle.

Joe fumbled around until he found the light switch. 'Grace?'

'Yeah.'

'Urgh. What is this?' Joe asked, mid-sip.

'Spumante.'

'Appropriately named.'

'You've changed out of the suit. Nice shirt.'

'Thanks. My grandmother gave it to me.'

'Is she visually impaired?'

'Very funny. What are you doing out here? Don't you have a room – like inside?'

'Yeah, less chance of being discovered out here.'

'And so much more ambience, too.'

'Exactly. So what are you doing out here then, Joe?'

'Your brother's in there. He's angry.'

'He's not really.'

'No, not "Hulk" angry but still angry. And he's right. But I didn't think he minded.'

'Minded what?'

'All of it. The bagging we give him at school, me cancelling on him all the time . . .'

'Why did you think he wouldn't mind that?'

Joe smiled. 'Because I wanted him not to. It was sort of easier that way.'

'He doesn't mind a joke. But no one wants to be the joke all the time.'

'I don't think he's a joke. Jokes don't get girlfriends as good-looking as his.'

'I know. Simone's beautiful.'

They sat in silence for a few moments, while a couple of party-goers got some soft drink from the fridge.

'What about you, Joe? Why's there no special lady in your life?' Grace asked, once the coast was clear.

'I have my mum. Besides, no time.'

'Is that right?'

'Yes. How's Harrison?'

'He moved onto Calista. I s'pose I wasn't glamorous enough.'

'Thus, the basis of your being out here. Any guy that re-pierces his ear at the age of fifty is a tool.'

'Harrison's not fifty and he doesn't have a pierced ear.'

'Harrison Lehmann, Harrison Ford. Any guy that's called Harrison is a tool.'

'Thanks.'

'Tool doesn't even cut it for Lehmann. He's a toolbox, a toolbar. The king of tools. Whereas I myself am the tool of Kings. Important distinction.'

'I appreciate the sentiment, Joe.'

'But he was *your* tool, right?'

'For five glorious dates.'

After they had emptied the contents of the bottle of Spumante, Grace retrieved another from her seemingly endless stash. 'Leftovers from the family Christmas party.'

'I might just have a Coke anyway, if you've got one,' Joe said, suddenly feeling a little light-headed.

'Here you go.' Grace tossed him a Pepsi. 'Same thing.'

Any chance that they'd had of initiating a lasting friendship was now lost. Everyone knew that Coke was by far the superior cola beverage, except of course, those who liked Pepsi better.

'I'm not usually in the habit of getting "pickled", as my father would say, at family occasions. I'm just a bit – stupid at the moment.'

'My father calls it "getting on the sauce". And I'm a bit stupid all the time, if it helps.'

Grace laughed. 'It sucks that there isn't some test you can do to see if someone's right for you. You could save yourself so much time and energy.'

'Ah, but it's all part of the journey, Grace.'

'A significantly longer journey since I failed my licence yesterday.'

'Oh. Sorry. Was it the parallel park?'

'No, it was more the near-miss with the pedestrian.'

'I have heard they're fussy like that.'

'Yeah. Do you know what I'm a big fan of? The whole avoiding humiliation thing.'

'Yeah, I'm a great fan of it myself.'

They sat in silence for a few moments then Grace said, 'It's kind of worse that Harrison's a tool. Why do I like a tool?'

'We could call him a turd if you like? Or a dickweed? Turd-burger – that's cutting.'

'I could never like a turd-burger.'

Joe pulled out a stash of lollies from his pocket. 'Do you like milk bottles?'

'Does anyone?' Grace opted for a couple of strawberries and creams.

'You know Harrison's glasses?'

'I loved his glasses,' she sighed.

'They're not prescription. The lenses are actual glass – you can see right through those babies. He wears them for street cred. Or to draw attention from his enormous forehead.'

'He does have a big forehead.'

A chorus of cheers erupted from the house, Joe surmising that the piñata had finally been conquered. 'I sort of know how you feel. I told a girl that I loved her last year. She had kind of a big forehead.'

'What did she say?'

'She laughed.'

'No?'

'Well, she thought I was joking.'

'Why would she think that?'

'I don't know. I do joke a fair bit.'

'I have noticed. So what happened? Are you still friends?'

'It was complicated. She's going out with Lawrence now.'

'Claudia. Hence the fight. Tim kind of told me.'

'I like to call it a feud.'

'And that's why you joined STC?'

'Not the only reason.'

'Of course. My brother being the other one.'

'Sort of.' Joe cringed, recalling his selfishness. 'Claudia thought the only reason I liked her was because I didn't know any other girls.'

'Harsh.'

'Maybe she was right. School aside, I don't really know any other girls our age, apart from a couple at work. But one of them is my brother's girlfriend and the other's unbelievably beautiful, like a veela.'

'Well, you know me, and I haven't even met your brother and I'm not a veela – I don't think.'

'Do you want to go out with me then?'

'No.

'Thanks.'

'God, I hate that I'm this person right now. Depressed over a boy. That's so unattractive. I hate girls who wallow. What's the point?'

'The wallowing. That's the exact point. I actually wallow spectacularly. So what reason did you get?'

'Reason?'

'From Harrison?'

'He just didn't think of me that way.'

'He didn't find you attractive?'

'I don't know. Probably not.'

'You are. You're really pretty. You could be a veela.'

'Yeah, thanks.'

'I just meant . . . in case you were thinking . . .'

'That I should wear a bag over my head?'

'No.'

'Why? Because of one idiot boy? And let's face it, he is an idiot because he passed me up.'

'Of course. But didn't you think maybe there was something . . . wrong with you? Even for a little while?'

'That sounds like wallowing to me, Joe. Do you not think you're attractive?'

'Well . . . I don't know.'

'Because of Claudia? You believe far too much of what other people say.'

'You are wallowing a bit though, aren't you?'

'A bit, yeah.'

'I reckon he was probably scared of you – Harrison, I mean.'

'Scared?'

'Yeah. I've seen you in class. You've got friends, lots of friends. But you can take or leave them. Harrison would want one of those needy chicks . . . girls to hang off him.'

'Needy's the go then?'

'Not for people with taste.'

Grace smiled. 'You're a good-looking guy. Once you grow out of your grungy high-school boy phase, you'll have a lot of potential.'

'Did you know potential is one word away from pot-hole in the dictionary.'

'And?'

'Don't you think that's symbolic or something? Just one word apart. If you were assigned one of the two to symbolise your life – I'd get pothole. What would you get?'

'Whatever I want. I'm not having only one word. I'm more than one thing. What about potentilla?'

'That's your word?'

'No. It's a plant. It comes after potential and before pothole.'

'Not in my dictionary.'

'Then you need to change dictionaries, Joe.'

'Maybe.'

Grace stretched her legs out, a mischievous smile spreading across her face. 'OK, if your life's such a pothole, how many girls have you kissed – despite your taste in fashion?'

'What? I don't know.'

'You don't know as in you've lost count, or you don't know as in you do know but you don't want me to know?'

'What was the first one again?'

'How many?'

'Kissing girls is a measure of success, is it?'

'Well?'

'Three.'

'There you go. Three's a lot, for your age.'

'Not when you hear the context.'

'There can be context for a kiss?'

'For mine, yeah. Kylie Watson kissed me because she didn't have her contacts in and thought I was Ben Oakes. Then there was Sarah O'Connor – a great kiss, which was slightly spoilt when I found out Lawrence had dared her to do it. And then . . . there was Celeste Green, who right before our lips met said, "You'll do".'

'Really?'

'Yes. I probably shouldn't have gone out with her for six weeks.'

'You're very funny, Joseph King.'

'I think that's the problem. Claudia chose Lawrence because I'm not going anywhere and he is.'

'Where's he going?'

'He's going to be an architect. They both are.'

'You don't think that maybe she chose him because they've got more in common.'

'Maybe.'

'I think it's as unsatisfyingly simple and clichéd as sometimes it's just not meant to be.'

'Yeah. So are you going somewhere, Grace?'

'Shit, who knows? I hope so. I want to get into the college of the arts next year – if that's going somewhere.'

He loved the way she swore. She didn't flinch at all, like he did, looking around to see if his mother had the soap and water on standby.

'What's your art of choice?'

'Ballet.'

'Seriously? Like Billy Elliot?'

'Like Dame Margot Fontaine. I want to float and – what was it? Soar like an eagle?'

'I think it was a falcon actually. You got my English piece.'

'And you got mine, hence the no reply.'

'I kind of lost it. Sorry.'

'Doesn't matter.'

'So you'd have to rehearse all the time – to dance?'

'Every day.'

'How do you know when you're doing enough? Doing what you're supposed to do?'

'It's a feeling, I think. You just know how much you have to do to be as good as you can be.'

'But even then, there might be someone better, right?'

'There'll always be someone better. That keeps me going.'

Joe played with the rim of his can. 'This sounds ridiculous but – I didn't know I was supposed to have a plan.

Lawrence and Brad were going along fine, so I thought I was too. Tim had his plan in utero, so he never really counted. So now I'm out on my own and I'm going to be left behind.'

'You're in charge of your reality. Which is only limited by your perception.'

Sometimes Grace's insight sent a shiver up Joe's spine, giving him what he'd once heard a Mexican exchange student refer to as chicken skin.

'Who said that, Freud?'

'Dr Phil.'

'Well, reality. That's a big job. I like the little jobs. I wouldn't hire me.'

'Are you really not friends with Lawrence because he went out with a girl you liked?'

'Like that's not enough? Betrayal, Grace. There's a reason it's a theme of plays and literature the world over.'

'So, not convenient excuse?'

'You're crazy, lady.'

'OK. My mistake.'

'I just felt so embarrassed when she rejected me, like such a loser. Why is it you never remember the good moments of your life in half as much detail as the worst moments?'

'Well, about 0.0001 percent of the world's population can draw from those harrowing moments and make very successful livings as actors and musicians. But the rest of us are stuffed.'

'I'd gone and told Lawrence all about it, and then

they'd probably spoken about it. So I was . . . once, twice . . . three times a loser. And when I saw them together, they were all "we didn't know how to tell you, Joe . . . we didn't mean for it to happen". And I hadn't even seen it coming. Loser.'

'You might feel like you lose sometimes, but no one loses and never wins again.'

He nodded as he took a sip of his drink. 'What about politicians?'

'Politicians?'

'When a leader of a party stands for election and loses, they don't get to stay the leader. They get ushered out a back door like an Olympic drug cheat and you never hear about them again until they get caught for drink driving.'

'OK, so maybe politicians lose. But that's probably karma anyway. No one wins all the time, either.'

'What about Harry Potter? He always wins. He worries and has to work hard and fight evil, but he wins all the time – in the end.'

'Hang on. He doesn't have parents.'

'Exactly.'

'Come on, who else then?'

'Lawrence Barry. He wins,' Joe said, after a few minutes.

'Lawrence?'

'I get a bike for Christmas – he gets a better one. I get a mongrel dog – he gets a pedigree from a breeder. I get a computer game – he gets a computer. We go to Rosebud on holidays – he goes to Queensland. My voice breaks – he grows facial hair. My dog dies – his lives for another two years.'

'I don't think that he had anything to do with those last two.'

'No? I'm not so . . . Grace, is the room spinning? Can you see that?'

'No, two-sip screamer. It's just you.' She clapped her hands with sudden excitement. 'Ooh. I've got one. You get Tim and me, he gets Claudia. I didn't know you had this rivalry with Lawrence.'

'It's always been there, sort of lurking, but I knew it was petty. I know that it's petty.'

'But now you're – embracing the pettiness?'

'I don't know. I know it's irrational. I'm wrong, but then, that makes him right, doesn't it? I lose again.'

'Joe, you're not a loser. You're only a loser if you think you are. And if you think you are – then you *are* a loser.'

'But why am I never the one that gets chosen? I'm always holding my breath, biding my time till I stuff up somehow.'

'That self-confidence is so attractive.'

'I'm just sick of feeling like the little brother. With Anthony, with Lawrence, Mum and Dad. Claudia even said I was like her little brother.'

Grace was temporarily outraged. 'That's just cruel. She didn't have to say that.'

'I'm the eternal quirky sidekick. Did you ever watch *Buffy*?'

'Yeah. I loved it.'

'There was this episode towards the end where Xander was talking to Dawn about how hard it was to be the only group members without special powers. He just had to hang around, trying to be useful in some other way, like providing the doughnuts. That's what I feel like. I'm Xander. There to hold Lawrence up. To be . . .'

'The wind beneath his wings?'

Joe laughed. 'Yeah. And it is cold there in his shadow, never having sunlight on my face.' He began tearing a Mintie wrapper he'd found in his pocket into a long strip.

'I saw that episode.' Grace said after a few minutes. 'Dawn told Xander that seeing was his power.'

'Yeah, not kick-arse karate moves, not witchcraft – not even x-ray vision. Just being able to see.'

'It's a good talent – like being able to tear Mintie wrappers.'

'Will it make me employable?'

'The Minties – no. The seeing – definitely.'

'What if I never find what I want to do and I just piss my life away? I could do something that I think I want to do and it could turn out not to be what I want. My dad did that and he's in the same job twenty-five years later.'

'So you do something else.'

'Why didn't he?'

'I don't know. But I do know you're not him. If I was my mother I'd have jumped off a cliff by now. She's nuts.'

Joe smiled, realising he hadn't enjoyed talking to some-one this much in a while. He felt comfortable but nervous at the same time. He didn't quite understand it.

'It's like *The Great Gatsby*. Jay Gatz never got what he wanted or wanted what he got or even wanted what he wanted really. And it turns out he wasn't so great. It terrifies me that my dad was once my age with hopes and ambitions. It's easier to believe he was always unhappy and middle-aged.'

'Gatsby turns out to be a shonky liar who had an obsession and affair with a married woman. Correct?'

'That's right.'

'And in the end he kills someone and gets killed himself?'

'Yeah.'

'Well, just don't do that and you'll be fine, Joe.'

'Good tip.'

'And don't call people "old sport" either. That annoyed the hell out of me.'

He laughed, adjusting the roll of carpet underlay he was sitting on.

'Move over,' Grace said, sitting next to him. 'You're going to be all right as soon as you stop deciding you're not going to be.'

'You really think so?'

'Yeah, and those sidekick characters are the reason I watched *Buffy*. Buffy herself – not so interesting.'

'Her leather pants were pretty interesting.'

Grace leaned in close, resting her head on his shoulder. 'Xander was my favourite character.'

'Really?'

She nodded, looking up at him. A shaft of light lit her face. She had never looked more beautiful to Joe, despite her slightly blurry appearance. He'd been here before. That second in which he had to decide whether to seize the moment. He decided not to think about it. He leant in towards Grace. She edged towards him. Their eyes met briefly and she smiled. So he kissed her – not on the nose, but directly on the lips – for what seemed like forever. At that moment thoughts were racing through his head, not least of which was that he had a sneaking suspicion he was something of a kissing genius.

'Well,' Grace said when they finally moved apart.

'Well good or well bad?'

Grace leant in and kissed Joe again, easing him back so they were both lying on the musty carpet underlay.

'What the bloody hell's going on here?' Tim asked, switching on the lights. 'Joe?'

'Ah . . . I . . . We . . .'

'Grace?'

Joe looked over at Grace pleadingly. It was up to her now to choose the most appropriate words to quell her brother's fears. She was nothing if not articulate.

Grace sat up, brushing some cobwebs off herself and looked Tim right in the eye. 'What now?

13

'Tim, hi,' Joe said hurriedly. 'And Simone. Hello, Simone.'

Tim shot Joe a look. Joe couldn't decide if it was quizzical or murderous.

'Hello again, Joe,' Simone said.

'Sorry to disturb you, I just wanted to see if Joe was staying tonight or going home,' Tim said, resting his hand awkwardly on a rake. 'But I see you've already taken care of the arrangements yourself.'

'What? Oh, no. We weren't doing anything,' Joe said.

'No, Tim, it's just like in that old song. What is it? You know, Joe . . . that old song with those two people and the mix-up . . .' Grace struggled.

'*Lola*?' Joe suggested, getting to his feet.

'No. Not *Lola*,' Grace didn't appreciate the suggestion that she was really a man. 'Help me up.'

Before he knew it, Joe had tripped on his Clayton's bottle and was right back on the underlay. Grace burst into hysterical laughter and Joe followed suit, causing the clearly identifiable pub-like smell to waft over to Tim and Simone.

'Have you two been drinking?' Tim asked.

Grace grew intensely serious for a moment. 'Well, Tim the thing is – yes.'

She let out a huge laugh. 'Just a little bit.'

'First I catch you doing . . . whatever you were doing and now this. Why? I mean, half the family's here for God's sake,' Tim said.

'Think you just answered your own question there, Timmy,' Joe added.

'Come on, Tim. I'm eighteen,' Grace said.

'Yeah. And I've only got a couple of months to go. You're always telling me to be more organised. The one time I do something a bit early, you're angry. You're sending me some very mixed signals, buddy,' Joe said, sending himself and Grace off again.

'*Wake Up Little Susie*. That's the song. They've fallen asleep and lost track of time. This is just like that,' Grace said proudly.

'Except we weren't asleep, were we?' Joe said.

Tim pursed his lips the way he did when Joe sent him notes during class. 'Joe, how are you getting home?'

'You can use my mobile,' Simone offered.

Joe's laughter ceased. His parents could not see him like this. He was one step away from singing *Khe Sahn* and vowing to strangers that he loved them.

'I s'pose I could put you on my floor,' Tim said reluctantly.

Joe stumbled over and slapped Tim on the back. 'You, my friend, are a champion.'

And so he was. Tim told Joe to leave a message at home letting his parents know that he was staying over and set Joe up in the spare room.

'Are you sure that aiding a law-breaking minor won't affect your police academy application, Tim?'

'I think it'll be OK. If Mum asks you in the morning, tell her you and Grace had some bad shellfish. In fact, tell *me* you had some bad shellfish – tell me something to explain tonight.'

'I don't know what to tell you.'

'I told Al that she shouldn't invite you. I knew it was a bad idea.'

'Why? Because I didn't come to your party?'

'Because I didn't think you'd enjoy yourself. I thought you'd think it was daggy, not really your style.'

'My style? Sure it was.'

'There was a piñata.'

'Yes, there was. But you're wrong about me.'

'Yeah, I should've known you'd make your own fun – what with hitting my uncle and swiping my dad's wine . . .'

'That first one wasn't my fault . . .'

'OK, involuntarily punching my uncle, but let's not forget the part where you got intoxicated with my sister . . .'

Joe winced. 'Can you please stop saying that word?'

'See. Not your style.'

'I don't even have a style.'

'Well, you should, Joe.'

'What's your style then? Deceit?'

'What?'

'You didn't tell me about Simone.'

'I'm sorry. I didn't want you to think I was rubbing your nose in it or anything.'

Joe smiled. 'I don't deserve a friend like you.'

'I know.'

'But you can talk about it, about her. It's fine. I'm happy for you.'

'So nothing happened between you and my sister? Really?' Tim said, handing Joe a vomit bucket. 'Just in case.'

'Thanks, but I don't think I'll need it. Would you hurt me if I told you that our lips met for several moments, and it wasn't strictly necessary for the preservation of life?'

'What?'

'We kissed.'

'I spotted that. Don't be worried about me,' Tim said.

'Thanks.'

'I'd be more worried about my dad.'

'You're not going to tell him, are you?'

'Are you mad? God, alcohol obviously kills more brain cells than we know. No. I won't say anything. This will die with the three of us – and Simone. Or Dad will find out and you'll die.'

'Very comforting.'

'You don't want to be going there, Joe. You're friends, we're friends – don't ruin everything. My sister's a nice girl.'

'I know. And I'm a nice guy.'

Tim's face grew serious. 'No, Joe. You're a top guy, when you want to be. But she's my sister and she's also very intense. She doesn't do things half-arsed. Don't start something you can't keep going.'

'Yeah. OK.'

'Goodnight.'

'Night.'

'Make sure you keep the bucket beside your bed.'

Joe lay there, wishing that what Tim had said was true. Maybe there had been a time when he had been a top person, but he hadn't been lately. And he wasn't sure whether it was a good or bad thing that Tim had seemed to overlook most of his jerky behaviour. Maybe that was what friends did. Embraced the good and forgave each other's faults. He hoped that Grace would be able to forgive him though, assuming there was something to be forgiven.

Joe's mind was buzzing. He started thinking about his Coles theory again. Grace was in another league of shopper altogether, he decided. She was the practical shopper, the kind of person who would work from a list like Tim, but rarely stray. She would shop on a full stomach so as not to fall prey to immediate cravings, and she would never be influenced by the manipulations of advertising. She was the informed shopper with a social conscience, the kind who bought the generic brand or items with ticks and Australian flags and declarations of friendliness to animals. She was the near-extinct breed of customer who obeyed the request of the sticker at the register, arranging her groceries into apartheid-like groups so that no deli items mingled with cleaning products or pet food.

And she would definitely be an exact change giver, rifling around in her purse until she found that twenty-five cents. This was the ultimate gesture of thoughtfulness. After he finished applying his theory to Grace, he tried to work out what sort of shopper Claudia would be, but after a few moment's deliberation, he couldn't quite place her. He really had no idea who she was, which made him realise that he wasn't actually annoyed with Lawrence any more for taking a girl he never had away from him. He was angry with himself because he was to blame for the whole mess. Joe wasn't Lawrence and never would be. And maybe it was the alcohol talking, but right now he felt all right about that.

Later the next day, Joe plonked himself in front of the television at home, ready for it to work its magic. He was relieved that he'd been able to avoid Tim's parents in the morning. Getting through breakfast without seeing Grace or kissing any more of Tim's relatives had been a huge plus. He'd sort of wanted to see Grace and attempt to redeem himself. But really his basis for seeking redemption was only because he wanted it, not because he necessarily deserved it. Then again, maybe redemption wasn't required if Grace actually liked him and he liked her. He did like her. And Grace was too good to be on the market for long. Not all boys were as stupid as Harrison Lehmann. It was only a matter of time before someone else snapped her up. He didn't like the thought of that. But short of a written declaration of Grace's ardent admiration for him, Joe felt he could not act. Rejection was such an acquired taste.

Mrs King sat down beside Joe, armed with a photo album full of pictures of him as a kid. She flipped it open and started pointing and smiling.

'Lawrence. Look at him. He was a beautiful little boy, wasn't he?'

'Adorable.'

'Chris's party. How old would he have been there?'

Joe looked at the cake in the picture, with its big red eight. 'No idea.'

'I remember those cord overalls, with their little pocket. Denise made those, you know. She made you navy ones. They're probably in here somewhere too.'

Joe looked back at the photo his mum was describing, careful to not appear too interested. 'Lawrence has got something in his pocket,' he said. 'What is it?'

She studied the photo more closely. 'I can't see.'

'Yeah, I see it. There's some sort of handle, and a pointy end . . . it's the knife he put in my back ten years later. How about that, Mum?'

She pushed him away. 'You just watch your show and keep your comments to yourself.' After a few more minutes, his mum closed the album and placed it on the coffee table in front of Joe. 'I'd better finish getting your dinner.'

I am not going to let her scheming work, Joe thought as he watched the last five minutes of *The Price is Right*. He thought it again as he turned the *M*A*S*H* repeat off, and he was still thinking it as he opened the album and began looking through.

There was one photo in particular that he hated. He was nine years old and he was wearing a pair of awful grey cord pants that had belonged to his brother, because his green school ones had been in the wash. He still vividly recalled the day the picture had been taken. They'd had a parade for 'book week' and there had been dancing and no work all day. Joe had got right into it, with Lawrence by his side. But midway through shaking his tail feather, the cords had given out and split right down the back. Lawrence had wrapped his jumper around Joe's waist, but half the class had seen, and had reacted in accordance with the instinctual rules of slapstick, laughing their heads off. That was where it had begun.

'How are you? That's good. How's work?' Joe heard his father in the den, obviously on the phone to Belinda. 'Any news?' Seconds later Mr King called out to his wife and dropped the phone like a hot potato.

'Your sister's on the phone,' Mr King said, sinking into his recliner beside Joe. 'Mum's chatting to her. Thought I'd better keep it short so she can save her pounds.'

'Yeah.' It occurred to Joe that he hadn't actually heard the phone ring. 'You called her, didn't you?'

'Sorry?'

'You called Belinda, so she doesn't save any money.'

Mr King shifted uneasily in his chair. 'Yes, so I did. I forgot about that.' He looked out at Jen as she giggled into the receiver. 'I don't like to keep her too long. Your mother always has so much to say.'

Joe smiled. 'Yeah.'

He was hit with a sudden uncomfortable feeling that extended to the pit of his stomach. It was the type of feeling that came from having information that you didn't want and didn't know what to do with. Like the time he had snooped until he'd found every one of his Christmas presents. He'd gone to his room afterwards and cried into his pillow because there was no recapturing the surprise come Christmas morning. He'd ruined the day and known that he'd only had himself to blame. He looked at his dad, wondering when exactly it had happened. When was the moment that his father had stopped knowing how to talk to his own daughter?

If his dad could just learn how to relax he wouldn't have been half as painful. He wasn't that bad as far as dads went. Unlike Brad's dad, he was there, so that went in his favour. And Joe knew that his father was a good person. But whenever they were close to having a good time, his dad always managed to botch it by being intense. When Joe and his siblings used to muck around as kids, his dad would sometimes come in, almost panicked by the noise, assuming that they were fighting. He'd feel compelled to add in a dad line about keeping it down and then the game would be over.

Joe pulled out a wad of twenty dollar notes from his pocket. 'Here's some money for the car, Dad.'

'Very good. I'll write it in the book later. *Seinfield* on yet, Joe?'

He had given up trying to correct his dad's pronunciation. He didn't even really hear it anymore. 'Yeah, in a couple of minutes.'

Joe had never seen his dad laugh as much as he did at nine o'clock every night, when they watched *Seinfeld* together. It was difficult to explain, but it made him feel good that his dad had connected with this show in the same way that he had.

Mr King laughed. 'That Kramer's out of control.'

'Yeah.'

14

Sometimes, Joe found, he uttered certain words so often in the course of his day that they became second nature to him. Words like 'How are you?/Did you want your potatoes in a bag?/Price check/Piss off, Brad/Cash out?/Ed's under the house' and 'Sorry I'm late, Mr Woods'.

'Four minutes. A personal best. What exactly kept you, Mr King?'

'I was performing an act of community service.'

'Is that right?'

'It was my neighbour, sir.'

'Go on.'

'We got chatting, as we do from time to time. She's an elderly lady, very affable, but I think quite lonely. Her children live a fair way away. Anyway, among other things, she asked me, in my capacity as a part-time supermarket employee, why it was that so often the pre-wash stain remover refills are more expensive than the package with the nozzle.'

'And?'

'I honestly couldn't say. Although, I'm sure you'll agree, it's madness, sir.'

'OK. Take a seat, Joe.'

'Seriously?'

'I could write a note home in your diary and I could give you a detention slip but that's all a bit predictable, isn't it? I correspond with your parents more than I do with my own. I think they're sick of hearing from me. I'm in a good mood. Put it down to mandarines being in season. Don't worry, it won't last. There's always tomorrow.'

'Hey, I heard you're not gay,' Brad said, as he passed Joe in the corridor before class.

'What?'

'Tim said you and Grace were hot and heavy the other night.'

'Hot and heavy? Who says that?'

'So, were you?'

'Piss off, Brad.'

'Oh, the gentleman never tells.'

'Hang on, you're basing me not being gay on the fact that I may have kissed Grace Kelly on Saturday night?'

'Well, yeah.'

'Information you got from Tim – which is at best hearsay.'

'Now I'm basing the gayness on you saying "hearsay".'

'Fair enough. But wouldn't the fact that you frequently refer to me in the feminine form mean that if I were to be attracted to a girl, that in itself would confirm, rather than disprove my homosexual status?'

'Hey?'

'You've undone your own argument, Brad. You're basically full of crap, aren't you?'

Brad cracked a smile. 'Footy practice. Bye.'

Joe surveyed the contents of his lunchbox. No chips again. Ever since Anthony had finished high school, his mother had stopped buying them every week. Chips had always been the one thing that he'd had to make his peers jealous. It was amazing, the envy a small packet of Twisties could generate from kids from less fortunate non-chip-buying families.

'Hi, Joe.'

'Grace. How's it going?'

'It's going great. You?'

'Fine.'

Brad ran back down the corridor, winking at Joe as he passed him.

'What's he on about?'

'He's been speaking to Tim. About, you know . . . the other night.'

'Oh. What's Tim been saying?'

'I don't know exactly. I'm sure it's nothing bad though.'

'It better not be if he values his life.'

Joe reached into his bag. 'Miss Elliot printed the news-letter for movie night. It looks great, doesn't it?'

Grace studied the newsletter. 'That's really good. There's a grammatical error, but that aside . . .'

'They're supposed to be going out tomorrow.'

'You've done well, Joe.'

'I've got the screen penned in. What do you think about the movies?'

'*Speed* and *About a Boy*. Good choices.'

'Thanks. I thought a comedy was the go. Keanu always makes me laugh.'

'So you're still doing the popcorn and drinks, too?'

'Yeah, based on previous candy-bar experience, I think we can raise a mother-lode just from that.'

'Probably.'

Joe looked around uneasily. 'I haven't said anything to anyone about . . . you know.'

'The other night,' she added.

'Yes. And I wanted to say I'm sorry if . . .'

'You don't have to be sorry, Joe. This doesn't have to be awkward. We're friends who went a bit stupid because we were . . .'

'All liquored up?'

'Exactly. It's no big deal really. We didn't do anything ridiculously stupid.'

'Yeah, we kissed a bit.'

'Quite a bit.'

'But it's not like we had a roll in the underlay or anything.'

'Right.' Grace smiled. 'So friends, Joe?'

He wanted to tell her how he felt. He wanted to tell her that he thought she was the best thing since toaster crumpets. That she was beautiful and witty and kind and made him feel like the best version of himself. But Brad was on his way back down the hall and he couldn't risk being interrupted during something this important. Plus, he was a great big wuss.

'Friends, Grace.'

Joe and Tim sat in the Kings' kitchen drinking one of Joe's specialty milkshakes. For some reason, milkshakes always tasted better right after school.

'It's not like I spill my sister's secrets all the time, Joe. You didn't hear the context.'

'What was the context then, Tim?'

'For one thing, let's not forget that I was defending you. I once took a bullet for you, man.'

'A paint bullet, but still a bullet. OK.'

'I was speaking to Brad and he made one of his usual comments about you being gay – I think it had something to do with your hair, which I can sort of see.'

Joe patted his hair. 'What about it?'

'I can't remember exactly. Something about gel.'

'The curls are unruly. But I barely even use any product.'

'He didn't go into detail. He just said you had the hair of a homosexual.'

'I've always had this hair. If I'd put streaks through it

or had it long like Beckham then maybe I could understand, but –'

'Your hair's fine.'

'Thank you. Sorry, go on. What did you say to him?'

'I said . . .' Tim paused for effect. 'Do gay people go around kissing girls?'

'They do actually.'

'What?'

'If they're gay women, they do.'

'That's a point. Luckily Brad didn't pick up on that. He's not a details man, is he?' Anyway, that's when I told him about Grace.'

'Right. Thanks, I think.'

'I just said you'd kissed. Grace is my sister, I wouldn't have said anything too . . .'

'I know. I appreciate it. You didn't have to say anything at all.'

'Well, it was Brad. I kind of had to disagree.'

'True.'

'Did I tell you he gave me a birthday present?'

'Brad?'

'Yes. I mean, it was food from the tuckshop bought with his counterfeit two dollar coins, but it was the thought that counted.'

'That's a heartwarming tale.'

'I saw him in the library during one of our studies today.'

'Not in the seminar room again?'

'Yeah.'

'In his continuing quest to be disgusting?'

Tim laughed. 'It started out that way, but now he's addicted to a German detective series.'

'Serious?'

'Yeah. The main character's a German Shepherd. He loves the shit.'

Joe made a mental note to commit the image to memory.

'Speaking of the library, are you going to start hiding there at lunchtime again?'

'What? I don't hide.'

'You said you were going to come with me today – talk to Lawrence, cop flack from Brad, familiar?'

'Yeah. I was feeling a bit – chicken. A lot chicken.'

'Tomorrow then?'

'I'll see how I go.'

Tim placed a firm hand on his shoulder. 'Tomorrow, Joe.'

'Yes, officer.'

'What do you reckon they call them in Germany?

'Call what?'

'German Shepherds.'

'I don't know. German Shepherds?'

'But they're in Germany, so maybe they're just shepherds.'

'Aren't they Alsations?'

'Are they?'

'I think so. Maybe you should ask Brad, Tim. I'm going to take Ed for a walk. Want to come?'

Tim looked around the room. 'Where is he?'

'Under the house, at a guess.'

'How do you get him out?'

'Bribery.'

'How long does it take?'

'Anywhere from a minute to an hour or two.'

'Think I'll pass.'

'Good decision.'

After he'd successfully enticed Ed out from under the house with a piece of dog chocolate, Joe took him for a walk. The previous day, he had spent more than an hour attempting to bribe him out from under the laundry sink, before he'd decided that it was too late to go for a walk. Ed had eventually come out and Joe's mum had said he really should give Ed some chocolate in fairness. In the end, Ed had wasted an hour of Joe's time, avoided a walk, and scored a piece of chocolate for his trouble. Something was not quite right in the animal training department. Joe's mum had theories that Ed had been mistreated in the past. And maybe she was right. But Joe had his suspicions that Ed might just be very lazy. There was such a thing as lazy people. Why did every dog have to like exercising? It didn't make sense.

He was growing tired of people stopping him to ask about Ed's peculiar behaviour, and then pointing out that they themselves had normal dogs who loved walking. Maybe Ed was a bit crazy. But if one dog year equalled seven human years, Ed was theoretically contending with the seven-year itch every year of his life. No wonder he was heading for nut-bag city limits.

This was what it came down to: Anthony had wanted a pet on a whim, and now Joe had inherited it, and all the responsibilities that went along with animal ownership. They needed to make cautionary bumper stickers: 'A dog is not just a trophy to rub in your underachieving brother's face every day before ultimately shirking all responsibility and leaving the training and care to the aforementioned underachieving brother'. Admittedly it was a little long, and needed some work to make it sound a bit more catchy.

Joe finally got Ed across the road, which was no mean feat. He soon realised that he'd forgotten to take a pooper-scooper or plastic bag with him. He looked around shiftily as Ed decorated a fern with his own special touch. The owner of the house just happened to be looking out his lounge-room window at the time and began violently tapping on the glass, yelling abuse. Joe tried to make Ed run, but Ed had decided that he didn't feel in the mood, and instead lay down in the middle of the road, refusing to move. When Joe pulled his lead harder, Ed did a move that could only be described as a head-boogie.

Joe had to think fast. The old man was on his feet. He realised that he had just seconds to devise a plan. And so he'd opted to run for his life with a dog in his outstretched arms. Thankfully, they lost old Mr Cranky Pants when he stepped his Zimmer frame in Ed's fresh business. They would never be able to walk down Herbert Street again.

Once he'd returned from walking Ed as far as Ed would

allow him to go, Joe turned on the television. He soon settled into his dad's lazy-boy, watching the tail end of a cable movie featuring a debonair yet troubled, unfulfilled man driving his child's babysitter home. He had seen the start of this particular movie about four times, as was the cable owner's wont, and it was pretty exciting to think that he might finally get to see the end, after all the time he had invested in it. If Lawrence had been there they would have laid bets on the plot. They'd kept a book over the last holidays, and Joe's accuracy was second to none. This was the real tragedy of their feud: it was spoiling a perfectly good betting opportunity. Joe opened the book and began writing in the 'Joe's proposed plot' column. *Mr Cable-knit beds babysitter. Babysitter forms obsession. Wife kills babysitter.*

'Please, Stacey, call me Matt. Mr Montgomery sounds so formal,' Mr Cable-knit said, reaching over to open Stacey's car door.

Joe had a good feeling about this one. Fifteen minutes later, however, Cable-knit's wife had gone missing and Stacey's car had broken down. Cable-knit came to the rescue, as he just happened to be passing by. Cable-knit burst into tears, apparently distraught by his wife's disappearance. And naïve, impressionable, extremely familiar-looking Stacey had offered to drive him home. Joe had just placed the actress playing Stacey when the phone rang.

Things were just beginning to hot up. Stacey had agreed to go inside for a coffee with Cable-knit. The phone continued to ring. Usually Joe would successfully psych out whichever family members were home. He had only had to answer the phone about twice the previous year. And that was just because there was no one else home besides Anthony at the time.

'Matt – Mr Montgomery. I think I should go home now,' Stacey said uneasily.

'Oh. I've made you uncomfortable. I'm sorry, Stacey, but you're a beautiful girl. Does your boyfriend really understand you?' Cable-knit said.

With no one to psych out, Joe reluctantly reached for the phone.

'Hello.'

'Joe, can you get Mum or Dad? Mum. Can you get Mum, please?'

'Anthony?'

'Yeah. Please Joe, I need to tell . . .'

'Bored already?'

Joe looked back at the television.

'That's better, Stacey. Nice and relaxed. You were so tense. Now that coffee, how do you take it?'

'Joe, I mean it,' Anthony yelled. 'I don't know what to do. I need to speak to Mum or Dad.'

Joe hit the mute button on the TV. His brother was serious.

'They're not here. They're still at work. Dad shouldn't be too . . .'

'Shit. Shit. What am I going to do?'

'What's going on, Anthony? What's wrong?'

Anthony's voice wavered. It sounded like he had begun to cry. But surely that wasn't right. This was Anthony, after all.

'There was an accident. We were whitewater rafting and it was really rough and stormy. It was too rough. We didn't know what we were doing. We tipped and . . .'

'What?'

'They're still looking for people.'

'But you're all right?'

'Yeah. But there are a few people missing.'

'Bloody hell, Anth. What about Chris? Is he with you?'

'No. He's not.'

'But he's OK. He's there somewhere, right?'

'No. They haven't found him.'

'But he'll be fine. I mean, he's not . . . they don't think he's . . . he couldn't be . . .'

'I don't know. I don't know anything. They're saying it's bad. He might be. I don't know what to do.'

The phone went quiet.

'Anthony. Anth, are you still there?'

The crying grew louder.

'Anthony, listen to me. It'll be all right. Don't worry. Is there someone there who you can talk to until I can get Mum or Dad?'

'Yeah. There are lots of people. Don't worry, I'm fine.'

'That's good. Because you shouldn't be alone. But, yeah, you sound OK, so that's good. Just hang in there.'

The line was quiet again.

'Anthony? Say something, will you?'

'I'm scared, Joe.'

'I'll find someone. I'll get Dad to come home.'

Once Anthony had hung up, Joe called his father's mobile.

'I'm just turning into our street now. What's –'

Joe ran outside, down the driveway, onto the street. He knew it wouldn't get his dad home any quicker, but moving made him feel more useful.

'Dad. There was an accident. It's Chris. He's missing.'

15

Joe and his dad sat watching the muted television in scared silence, waiting for Anthony to call back.

'And you definitely told him to call?'

'Yeah. He couldn't give me a number so he said he'd ring.'

'Right. So it's been – what? Twenty minutes or so?'

'About that.'

'Do you think we should call the Barrys, Joe?'

Joe was taken aback. He couldn't recall any other time that his dad had asked him for his opinion. He was struck by the earnestness of his father's face. 'I don't know, Dad. Maybe someone else will. We can't tell them anything. It might be better not to right now.'

'But what if – if it's bad, wouldn't you want to know right away? I don't know if it's right to keep it from them.'

'Let's give Anthony ten more minutes. Mum was leaving when you called her, wasn't she? She'll be here soon. Let's just wait at least till then.'

The phone rang. Mr King and Joe jumped to their feet and Mr King grabbed the phone. Joe watched as his dad spoke, looking for the slightest clue.

'Where exactly are you, Anth? Right, and who's with you? Have you eaten anything? What are you doing when you're not on the phone?'

At first Joe was annoyed by his father's insistence on confirming seemingly irrelevant details, but as the phone call went on, Joe was quietly amazed by his father's capacity to calm his brother. 'Make sure you stay put, mate. You need to concentrate on keeping warm and eat something.' And then it occurred to Joe that these things may have sounded irrelevant, but all alone in turmoil and in another country, Anthony needed to hear them.

Since Joe had spoken to his brother, they had found the body of one of the boys' hostel room-mates. Mr King made Anthony put one of the counsellors on the phone so he could make sure Anthony was being looked after. He asked the woman whether he should get on a plane and join Anthony, but she said that it wasn't necessary at this stage.

'Then it's necessary that you give my son the best bloody care you can,' Mr King yelled, his voice not needing the aid of a phone to reach New Zealand. Mr King told Anthony to stay put and keep calling reverse charges, and vowed he'd be on the first plane over, regardless of what anyone said.

Joe wondered whether his dad would ever realise the power that he had over his children. If he told you to put a jacket on to keep warm, then you would. If he told you that you needed to eat something, then you ate something. If he told you that there was no bogeyman, then there was no bogeyman. If Graeme King told you that it was all going to be all right, then it was all going to be all right. And right now Joe was waiting to hear those words.

'Right. I'll just write a note to your mum. Grab a jumper Joe, we're going to the Barrys''

'Me? Are you sure that's really . . .'

'Come on, son.'

He didn't recall his father ever calling him that. It had to be a bad sign. He picked up his hooded jumper from his bedroom floor, along with his lolly stash and followed his father to the car, wondering why he had to go too, and hoping that he could at least be of some help. Joe wanted some sort of reassurance from his father that things would turn out all right. Things had to be OK. Nothing could happen to Chris. Nothing like this ever happened to people that Joe knew. He looked at his father, waiting for some sign that this wasn't real. That there wasn't anything to worry about. But the only words that his father spoke on the way to the Barrys' put the biggest fear into him that he had ever known.

'Now would be a good time to pray, Joe.'

They knocked on the Barrys' back door, like two police-men ready to deliver the worst imaginable news. Jim Barry took one look at Joe and Mr King and his face fell.

'What's happened?'

Right there and then Joe knew that his father had to do one of the hardest things that he would ever have to do in his life. He had to tell Jim and Denise Barry, two people he had known for over fifteen years, that their son was miss-ing, possibly drowned, while his own boys were safe.

They headed inside and boiled the kettle for the manda-tory cup of coffee that was required in these situations.

'It's white with one, isn't it, Graeme?' Mrs Barry said.

Mr King nodded. 'Look, I can do that, if you like, Denise.'

'No, it's fine thanks, Graeme. Joe?'

'Yes?'

'Your coffee. How do you take it, love?'

'Umm . . . same as Dad please.' The truth was Joe didn't know how he took his coffee. He never really drank it. It was something that his sister teased him about: his lack of sophistication in the realm of the hot beverage. He'd always been confused by coffee. From what he could tell, it only had three real purposes: it was either used as a tool of seduction, like in the babysitter film, a tool of study, like Anthony used it, or for comfort and condolence, like now.

It was when Lawrence appeared that the dull aching in Joe's stomach turned into a sudden need to purge. He went to the bathroom and vomited. His hands were clammy and his legs felt shaky. He'd seen a guy sever his hand, blood oozing from everywhere, and not even blinked. But now he struggled to keep it together. He needed to sit down. He perched on the edge of the bath, praying as his father had suggested, and in between, reciting his times tables. He hoped that God wouldn't mind the interruption. Times tables were like Joe's nervous tick. And if you got down to it, God had made Joe, warts and all, so it was really his fault.

He began by making his standard apology to God, for only praying when he needed something, promising again to keep in touch through the good times, if God did him this one favour. Deciding that a bit of back-praying couldn't hurt, he thanked God for the nice weather on his last birthday, for giving him Ed and for the cancellation of the proposed *Big Brother* reunion show. Back-praying over, Joe moved on to bargaining.

'Now, I know I didn't buy *Crash Bandicoot* to share with Anthony after I'd prayed I'd get the winning Melbourne Cup horse and I did. But that was only because Dad ended up buying it. I still feel guilty. And I know I've been petty with Lawrence and a bit mean to Tim and Lawrence and there was that whole thing with Grace . . . But I said sorry, and I meant it. But if you make Chris be OK, I'll do anything. Please, God. Don't do this to us. Don't do it to Anthony. $7 \times 8 = 56$.'

Things had only become worse when Joe re-entered the lounge room. Lawrence looked like he'd just been hit by a truck and finished of by a steamroller. $9 \times 6 = 54$.

Joe sat in the armchair next to Lawrence. 4 × 12 = 48.

'Sorry.'

'Yeah.'

'He'll be OK.' 12, 18, 24, 30, 36, 42 . . .

'Yeah.'

Joe fished around in his lolly stash until he found a piece of Hubba Bubba. He put it in Lawrence's hand. Lawrence held it tightly. Suddenly remembering something important, Joe excused himself again, and headed back to the bathroom.

'God. Just a couple more things. First, it was *me* who put the hole in the kitchen lino with Dad's nine iron. But you probably knew that. And also, I didn't put the petrol cap back on the tin properly after I mowed the lawn once, and Belinda knocked the can over and it melted Anthony's remote control Jeep, and I sort of let her take the blame. And I sort of let Anthony take the blame too, when I put a hole in the couch with another one of Dad's golf clubs – but he did put the hole in the wall. That was him. So, I think that's it. I just wanted to say sorry. But God, Chris is one of the best people I know.'

Joe's version of praying was interrupted by the phone ringing. Joe ran back out to the living room as Denise picked it up, eagerly. It was a telemarketer. She hung up and sat back down with her coffee. Joe sat next to Lawrence, never more aware of the inadequate nature of words.

'Woods told me off for my shorts again today,' Lawrence said absently.

Joe looked at Lawrence. There was nothing appropriate to talk about at this moment, and at the same time, the silence was so forbidding that there was nothing too inappropriate to say either, if it helped drown out the quiet for a moment. 'Did the vein in his forehead pop?'

Lawrence fiddled with the cuff on his jumper. 'Yeah. Brad reckons he's found a loophole in the uniform bit of the school handbook so we can't get detention.'

'Brad?'

'Yeah.'

'He can read?'

'Looks like it. Did you hear what he got Tim for his birthday?'

Joe nodded. 'I'm surprised Tim didn't make him take it all back.'

'You know who Brad's going out with, don't you?'

'Who?'

'I'll give you a clue: it'll be the best two weeks of his life.'

'Jade Pryce?'

'Bingo.'

This was probably the weirdest moment Joe had ever been in. It was such a relief to be talking to Lawrence again, but so awful that it was under the worst possible circumstances.

'I wanted to tape a show on channel nine,' Lawrence said, suddenly sounding distant.

'Have you got a tape?'

'Yeah, but should I? Is that wrong right now?'

'Pop your tape in, Laws.'

Lawrence set up his recording. 'I should finish my science write-up.'

'No, I reckon that's wrong right now,' Joe smiled. 'Anyway, I've done mine. It won't take you long.'

They sat pretending to watch *All Saints* for the next half an hour while Lawrence's parents and Joe's dad sat in the dining room drinking their fifth cup of coffee.

'Wasn't that doctor just doing plastic surgery?' Lawrence asked.

'Yeah.'

'And now he's doing a cancer scan and is about to operate on that kid's eye?'

'He's a jack of all trades, apparently. You should hear Anthony go on about the inaccuracy of it.'

The mention of his brother's name suddenly felt strange. Even though Joe had been told that Anthony was safe, he wouldn't quite be able to believe it until he saw him. It was as though Chris and Anthony had become a kind of abstract concept as soon as they'd left the country. They wouldn't really have their brothers back until they saw them again. Joe hoped that Lawrence would get that chance.

The phone rang. It was Mrs King asking if there was any news. Joe watched anxiously as Mrs Barry nodded her head and smiled through her tears . . . 7, 14, 21, 28, 35, 42, 49, 56, 63, 70, 77, 84.

The phone rang again.

'Oh, thank God,' Mrs Barry sobbed. They had found

Chris and taken him to hospital. He was alive. He had a broken wrist and suspected fractured ribs, but he was alive.

Within minutes, Mr Barry had booked himself, his wife and Joe's parents onto the first available New Zealand flight.

'Can I stay the night at your place, Mr King?' Lawrence asked.

'Course you can. Joe, help Lawrence.'

The gathering moved to the Kings' house, so that Mr King could pack whatever his wife hadn't and they could all head off. Joe watched his mum and Mrs Barry hug each other with such intense emotion and relief that he found it difficult not to shed a tear.

In their absence, Mrs King had taken care of the refreshments, baking some canolli in the midst of the uncertainty and she insisted that the boys have some of her spag bol for sustenance before they went to sleep. Some cried and panicked in a crisis, Jen King cooked. As soon as Joe was able to detach himself from his mother's hug, the King and Barry parents were on their way. Joe was exhausted but he called Belinda before he went to bed and told her what had happened and that he missed her. He hoped there'd be a time when they'd all be together in one place again.

They made up Lawrence's trundle on Joe's floor.

'Are you comfortable?' Joe asked, as he looked up at his ceiling of glow-in-the-dark stars.

'Yeah, fine.'

Joe had never been more tired. But he'd also never been so full of adrenaline. He could feel and hear his heart beating. It felt like it was getting faster. 'Could I be having a heart attack?'

'No, Joe.'

'My heart's beating really fast.'

'You're not having a heart attack.'

'OK. So you don't need another pillow or blanket or anything?'

'Nah. I'm fine, really.'

'Because if you want, you can sleep in Anthony's room.'

'No, I'm all right.'

'OK. Goodnight, Lawrence. I'm glad Chris is OK.'

'Me, too.'

'And I wanted to tell you that I'm . . .'

'What?'

'Sorry for . . . you know?'

'For what?'

'For the whole Claudia thing and . . .'

Lawrence laughed. 'Joe, you're a dickhead.'

'I know.'

'You're very good at it.'

'It wasn't really about her, you know.'

'Yeah. What was it about?'

'It sort of hit me that I was going to get left behind next year. It wouldn't be you and me any more and I didn't know if I'd be all right.'

'Of course you'll be all right.'

'I kind of morphed you and Anthony into one – the

achieving school captains. I'd started to feel like a loser little brother around you – which wasn't your fault.'

'You're not a loser. Lose the complex, Joey.'

'Do you remember the day I split my pants in grade four?'

Lawrence laughed. 'That was a classic.'

'You gave me your jumper to hide my bum and then you took me out and loaned me some tracky pants and we went back into the hall.'

'I remember that.'

'It sort of became a pattern. I didn't do my work, you'd do it for me. You get a job at Coles and get me one.'

'That's what mates do.'

'I know. But what did I ever do for you? I mean, do mates copy mates' subjects, too? I relied on you too much. Sometimes I feel like I never gave back the pants.'

'What?'

'Your pants. I've always basically wanted to be you, Lawrence. And I'm not, and never will be and now I'm fine with that. But I think this whole – incredibly stupid fight kind of had to happen for me to realise that.'

'Jeeze, I'm sorry. I don't know what I should say.'

'It wasn't your fault.'

'Maybe it was a bit. I don't think you ever did give those pants back, you know.'

Joe laughed.

'No, seriously.'

'Why do you hang around with me, Laws? What do you get out of it?'

'I like you. We have a laugh.'

'You can laugh with anyone.'

'That's crap. When we went back into the hall that day, you wearing my pants – that you stole – you put those cords, with the huge hole in the arse, on your head and danced like a dickhead and cracked everyone up. In the end no one cared that your pants had busted because you were hilarious.'

'I don't remember that.'

'You're a pretty easy person to like, Joe – when you're not trying to convince people they shouldn't like you.'

'So you don't hang around with me just to feel better about yourself then?'

'Shit, yeah.'

'Thought so.'

The boys were quiet for a few moments, Joe looking up at his sticker galaxy, Lawrence fiddling with his glow-in-the-dark watch. It was that familiar comfortable feeling that they'd always had. It made Joe realise how much he'd missed it.

'I hang around with you to feel better about every-thing, Joe.'

Though there was silence in the house and in the street, somehow Joe felt that everything was louder than ever. His head was buzzing, filled with unpleasant thoughts that would not leave him alone. Even the sheep that he'd tried to count had been taken off to the abattoir.

'Laws, are you awake?'

'No.'

'Sorry. I just can't stop thinking.'

'I know.'

'I did try to call you a few times. And I went round to your place but . . .'

'It's forgotten.'

'Thanks. So, are you and Claudia still . . .'

'No we finished it. Every time I looked into her eyes, I was reminded of the heinous act of betrayal that I'd committed. The hurt I'd caused my friend, Joseph Leslie King. The guilt was too much.'

'Really?' Joe asked, a little excited.

'No. We're still together. But we did feel bad.'

'I'm glad it's worked out. Don't ever use my middle name again.'

'Thanks. I really like her.'

'I think I liked the idea of her,' Joe said thoughtfully. 'Like if I was with her, I wouldn't have to worry about anything else.'

There was a moment of silence, which allowed Joe's troubling thoughts to creep back into the forefront of his mind.

'Shit, Laws. Chris and Anthony. Imagine if . . .'

'Yeah.'

'I mean, how would you handle something like that?'

'Who the hell knows?'

'Do you know what my last word to my brother would have been? "Bye".'

'Some would argue that's actually a perfect last word.'

'Not the way I said it, what I meant by it. I've never

known anyone who's died. I didn't think it would ever really happen. I know it's stupid, but I still hope it won't.'

'I've only lost my granddad.'

'I remember. How old were we? Ten?'

'Yeah. Mum and I stayed with Grandma the night that he died, and Mum made me sleep in Grandma's bed with her. She just about smothered me. The next morning I woke up and she thanked me. I didn't really get it. But now I kind of do.'

'You kept her company?'

'She hadn't slept alone in thirty-five years. There's not a lot you can do in these situations. But I'm glad that I could do that for her.'

'Actually my great uncle Bob died about six years ago.'

'Sorry.'

'From what I recall, there wasn't anything that great about him. All Anthony and I remembered was him peeing with the door open.'

'That's a comforting memory.'

'It's not like it was wide open or anything. It was just ajar. Anthony thought that was the laziest thing he'd ever seen. But I just thought it was sad.'

'I'm with Anthony on that one.'

'But it was a habit. He'd lived alone so long that he'd got used to not having to close it. Why would you if you were on your own?'

'Only you could come up with that, Joey.'

'Yeah. You know, I reckon my grumps will be around forever.'

'God willing, yeah.'

'No, seriously. I reckon he'll stay around just to spite us.'

'He's not that bad.'

'He's not that good, either. I don't know how my dad put up with him growing up. He would have been an absolute bastard.'

'He is very scary. Remember how he told us that those plastic boys moulded onto the windmill at his place used to be real boys, the same age as we were?'

Joe laughed. 'Yeah, and what did he say? He put them up there because they gave him trouble. They didn't eat their crusts?'

'In my family you just got told you'd get curly hair.'

'I can't believe we fell for it.'

'In our defence, the man had a rifle and a stuffed duck sitting on his bar.'

Lawrence fell asleep very quickly, as he always did. And Joe lay awake staring up at the sticker galaxy. Out of one of the worst moments of his life had come the realisation that he cared and other people cared. It was amazing how good people like his father could be in these bad times. He had no doubt that his dad would quickly revert to annoying him, but he'd definitely had his moment that night.

There was a strange hybrid of meaning and sadness that came out of a crisis. It was more confronting and real than anything Joe'd ever experienced, and at later times in his life, he was sure he would long for the feeling of solidarity and togetherness brought on by such moments. In the midst of the crisis that evening, Joe hadn't been able to imagine going back to school or doing anything as mundane and meaningless as homework – even though that this had been his pre-crisis stance as well. It had really felt like things would never go back to normal. All that had mattered to him was that moment and the people in it. Things were starting to become clearer. For better or worse, mainly worse, he feared, he was growing up.

16

Joe hadn't exactly been expecting an emotional teary scene when they met Anthony and his parents at the airport, but he had thought that maybe somehow things would have changed between him and his brother – even if just a little.

He'd got a 'hey' when he'd greeted Anthony, which was a lot more than he'd got on other occasions, but for some reason, Joe was really disappointed. He was sure that Anthony's lack of enthusiasm had something to do with the fact that Isabelle wasn't there.

'Isabelle's been caught up at uni. She said to tell you she'd probably drop around later,' Joe said.

'Whatever,' Anthony said.

Joe looked over at the Barrys, who were hugging and wiping away tears, huddling like a basketball team in a time-out with seconds to spare. He was confused. He'd surprised himself earlier, by realising that he was actually looking forward to going to the airport to collect his loved ones – and not just because of the film-like quality evoked by the airport setting. He had to admit that he'd really missed them – his dad, his mum and even Anthony. But their arrival had felt like as big an anticlimax as New Years Eve 1999.

And then Joe was hit with another realisation. He had wanted to hug his brother. He'd wanted to hug his brother the way that Lawrence had hugged Chris. They'd managed to keep the hug strictly manly, by incorporating random firm pats on each other's backs. And Joe felt that he could have very easily done the same. But the men didn't really do hugs in his family.

For some reason, it had just felt too contrived. So he'd withdrawn his hug at the last minute, overbalancing and nearly landing on the baggage carousel as a result. He cursed his stoic Scottish ancestry. And he cursed Mrs Barry's part Greek heritage. Joe watched the Barrys' hugging session with admiration and jealousy.

'Good to see you, mate,' Lawrence said to Chris, causing Joe further insult.

'Now, Anthony, you can come with us unless you'd prefer to go with Lawrence and Joe?' Mrs King said.

'Whatever,' Anthony said.

'Don't worry if Anthony's a bit short with you, darling. He's been through a lot. He's just very tired. Needs to get home and readjust,' Mrs King said a little later, as Joe struggled to decode the workings of the airport trolley. 'He'll soon cheer up.'

As they loaded the bags into the car boot, this time it was Mr King who had a parental word in Joe's ear. 'If your brother's a bit out of sorts, try not to take it to heart. Cut him a bit of slack, hey? After a good night's rest in his own bed, he'll be his old self again – good as gold.'

He wondered what his parents were on about with their theories on his brother. His old self? Moody, despondent, reluctant to elaborate on one-word sentences? As far as Joe could see, Anthony already was his old self. And Joe found it difficult to stretch to his father's notion that his brother was usually akin to a precious metal. Anthony wasn't even gold-plated, let alone solid gold. Fool's gold, maybe.

As it turned out, for the first time since around 1991, Joe's parents had been right. After a few weeks, things had gone back to normal – a better sort of normal than Joe could have hoped for. Anthony and Chris were back at uni, making Anthony's infrequent presence at home very tolerable indeed. And Joe was well and truly back in the fold with Lawrence, Brad and Tim. He had also been featured in the local paper for his first-aid exploits at Coles, which he casually displayed on his table, as they sat waiting for their English teacher.

'I might go to the library. There's no way I'm writing on this for the exam,' Lawrence said, not convinced of the merits of *The Great Gatsby*.

'I don't think it's that bad.'

'Joe, thinness does not equal good.'

'Come on, old sport. *The Great Gatsby is a consummate summary of the "roaring twenties" and a devastating expose of the "Jazz Age",* Joe said, reading the back of his copy.

Lawrence grabbed the newspaper article from Joe's table and began reading select passages. '*"It was no big deal," Mr King said. "I remembered what to do from first-aid lessons and I just did it. The ambulance came really quickly anyway."* So modest, Mr King.'

'Give me the bloody paper, Larry Barry.'

Lawrence continued, undeterred. '*When asked whether the incident had prompted him to think about a career in the medical profession, Mr King said that he was considering becoming a paramedic.*'

'Is that true, Joe?' asked Grace, who was sitting nearby.

'I don't know. Yeah. It is actually.'

'That ambo's joke about ordering ham, not hand – hilarious,' Lawrence said.

Grace was intrigued by Joe's newfound ambition. 'Have you ever thought about being a paramedic before?'

'No. Probably because I've never been in that sort of situation before – except when we had to revive resusci-Annie. I think it was one of those defining moments.'

Lawrence tossed the article back on the desk. 'Well, what does your paramedic do exactly?'

'Save people's lives,' Grace said promptly.

'Ambulance driver, Laws. It's just another word.'

'What do you need to do for that?' Grace asked.

Joe pulled out a crumpled piece of paper from his pocket. 'I'm looking into it. I've got one of those careers appointment thingys this afternoon with – Miss Davis?'

Lawrence laughed. 'Mrs Davidson. We'll show you the room, Joey.'

'Good morning, everyone,' Mr Woods said. 'Miss Barker is unwell so I will be taking you this lesson. First of all, Mr Barry and Mr King, get out of my classroom.'

Lawrence stood up. 'Sir?'

'Go home and get changed, the pair of you. I don't care what your excuses are. You've both been warned. You are only to come back to school when you are correctly attired. And report to me. Off you go.'

'You beauty,' Joe said, as he and Lawrence walked to their lockers. 'What do you want to do? Maccas? Movie?'

Lawrence pulled a pair of pants out of his bag. 'I've got some here. In case – this happened.'

'So? Woods doesn't know that. Let's go.'

'I've got a meeting at lunch with some of the teachers. I can't miss it.'

Joe could tell that Lawrence was disappointed by his own inability to contravene school rules so he decided to let him off the hook. 'That's OK. You go to your meeting and I'll waste a bit of time and be back myself. So much for Brad's loophole.'

'Yeah. Are we really surprised though?' Lawrence laughed.

'I think we're agreed that I win the bet?'

'How's that?'

'Technically I will be in the shorts for longer.'

'OK, Joe. And now we'll officially never have to do it again.'

'That being the best thing about completing our high school education.'

Joe went home and let Ed inside. But when Ed noticed Joe changing his clothes, he grew suspicious that a walk was afoot and hid in the bathroom, so Joe let him back outside, putting him out of his misery. He put the TV on briefly, while he ate the remainder of the previous evening's spaghetti bolognaise, but after a while became bored and decided to head back to school.

His bus came right away and when he disembarked at the other end, he went on a slight detour through the shopping centre, the mecca of time-wastage. He briefly debated going to Adam Sandler's latest film, but even going back to school looked more attractive, so he bought himself a chocolate milkshake and wandered through the centre.

'What are you doing?' Anthony asked, coming up behind Joe as he inspected a 'nice price' stand at the music shop.

'Oh, hi. Just a bit of "me time", you know, while the kids are at school.'

'When I went to school it used to go till ten past three. It's ten past one, Joe.'

'I got sent home.'

'Why?'

'To change into pants. What about you? Don't you have one of your full days on Thursdays?'

'We don't have class today.'

'Really? You don't have any classes at all?'

'Not this afternoon. There's a strike. Don't tell Mum and Dad about this. They'll only blow it out of proportion. Some stuff they don't need to know.'

'I agree. So you won't be telling them about seeing me either?'

'I didn't see you.'

'Fine. And I didn't see you.'

'Who's making you change? Woods?'

'Yep. The guy's a Nazi. Curse these rugged, non-Aryan looks of mine.'

Joe swore that he almost got a smile out of Anthony. He thought about asking Anthony if he wanted to hang around and do something, but it felt too weird. He probably had his own things to do anyway. And if Joe was honest, he wanted to go to his careers appointment that afternoon. He was scared that he would be laughed out of Mrs Davidson's office, but he had to give it a go anyway. He had to start somewhere.

'I'd better go, I'm meeting Isabelle.'

'Right.'

'So I'll see you at home, Joe.'

'OK.'

Mrs Davidson turned out to be very helpful, and as a bonus, devoid of humour, which meant there was no laughing at Joe's ambition – hypothetical ambition, that was. She had consulted a pile of books about the best strategy for a hypothetical entry into a paramedic course. And by the time Joe had left her office, it didn't feel quite so hypothetical any more. Maybe his mother had been right. Maybe there weren't trumpets when the big moments happened in life. Maybe, for Joe, there were sirens.

Joe couldn't explain it, but as he walked to work after school that afternoon, he felt – light, as if having just one possible plan up his sleeve somehow lessened the load. At work the annoying customers annoyed him less and the time felt like it passed more quickly than usual. He was aware that his plan was not the solution to everything, that there was every chance that it might not even work out. And for now he was glad not to know which way it would go. He'd deal with whatever eventuated, but maybe this hoping and planning and feeling that anything was possible was the nicest part of all.

'Hi guys,' Isabelle said to Joe and Lawrence, as they sat in the break room at work. 'Do you want my Saturday shift, Joe?'

'No. I'd better not. I've got heaps of work at the moment. Dad said I could ease off on the repayments, too.'

'OK. Know anyone who does?'

'I think Dave wants some more shifts.'

'Cool. Is he around?'

'I think he's on register three.'

'She got another warning,' Lawrence said, after Isabelle had gone.

'What for?'

'Wearing her nose-ring again.'

'Isn't that about three warnings now?'

'Two . . . They're not sacking her 'cause they need the staff, but Oliver reckons they'll get rid of her soon. No offence, Joe, but I don't know what your brother sees in her.'

Lately, Joe didn't know either. From what he could tell, things weren't looking too hopeful for Anthony and Isabelle, largely owing to the fact that Isabelle was fast becoming a professional university protester, sleeping out or sitting-in at any opportunity. She was all about the cause, mouthing off about injustice, citing statistics and demonstrating her love of primary colours by applying them to her hair.

She'd berated Joe one afternoon for buying a pair of Nike runners, going on about exploitation and slave labour. She'd also nearly had a stroke when she'd seen Anthony's new Nike watch, but he'd firmly indicated that debate concerning his shopping habits was strictly off limits. Joe worried about Isabelle's future as a checkout chick, given that she was on her second warning at Coles. The first warning had been for coming to work with her hair dyed bright green, and the second was for refusing to wear a name badge because she'd felt that it insinu-ated that she, the exploited proletariat, was somehow the property of the evil corporate empire of Coles Myer.

'You don't mind it when you get your pay cheque every week though, do you?' Joe had said during one of her recent tirades.

'But the job's soulless. We, the proletariats, toil tire-lessly with little thanks and great pain. Why do we do it? So that the bourgeoisie can get richer and fatter, laughing all the way to the bank, while we choke on the oppression. Communism had its merits. But then, we're lucky, comparatively speaking. Women of some cultures can't even leave the house.'

Sociology 101 had so much to answer for.

Not surprisingly, Joe had recently taken to spending his breaks with the smoking members of the Coles team whenever Isabelle was working with him, preferring the risk of long-term health problems to the short-term effects of ear bashing. He admired Isabelle for getting involved in social justice, but he didn't understand why she had to become boring. Sir Bob Geldof was into a bit of justice, and he was a lively sort of bloke who even swore a lot – and then there was Grace. She was into justice and she was great: funny, pretty, clever . . . There was nothing *ungreat* about that girl.

'Joe.' Lawrence said.

'What?'

'Are you coming?'

'Where?'

'Xanadu. Where do you reckon? Back to work.'

'Oh. Yeah. OK.'

'What are you thinking about?'

'Stuff.'

'Good stuff or bad stuff?'

Joe smiled. 'All good stuff.'

'Only an hour and a half to go, add that to your list.'

They headed back onto the floor. 'Would be cool though, wouldn't it?' Joe said. 'If we got to wear roller skates?'

Joe's brother's relationship was officially on the rocks, especially now that Isabelle had disposed of her mobile phone, due to its capitalist-enabling nature. Getting in contact with her was proving to be increasingly difficult. Joe had witnessed several heated telephone conversations between Anthony and Isabelle in the last few days. Both were apparently unhappy with the other's level of support and understanding.

But at least one area of Anthony's life was on the up and up. Each night he came home and dazzled the family with anatomical facts and stories of rare terminal illnesses – the usual dinner conversation. And it seemed that he would also never tire of talking about Betty, the cadaver that he and his group had been assigned for the year. Mr King sat listening to his son, beaming with pride. He was still telling everyone that he had a son who was studying medicine – long-lost relatives, neighbours, telemarketers, and on one occasion, a pair of Mormons – anyone who would listen.

'I'm begging you, anyone, please let me come to your place for tea tonight? It's *Medic Alert* night. I can't bear Dr Tony's analysis again,' Joe implored as they sat in the common room in their second last lesson for the day, watching Brad run round and round the oval, for no apparent reason.

Grace seemed unmoved. 'Anthony's a first year medical student. He hasn't even been in a hospital yet, has he?'

'No. But you should see him. The way he laughs smugly and points out faults with medical procedures. If I hear him question Dr Cartwright's methods one more time I'll . . . well, I'll just keep complaining, probably. But it'll be very unpleasant for a lot of people, you three included.'

'Sorry, I'm out tonight, Joe,' Tim said. 'Gym then swim.'

'Damn your commitment to entering the police force.'

'At least it sounds like Anthony likes his course,' Grace said.

'Chris likes graphics, doesn't he, Larry Barry?'

'Yeah, really likes it.'

'But it's not as if he gives a running commentary of the misuse of colours on *Changing Rooms* or anything, is it?'

'He's not home that much, actually. He has to do heaps of stuff at the studios and he's made lots of friends so there's always something going on. Mum and Dad have even started using the "you treat this place like a hotel" line.'

'I'm familiar with it. Do you know if Anthony gave Chris that CD I wanted him to burn?' Joe asked. 'I gave it to him last night but I knew it was risky.'

'Chris was out last night so I don't think he saw Anthony, unless they met up somewhere.'

'I don't know. I thought Anthony said he was going to your place for tea, but then I wasn't really listening, so he could have said anything. He'd better not have lost that CD, though.'

Joe turned to Grace with pleading eyes.

'Sorry. I've got ballet.'

'I love ballet.'

'You're not coming to my rehearsal, Joe,' Grace laughed.

'Fine. Et tu, Lawrence?'

'Sure. You can come to my place tonight if you want. Mum and Dad will be out, so I'll make something or we can get pizza.'

'Laws, old sport, your mercy will be rewarded in due course.'

'See ya,' Tim said, hopping in his father's police patrol car with as big a grin as he'd had on his face when he'd first done it in year seven.

'Bye, Timmy. Don't train too hard.'

Tim's dad gave Joe a wry smile. He hadn't bought the whole bad shellfish story after the party.

Joe waved to Grace as she put her schoolbag in the car boot. 'Bye, Grace.'

She smiled and waved.

'She's pretty cool, isn't she?' Lawrence said.

'Yeah. It's great. It's like we've got a new character on our show.'

'I reckon she likes you.'

'Have you been speaking to Tim?'

'Brad actually. But I have eyes, too. Joe, you went the pash. What's going on?'

'Nothing.'

'Yeah, but why?'

'You mean apart from her father owning a firearm?'

'I'm not going to push it. I just think you two need to talk.'

'We will.' Joe decided a subject change was long overdue. 'So how was Woods' form this arvo?'

Lawrence laughed, unable to hide his absolute shock and amusement. 'He called you "buddy". Must have been the magnesium.'

'It was not the magnesium. Woods has a new respect for me.'

'You ran an errand, Joe,' Lawrence teased.

'Yes, I did. And very well, might I say.'

'Saturday night. Two weeks. Keep it open,' Brad said, pausing briefly before he jogged up the street with Mr Sturt and the cross-country team. 'Get your girlfriends to come, too.'

'Is it his birthday?' Lawrence asked.

'I thought it was in January. Tim's is in July. I was sure it was Jan . . .'

'Isn't that Anthony?' Lawrence interrupted.

'Anthony who?'

'Your brother, loser. It is. He's . . . he appears to be – waving, Joe. It *is* Anthony,' Lawrence said in disbelief.

Joe looked at his brother. 'What's he want?'

'You'd better ask him, Joseph.'

Joe approached his brother with great caution. The Crocodile Hunter had less to fear from hungry ten-foot long crocs than Joe did from this situation. 'Hi,' he said, maintaining a safe distance.

'Mum said I had to pick you up sometimes when it's raining or whatever. You know, when I've got the afternoon off. It's like a condition of them lending me the money for the car.'

'Oh. Right.'

'Are you coming then?'

'Actually I'm going over to Lawrence's place for tea. We were just going straight there.'

'OK.'

'But – thanks. You can drive us over there if you like. Chris might be home.'

'Nah. I was at his place last night. I've gotta go.'

'So you drive me home or nowhere?'

'Basically.'

'Thanks. Well, can you at least tell Mum where I've gone?'

'If I remember.'

'Great. So it's the game of chance, then. Will you remember or not? Because I'll ring her myself.'

'Whatever. I'll tell her.'

'You're tops, Anth,' Joe said, walking away.

Anthony hopped back in the car, and drove off, his attempt at a burn-off to demonstrate his annoyance thwarted by the crossing lady stepping onto the road with her big orange stop sign.

'It's not even bloody raining,' Joe called after him.

Lawrence shared Joe's disbelief. 'What was that about?'

'There's no certainty anymore. I'm Woods' buddy. Anthony's trying to pick me up from school as if he was – my brother. The world's gone mad.'

Chris dropped Joe home after *Medic Alert*, because Lawrence had been caught up helping his father with a computer-related question – namely, how to turn it on.

'Thanks for the ride, Chris. I could have walked.'

'And risked damaging your precious art work?'

'Yeah. I appreciated the art advice, too. What was it again? Give up?'

'I was joking. Honestly, your collage stuff is pretty good. I'm glad you and LB are mates again. He says you've got yourselves a bit of a posse.'

Joe laughed. 'Yeah, I s'pose we have a bit.'

'Joe?'

'Yeah?'

'How's Anthony going?'

'Same as when you last saw him – a whole what? Twenty-four hours ago?'

'Sorry? I haven't seen him for a while. We kind of keep missing each other.'

'Oh. I wondered why your mum was asking about him. He's meant to have been at your house a fair bit. Maybe he's joined ASIO or something.'

Chris laughed. 'So he's good then?'

'Yeah. He's OK, I think.'

'He seems OK. Probably just busy at uni and with Isabelle. I've had lots on, too.'

'So is your wrist OK?'

'Yeah. It's fine. It wasn't broken so I was lucky.'

'I'm sorry about what happened in New Zealand, Chris. I didn't really get a chance to say so.'

'Ta. But it's history. What's there to say really? I'm not one of the poor guys who died. Mum's still all concerned, but I'm fine. '

'She's a mum. They haven't quite got the whole not-worrying thing down.'

'Yeah.'

'It was pretty bad though.'

'I s'pose. But not for me. I keep hearing that it was this tragedy – young people out for an adventure killed. I wasn't. So it wasn't my tragedy.'

'Maybe. But just 'cause you didn't die doesn't mean . . .'

Chris was suddenly annoyed. 'Did you see the people on the news talking about rafting with the same company a couple of days earlier, like they'd had a near-miss?'

'Yeah, that was kind of desperate.'

'It shits me that people line up to make it all about them. It's not. It's about the people who ended up in the ground and the people who had to bury them.'

'I get what you mean, but you were there.'

'Yeah, but now I'm here. And I'm fine.'

'That's good, then.'

'Yeah. And Anth's OK, too. That's the main thing, isn't it?'

'I s'pose so.'

'We're lucky, he and I. Really lucky. Right,' he said abruptly. 'I've got an assignment to finish. I'll see you, Joey.'

Joe had half-expected to walk into a barrage of questions from his mother, doubtful that Anthony would have passed on his message.

'Hello, Joe, love,' Mrs King said.

The attachment of a term of endearment to his name was generally an indication that all was not well.

'Am I in trouble?'

'No, why?' Mrs King said. 'Come and sit down. Nice night, darling?'

'Yeah, fine. Anthony did tell you where I was, didn't he?'

'Yes, of course he did.'

'Mum, I know there have to be certain conditions for you and Dad lending him the money for his car, but can you tell him not to worry about picking me up? It wasn't even raining today. It was balmy. Shorts weather.'

'He picked you up?'

'Yeah, well, tried to.'

'That was a nice idea, wasn't it?'

'It was your idea, Mum.'

'I never said anything about picking you up. Come to think of it, I should have, but Anthony's not even home most afternoons.'

Anthony entered the room, hoeing into a bowl of ice-cream.

'That was nice of you to pick your brother up from school, love. Do you have Thursday afternoons free this semester?'

'Ah, not usually. It was kind of a one-off thing and . . . Ed ran away, Joe,' Anthony blurted out.

'Anthony, I was going to tell him in my own way,' Mrs King said in a cross voice.

'What? He needs to know. No point sugar-coating it.'

'When?' Joe demanded. 'Where?'

'Your brother was walking him down at the creek and he got off the lead in the scrub up the top of the track.'

'What were you doing walking him? You don't even like him and now he's gone? You need the harness. There's a knack to it.'

'I had the harness. He got out of it. That dog's like bloody David Copperfield.'

'He gets scared. Where did you last see him? Why didn't you call me? I could have helped look. I can't believe you, Anthony.'

'Clearly, I did it on purpose. I thought, here's a laugh.'

Joe caught a glimpse of his father pretending to watch TV in the other room – his usual response to conflict resolution.

'Joe, darling. I know you're upset but it's not what you think.'

'I got him back,' Anthony said. 'It took me three hours but I waited till he came back to me. He was just running up and down in the scrub. Didn't go near the road. A guy with a labrador helped me corner him.'

'Oh. Where is he?'

'He's in the backyard chewing one of his festy bones,' Anthony said.

'So he's OK?'

'Yeah, fine.'

'Sorry then.'

'That's not the end of it though, Joe, sweetheart,' Mrs King said. 'Your dad and I aren't sure whether Ed's going to be happy here with us. He hates walking and he's digging trenches in the backyard like he's preparing for a war. He ate Dad's slippers and the spare room doona. He goes crazy every night at nine o'clock for some unknown reason. I don't know if he'll ever get any better.'

'What are you saying?'

Joe heard his dad slide the TV room door shut.

'I think you and Anthony should go back to the shelter after school tomorrow to ask them what we can do about him.'

'What we can do?'

'If he can be trained or anything.'

'Of course he can be trained. He's a dog.'

'But he's very damaged, love.'

'So if he can't be?'

'Then Ed's gonna have to go back.'

'Anthony, I was going to tell him in my own way.'

'Mum, what difference does it make?'

'You're definitely going to need to work on your bedside manner if you want to make any kind of doctor,' Mrs King said, heading into the lounge room.

'Mum, can't we just wait for a while and see if he improves?' Joe asked.

'I'm sorry, Joe, honey, the decision's been made. It's not working. If he can't be trained, he can't stay.'

Anthony put his bowl in the sink.

'Just put it in the dishwasher,' Joe said.

'Fine. So are you coming tomorrow?'

'I s'pose there's no choice.'

'Right. Then I'll meet you where I did today.'

'All right.'

'I am sorry about this you know, Joe. He's a nice dog.'

'Yeah.'

Later that night, after he'd got in some bonding with his possibly condemned animal, Joe called Grace, knowing she'd be equally outraged by his parents' treatment of his canine friend. But her phone was engaged. A few minutes later he decided to try Lawrence. But when he picked up the receiver, he heard Anthony's voice on the other end. His first instinct was to put it back down immediately out of fear of his brother's wrath. Anthony had a sixth sense when it came to eavesdroppers. Joe was sure that Anthony must have heard the click and realised that he was listening, but after a few seconds, it seemed that Anthony was none the wiser. So listen, Joe did.

'But it can't be. Different directions, what's that about? It's a cop out, Belle. Of course things are different. We don't see each other every day. It's changed, but that doesn't mean it can't work,' Anthony pleaded. 'It's not like we're living in different countries.'

'I'm sorry, Anth. I really like you, it's just not the same.'

'As opposed to being different? We're going around in circles. Maybe we should think about this and talk tomorrow. We're both tired. It's not the best time to be . . .'

'Tomorrow won't change anything, Anthony. It's over. It happens.'

'It happens? What does that mean? Please, Belle. Let's just talk tomorrow?'

'No. Don't make me feel like the big bad wolf here. If you really want to know the truth, it's not me – it's you.'

'Great, can't even get your clichés right. Isn't it supposed to be "it's not you – it's me"?' Anthony grunted.

'No, Anthony.'

'Right,' Anthony said in a crushed voice Joe had only heard him use when the man at the computer shop had said that Belinda's Commodore 64 computer was irreversibly damaged, stripping him of his ability to play summer or winter games. 'Well, say hello to the three little pigs for me.' With that, Anthony slammed down the receiver and, from what Joe could tell, threw something across the room, causing a loud thud.

Joe was very impressed by his brother's ability to carry on the fairytale analogy in such a testing moment. But fairytales aside, Anthony was in a bad way – he'd been dumped by the love of his life. The only other lady with whom his brother spent as much time was a seventy-four-year-old cadaver named Betty. He really was up the shitter. And Joe didn't have a clue what to do.

But he was nothing if not sensitive and discreet. If anyone could help his brother heal his broken heart, it was him. In his first touching gesture of support, Joe picked up the phone and began dialling.

'Hey, Lawrence, it's me.'

'Hello, old sport,' Lawrence laughed. 'What did you forget to tell me in the twelve and a half hours that we were together today?'

'Listen, old sport, I've news. Isabelle just gave Anthony the old arse.'

18

The final afternoon bell fittingly tolled to the tune of the death march. Or at least it did in Joe's mind. He looked at his watch. There were still four minutes of school remaining, according to his Casio. He'd make sure he brought that to the office lady's attention on some other occasion. Perhaps when hell froze over. Judging from the discussion that he'd had with his mother that morning, his time with Ed looked like being cut tragically short. Actually, it hadn't been a conversation so much as a sort of Shakespearian monologue, in which Mrs King had listed, chronologically, all of Ed's misdemeanours since his arrival at Liberty Avenue.

'We've been over it. It's simple. If they say he can be trained, he can stay,' Mrs King had said. 'Otherwise, it's just going to be too much trouble. You do understand, don't you, Joe, love?'

'I understand. He's not perfect, so he gets the flick.'

'It's not that black and white.'

'Maybe I should start packing, myself. I'm not perfect either. I should have known. What do they say? A boy and his dog are soon parted?'

'Stop exaggerating, Joe. It's "a fool and his money", anyway.'

'I wouldn't know. I don't have any of that either, do I?'

'We never signed on for a special needs dog. I have enough trouble with the people in this house.'

'Can I at least stay home from school? I'm not going to be able to concentrate. I'll be thinking of Ed the whole time, wondering what's going to happen.'

'You're going to school, Joe. I'm sure you'll be able to keep your mind off the dog for six hours.'

'Everything will make me think of him – the picture of dogs playing poker in the common room, the hot dogs at lunchtime . . .'

'Here, don't forget your book,' Mrs King had said, handing Joe his copy of *The Great Gatsby*.

'Oh, no,' Joe said, feigning an emotional breakdown.

'What now?'

'It's dog-eared.'

Joe transferred the contents of his schoolbag into his locker, unable to contemplate doing homework in his troubled state. As he did so, a sort of montage of the good times that he had shared with Ed began to flash before his eyes.

He thought of all the occasions when Ed had hidden: in the laundry, under the house and in his favourite spot, the toilet. He smiled as he remembered the time that Ed had eaten his mother's Toblerone, packet and all, after taking it from her bedside table, which he had thought was alive when Joe had moved it. Then there was the night that he'd jumped on the kitchen table to eat the flowers. And who could ever forget the day that Joe's beloved dog had stood in the middle of the creek, refusing to move, later attempting to hop into a stranger's car, not keen on the walk home. 'Good times, good times,' Joe mused.

Joe headed down the corridor, hoping that perhaps Anthony had forgotten about their rendezvous. But Anthony was waiting across the road. Joe looked at his watch. Right on time. Ed stood on the back seat, his tail thumping against the window in excitement as he watched Joe approaching.

'Hi,' Anthony said.

'Hi.'

This was to be the only conversation in the seven or so minutes to the shelter. Somehow, it didn't seem right to say anything else. There were certain situations where talking really was cheap, where you could say any amount of words, but they wouldn't make a bit of difference. As they turned into the animal shelter carpark, Joe wondered whether undertakers ever made conversation. Or executioners. How would executioners chew the fat? What did one talk about before or after one had ended a person's life?

'Have you got him?' Anthony asked.

'Yeah,' Joe said, grabbing hold of Ed's lead.

They went inside and took a number. Ed lay his head down on Anthony's feet as they sat waiting, looking up with his big brown eyes as if to say 'See, I'm cute. I can be good. I can change . . .' Joe looked around the room. He noticed a young couple who appeared to be in the final stages of adopting a pair of kittens. Joe caught snippets of the shelter lady's instructions. 'So you'll need to get them vaccinated for that in a couple of months . . . It's all written down in the paperwork . . . They're great around children . . . This breed has a lovely nature . . .'

Joe never once heard the lady warn the unsuspecting couple that the animals wouldn't stay this cute forever, that it was also in their nature to actually grow and become cats. A man had brought in a rabbit he'd found in his front yard and Joe could see the look of annoyance on the reception woman's face as she thanked him and informed him that about two rabbits a day were handed in.

'Number eleven,' the rabbit lady's voice called.

Joe and Anthony walked Ed over to the desk.

'Hi. We got this dog from here . . . what would it be . . . a couple of months ago?' Joe began.

'And who's this?' the lady asked, walking around the front to meet Ed.

'His name's Ed,' Joe said. 'But we've . . .'

'Hello, Ed. You're a beautiful fella, aren't you? He's so soft, isn't he?'

'Ah, yeah, he is, but . . .' Joe started again.

'After Mr Ed?'

'Sorry?' Joe said.

'His name.'

'Oh, no. No real reason.'

'Mr Ed was a great show.'

'Yeah, I s'pose.'

Joe elbowed his brother in attempt to initiate some action. Or even some conversation. Anthony hadn't said a word since they'd got here.

'You're not sick are you, Eddie?' the woman said. 'No, you look good. You're a healthy boy, aren't you? Yes, you are.'

'No, he's healthy enough. It's just, we've had some problems. He's kind of a – special needs dog,' Joe explained.

'All dogs have special needs, really.'

'Yeah, but we were told he was active but he hates walking and yesterday he got off the lead and ran away and wouldn't come back for hours. He hides so he won't have to go out. He goes crazy every night around nine, nicking socks and shoes and hiding them. He thinks furniture's alive when you move it and one time he got on the kitchen table and tried to eat Mum's flowers. Oh, and he digs holes in the backyard . . .'

'Digging's very common. Normal dog behaviour.'

'No, I mean digging trenches. He also eats the hose . . .'

'A lot of this is very common puppy behaviour.'

'He's four and a half.'

'Do you know anything about his old home?' the lady asked.

'No. We were hoping you might be able to help us with that. Maybe that way we could get some idea of what to do.'

'OK, I'll look him up on the computer.'

'Thanks.'

A couple of minutes later the lady came back with precisely no information.

'I'm sorry, sometimes that happens. He might have just been dumped. I don't think he was seized. It's going to be a case of a bit of detective work on your part. And a lot of patience.'

'How much patience? Do you think he could get better with training?'

'A lot of the time training helps, yes. But I couldn't say for sure. I can give you the name of a trainer, if you like. Or you might like to consider behavioural therapy.'

'Mum doesn't really want to spend a lot of money.'

'I see,' the lady said, with a note of disapproval in her voice.

'No, she's a nice lady. We're nice people. Responsible people. My brother here's going to be a doctor. Responsible profession. It's just that Ed's been very demanding. Mum thinks maybe he'd be better off with someone else. Is . . . giving him back an option?'

Anthony looked away uncomfortably. Joe began to get annoyed by his brother's total silence throughout Ed's ordeal. Particularly as Ed was supposed to be Anthony's dog.

'Look, it is an option, we understand that it doesn't always work out, but I'll be honest – the chances of Ed

being re-housed aren't good. I don't mean to emotion-
ally blackmail you or anything, but that's the way it is
unfortunately.'

'Right.'

'But it's up to you. No pressure.'

'Of course, no pressure,' Joe said, feeling more pres-
sured in his life than he ever had before.

'Did you want to try the trainer?'

'I'm not sure. I really don't know if Mum will want . . .'

'Give us the trainer's number,' Anthony interrupted.
'We're not giving him back.'

'If you're sure,' the lady said, handing them a card and
virtually ushering them out the door.

Anthony grabbed Ed's lead. 'Thanks. Let's go.'

Joe had to hand it to his brother, when he did speak,
he spoke good.

'What do you reckon Mum's gonna say?' Joe asked,
as they turned out of the car park, Ed safely in the back
seat.

'Doesn't matter. She wouldn't want him heading for
death row.'

'Death row. That's good. Make sure we use that line on
Mum.'

'Training might work. I'm going to have a bit of time.
I know he was supposed to be my dog, so I appreciate
this, Joe.'

'He's a nice dog most of the time.'

'So will you help me with the training?'

'Yeah, I'll do anything for Eddie.'

Anthony was quiet for a moment. 'He just looked so alone, you know?'

'Yeah, I know.' Suddenly Joe realised that his brother had seen the same thing in Ed that Joe had seen that first day they'd brought him home: himself.

'I'm stopping at Maccas. You want anything?'

'I've only got a buck on me,' Joe said, feeling around in his pocket.

'I'll spot you.'

Joe attempted to feign nonchalance. 'Ta. I'll have a cheeseburger meal.' Obviously Anthony's break-up was affecting him in pretty major ways.

'Page two of the paper. It's you, isn't it?' the McDonald's drive-through girl said to Joe.

'Yeah, it is.'

'Thought so. We've got a pile of papers on the counter. I flick through them in the quieter times, so . . .'

'Do we get something free then?' Joe asked.

'I shouldn't, but . . . here,' the girl said, handing over a box of McDonald land cookies.

'They still make these? Great. Thanks.'

'When are you going to work next?' Anthony asked as he and Joe sat in the park with Ed, eating their food.

'Thursday night. Why?'

'Isabelle works Thursdays, right?'

'I think she still does.'

'I've got some stuff of hers. Could you give it back to her for me?'

'OK.'

'You'll hear it sooner or later so I may as well tell you – we broke up.' Anthony made it sound like he was only passing the information on to Joe out of courtesy because one of the tabloids would most likely run it on page one any day now.

'Oh, sorry about that.'

'Yeah, we were going different ways, you know. We hardly ever saw each other, so I just said there's no point shooting a dead dog – sorry, Ed. I said we should finish it.'

Joe carefully studied his brother's face, trying to see if he looked any different when he was lying through his teeth.

'How'd she take it?'

'She was all right. A bit disappointed, I think. But she agreed it was the right thing to do. So . . . anyway . . .' Anthony trailed off and looked over at Ed who was barking at a magpie.

'I've got so much work to do,' Joe said, sensing that his brother was in search of a subject change. 'Mrs Barry stays up with Lawrence at night when he's doing home-work, makes him coffee and cake. Good old Mum doesn't even make good with a cuppa . . .'

'Yeah,' Anthony laughed.

'Did you notice the pissy celebrities we get for McHappy Day? A guy who played about four AFL games and the local MP. Tim reckons his cousin had Russell Crowe at his Maccas one year. Can you imagine the attitude he'd give you?'

'You did well with that Scott guy, Joe.'

'I know,' he said, holding up his complementary cookies.

'Weren't you stressed?'

'I didn't have time to think about it. And Oliver was shitting me so much I s'pose I just did the opposite of what he did.'

'How did you remember to do all that stuff – like with the finger?'

'I don't know. It was like I could see that page of the first-aid book right in front of me. It wasn't that spectacular. You would have known what to do.'

'Yeah, but knowing and doing are two different things.'

'As someone who knows a lot about this stuff . . . Anth, do you think that I . . .'

'You what?'

'Do you reckon I could be a paramedic? I know it's hard to get into, but if I worked as hard as I can, do you think I'd have a chance?'

'What if I said I didn't think you could?'

'You don't think I can?'

'I didn't say that. But what if I did?'

Joe thought for a moment. 'I'd want to try anyway.'

'Then there's your answer. The only one that matters.'

'But you still didn't say . . .'

'Joe, I've dropped out of uni,' Anthony said suddenly.

'What?'

'I've deferred.'

'Since yesterday?'

'Since three weeks ago.'

'But you've been going every day. You tell Mum and Dad about it every night.'

'I make it up, Joe. It's easier to pretend that it's all OK while I work out what I'm doing.'

'Where have you been going all day then?'

'Work. The movies. The beach. The Glen food court. And the gym – I'm at peak fitness. I also went bowling once but that was a bit depressing.'

Joe could not have been more surprised if his brother had told him that he had decided to become a woman. Though Anthony did have very long eyelashes and delicate-looking hands.

'You won't tell Mum and Dad, will you? Dad'll hate me.'

'He's got me for that. But I won't say anything. So you've done the paperwork and everything?'

'Yeah. The Dean even asked me if I wanted to transfer to law.'

'But you didn't?'

'It's so boring.'

'What do you want to do, Anth?'

He thought for a moment. 'I don't want to do anything.'

'Oh.'

'But at the same time, I want to do everything. I can't explain it.'

'It makes sense. You don't want to waste time doing something you're not sure about?'

'I s'pose.'

'Maybe you'll find something you really like. It might

just take a bit more time. People change jobs all the time. It's probably the same with courses.'

'Maybe.'

'So you're sure about this, then?'

'No.'

'Right.'

'Joe, how do you even know that you're sure about something?'

'I'm probably not the one to ask but I'm a big believer in the gut. Maybe it just feels right.'

'I can't imagine having that feeling again. I planned my whole year last year, mapped out the marks I'd need, read medical journals, did extra courses and I got where I wanted to go. Where I thought I wanted to go. But now I don't know.'

'So change plans. Make another one. That's what Mum says, anyway. You'll get there.'

'Robbie Williams has got this song that says God laughs at the plans you make for yourself. Like it's a sort of arrogance to assume that you call the shots.'

'I didn't think you believed in God.'

'I don't.'

'That's a good song.'

'I know. And Robbie Williams is a prat.'

'But don't you think God – or whatever you believe in – would get pissed off with people who sit around waiting, doing nothing, not making any plans at all?'

'Probably.'

'So we can't win.'

'Looks like it.'

'Can I ask you something?'

Anthony nodded, scratching Ed's ears.

'Is this because of New Zealand? What happened?'

'Nah, it's nothing really. It's more like the little fish, big pond problem. The transition's a bit hard. They warned us at school, but I thought I'd be fine.'

Joe was confused. 'But you haven't just missed a few classes, Anth, you've deferred. There's isn't any transition any more – you knocked it on the head. So how can that be the problem?'

Anthony looked at his watch. 'We'd better go. Just tell me, either way, are you telling Mum and Dad – or what?'

'What? No, I said I won't, so I won't.'

'I'm sorry. I shouldn't have said anything till I've worked out what I'm doing. It's just that, you know . . .'

Joe did know. He was the only person that his brother had to talk to at the moment. Isabelle was gone and Chris was never around. It was slim pickings for poor Anthony.

'Dad's going to do his block.'

'I'd be more worried about telling them we had Maccas before tea,' Joe laughed. 'Remember what happened last time Mum found out we'd had a Big Mac meal after school?'

'My ears are still recovering from the shrieking.'

'So we'll both keep quiet about both things.'

'OK.'

Once he'd recovered from the shock of his brother's

news, Joe was secretly thrilled to be a part of the decep-
tion. It was the first time he remembered Anthony ever
sharing anything with him. Even as kids, when they'd
played games, they'd always played by Anthony's rules.
Rule number one being that Anthony never shared. Maybe
things were finally changing.

'It's a matter of adjusting. The lady reckons he'll be fine,'
said Anthony, doing all the talking for once in his life.
'Says it happens all the time.'

'Did she tell you how long it might take for him to
resemble a normal dog?' Mrs King asked, serving up some
broccoli.

'Not long. She's given us the name of an animal trainer,
though. Best in the business, right, Joe?'

'Yeah. That's what she said.'

'Well, that is good news, isn't it?' Mr King said, recog-
nising the resolution of conflict. 'How about some salt,
Doc?'

Joe nudged Anthony.

'Oh, sorry. Here, Dad,' Anthony said, taking the salt
from Joe.

'How was uni, Anth? Learn anything interesting?' Mr
King asked.

'Good. Um, not really, just . . . about ah . . .'

'Heart disease, wasn't it?' Joe asked. 'What was it?
Twenty Australians die from heart disease every day?'

'Yeah, about that,' Anthony lied.

'It's a frightening statistic. I couldn't quite believe it

when Anthony told me. Apparently there's a reason they call salt white death. You'd want to ease off it a bit, Dad. Stop being such a cowboy,' Joe continued, grabbing the salt from his baffled father.

'Uncle Phil's got heart disease, you know,' Mrs King said.

'Well, there you go. Everyone's touched by it,' Joe said.

'Yeah, it is very common,' Anthony added, feeling it necessary to authenticate his university anecdote *du jour*.

'Mind you, that man has every condition known to man,' Mrs King said. 'Hypertension, diabetes, asthma, hay fever. It'd be easier to list the conditions that he doesn't have.'

'He certainly doesn't suffer from good taste,' Joe added.

'Oh, Joseph,' Mrs King said, stifling a laugh.

'So what classes did you have, Anth? Was it anatomy today?' Mr King asked.

'No, anatomy was yesterday.'

'That's right. I can't keep up. Come to think of it, your Mum and I were talking the other day, and we thought that it might be easier if you write us up a copy of your timetable and pop it on the fridge. Just so we know when your late classes are. It'd be a lot easier. What do you think, mate?'

Even Mr King could pull of the 'mate'.

'Yeah, OK.'

'I ran into Sue Brooks today, from the school office,' Mrs King said. 'She said there's going to be a day where some of last year's year twelves come and speak to this year's year twelves about uni.'

'Right. We had that last year,' Anthony said, uncomfortably.

'You won't be surprised to hear that your name's been floating around the staffroom,' Mrs King boasted. 'I hope you can fit it in.'

Parents could be great people. But they could also be an absolute nightmare. It was like they had an in-built radar that detected when their offspring were lying, and immediately honed in on it. They thought that they were simply being interested in their children's lives, asking thoughtful questions, while their kids thought that perhaps their mothers hadn't been joking when they'd said they had eyes in the back of their head and knew everything that was going on.

Anthony looked at Joe in sheer desperation. Suddenly, he was sweating profusely, as if the kitchen light had become unbearably hot. Joe could see that Anthony was worried about tripping up, giving something away. He had a look that said he needed to buy a bit more time to get his story straight, and didn't want to answer any more of his parents' questions without a lawyer present.

'Man, I've got an absolute doozy of a biology assignment,' Joe said, suddenly.

'Another one?' Mr King asked.

'No, the same one I told you about last night. But the

volume of work involved. Ten criteria. Do you know I only found out today that criterion is the singular of criteria?'

'That's right,' Mrs King said.

'Criteria being the plural, of course,' Joe rambled. 'My movie night's filling up fast, too.'

'You said so, love. That's great. How's Isabelle, Anth?' Mrs King asked, smiling – sweetly to the impartial observer, but menacingly to those in the know.

'There's a name I haven't heard in a while,' Mr King added helpfully. 'She enjoying uni?'

'Yeah, she is,' Anthony managed to say.

'She's very busy, isn't she?' Joe said. 'Thirty-seven contact hours, would you believe?'

Anthony frowned warningly at Joe.

'Really? That's more than Anthony, isn't it? Times have changed since I did my Arts degree,' Mrs King said.

Joe patted his mother's shoulder. 'Yes, indeed they have, mother,' he said, making a good recovery.

'Tell her to come around for dinner one night soon,' Mrs King said, yet again honing in on her son's web of lies.

'I will,' Anthony said. 'When I see her.'

'When do you think that might be?' Mrs King asked.

When would the probing desist? Andy Sipowicz asked less questions. Joe sensed that his brother was now at breaking point. Something drastic was needed to divert his parents' attention from Anthony's university studies and love life. Like Abraham mounting the cliff-top to sacrifice his only son, Joe pushed his meal away.

'I can't eat my tea, Mum. Sorry, but I had McDonalds after school. I'm full as a goog. Could not fit another thing in.'

'You had what?' Mrs King said angrily. 'You know that Tuesday is roast night, Joseph. Did you both have McDonalds?'

'Nah, just me. I knew it was roast night, but what can I say? I really wanted it. When the Mac-attack hits . . . it was delicious.'

Mr King threw his serviette down. 'Joe, your mother doesn't cook for her health, you know. That was thoughtless. When are you going to grow up?'

'Yeah, I'm sorry.'

'Sorry doesn't change it, Joe,' Mrs King said, clearing the table, crashing plates around furiously. 'McDonalds? I can't believe . . . words fail me.'

The boys' parents headed huffily into the family room for some television therapy.

'Hey, thanks, Joe,' Anthony said a few minutes later when their mum and dad were happily installed in front of a not remotely amusing BBC sitcom.

'It's OK.'

'You were cool.'

'Nah. Well, yeah, I can't lie. I was pretty cool, wasn't I?'

Anthony smiled and headed to his room with Ed trailing behind, to watch the soccer in blissful peace. Joe went to his room to make a dent in his homework. It really had been an afternoon and evening of firsts.

19

'I am not going to say that to Dad.'

'Come on, Anth, it's the perfect opener.'

'"Dad, funny thing, I quit uni" is not the perfect opener,' Anthony said as he and Joe sat in front of the television.

'Well, you can paraphrase. But you do have to tell him and Mum soon.'

'I know. I will.' Ed came bounding into the lounge room, dropping a sock at Joe's feet.

'I know it's only been a week but he's more normal, isn't he?'

'Yeah, definitely,' Anthony agreed.

Joe got up and headed to the kitchen. 'Want a drink?'

'Yeah. Ta.'

Suddenly, Ed sprinted past Joe, nearly bowling him over.

'Joe, he's gone psycho. He's trying to attack me,' Anthony yelled.

Joe came back with their drinks and observed their dog. 'Nah, he's fine. He does this. He's trying to kill the fly.'

'Really?'

'Yeah, watch him. He's like a venus fly trap.'

They watched Ed pounce at the window, pawing at a pair of blowflies. He captured one and spat it out on the floor once the kill was complete.

'Good boy,' Anthony said. 'And he didn't even eat it. Our boy's wicked smart.'

'Joe laughed. 'They said he'd never be normal.'

'We should probably teach him to distinguish between bees and flies though. He could do some real damage to himself. Good boy, Ed. Fly. That was a fly,' Anthony said, giving him a treat.

Joe settled back on the couch. 'He was good on his walk today, wasn't he? Once he worked out that the log wasn't alive. I reckon we can let him off the lead at the creek soon.'

'Do you think that's smart? What if he does what he did last time?'

'We'll get him back. He can't stay on the lead forever.'

'I don't know if he's ready, Joe.'

'We can wait a bit longer.'

Ed pounced at the other fly, landing heavily on the window pane.

'He's got it. It's dead,' Anthony marvelled. 'Fly, Ed. It's a fly, boy.'

'It's not the only thing that's dead, Anth,' Joe said, pulling back the curtain to reveal a crack in the window.

'Oh, shit. Dad's going to go mental. We can't say it was Ed. They'll definitely make us take him back then.'

'Good point.'

Joe couldn't believe it. His brother was carrying on as if he were nine years old.

'So what do we say happened?'

'Relax, Anth.'

'How? Dad's already going to hate me – and he doesn't like Ed.'

'We'll tell him I did it.'

'What? What would we say you did?'

'We say, Dad, funny story, and then tell him I was playing football or basketball or juggling firesticks – whatever. And he won't hate you.'

'I might go back, you know.'

'To medicine?'

'Yeah.'

'Because of Dad?'

'No.'

'Really?'

'No.'

'You can't do something you hate.'

'But what's the alternative?'

'Becoming me, I s'pose.'

Anthony looked at Joe with a strange expression that Joe realised, after a few moments, was admiration. 'You don't care what he thinks, do you? What's that like?'

'I know what he thinks. But what I've figured out is you can't care when you know it's wrong.'

'You're right. I'm going to have to tell him.'

'Just make sure you tell him exactly what you want to tell him, Anth. Don't let him make you change your mind.'

Mr King barely batted an eyelid at Joe's latest confession. He just got the book out and added in the cost of a new window. Anthony insisted on paying Joe for it in an attempt to assuage his guilt.

'I still don't understand what you were doing. I didn't know you even had numchucks, Joe.'

'It really doesn't matter, Dad. I just stuffed up, I s'pose.'

'Ah, Joey.' There was almost a gentleness to Mr King's tone, as if Joe's confession was not at all unexpected. It almost seemed to cheer him up.

'Hey, Dad, there's another *Seinfeld* marathon on tomorrow night if you're interested.'

'We might have to have a look at that, Joe.'

Later, Anthony drove Joe back to school to make the final preparations for his movie night. 'Looks pretty good,' Anthony said as they finished setting up the screen.

'Yeah.'

'So who was that girl?'

'Which one?'

'The one who went to get the cushions?'

'Oh. Grace. Tim's sister.'

'That's Tim's sister?'

'Yeah. Not the one I did the deb with – that's Alice.'

'She's all right.'

'She's nice.'

'Easy on the eye, too.'

'Who are you? Uncle Phil?'

'What? She's good-looking.'

'I'm not introducing you.'

Anthony smiled. 'I get it. What time do you reckon you'll finish?'

'It'll be about 11:30 by the time we pack up. But I'll get a lift with Lawrence.'

'OK. Have a good night.'

Joe processed what his brother had just said. 'What do you mean you get it? Get what?' he called after him.

People soon piled into the school gym, armed with cushions, pillows, beanbags and whatever else they required for a comfortable night's viewing. Brad and Tim hijacked the common-room couch for the evening and fought for twenty minutes over its position, until one of the arms fell off and they came to the shared conclusion that it would go best back in the common room.

Lawrence manned the popcorn stand with Claudia, who he'd roped in as an honorary Hillview Secondary College student for the evening. Grace and some of the others from STC took the money at the door. In his role as event manager, Joe spread himself across the different jobs, pitching in as needed.

'This is all very impressive, Joe,' Mr Woods said, snacking on popcorn and weak orange cordial as part of his role as chaperone.

'Thanks for coming, sir.'

'It's amazing what people can do when they put their minds to it.'

'Yeah, it's just like Costner said, "if you build it, they will come".'

Miss Barker passed through the hall with Mr Sturt. 'Joe, this looks great.'

Joe walked over to Grace. 'I think we're ready to put on the first movie,' Grace said. 'Just quietly, we're raking in the dough.'

They walked over to get their popcorn. 'Great turn-out,' Claudia said, handing over their change.

'Yeah, he's done well, hasn't he?' Grace said, linking her arm with Joe's.

Claudia leaned in closer towards Grace. 'Are you two . . . together?'

Joe felt the blood rush to his cheeks as Grace leaned in and touched Claudia on the arm. 'We're having our first date next week,' she confided. 'I'm very excited.'

Lawrence smiled a surprised smile at Joe, who saw his surprise and raised him.

'That's great,' Claudia smiled. 'Joe's a great guy.'

'I know,' said Grace. 'Bye.' And she pulled the still stunned Joe away.

As the movie started, Joe sat beside Grace, watching her out of the corner of his eye. He wanted to know why she had said that thing about dating to Claudia. Half an hour in, he'd had enough.

'Can I have a word?' he whispered.

Grace turned to face him. 'Now?'

'No, next week, I thought I'd warn you in advance, like you did – with our date.'

'It's coming up to a good bit.'

'Grace!'

'Shhhhh,' said a girl from a row behind.

'Hey, don't shoosh us. We're the reason you're here.' Grace got up to follow Joe out.

'What's going on?' Joe asked once they reached the gym foyer.

'You mean what I said to Claudia?'

'Yeah. I appreciate it if you were trying to make me look good, but you didn't have to. I'm all right.'

'I know. I just . . .'

'What?'

'Nothing, sorry.'

Joe could tell that Grace's nothing was really something. 'Come on, what is it?'

Grace screwed up her face. 'I don't like her.'

Joe smiled. 'You don't like her?'

'You don't find her a bit patronising?'

'Not really.'

'Maybe it's not patronising so much. It's more that she . . . I don't know. I can't put my finger on it and it's annoying the hell out of me.'

'You're shirty, aren't you? I've never seen you shirty apart from when Jade Pryce is around.'

'I'm not shirty, Joe.'

'Stroppy?'

'No.'

'Testy?'

'No. More like . . .'

'Toey?'

'I'm just not . . .'

'Of sound mind?'

'I think I'm jealous.'

Joe did a double take. 'Why? Jealous of what?'

Grace sighed. 'I don't know. I can't help it. It's so irrational. I don't even know the girl.'

Joe sat down on the stairs. 'It makes sense.'

'You think?'

'Yeah, you love my guts.'

'Of course.'

'You're not to blame. The looks, the charm, the green hue in my eyes.'

'They're blue.'

'With this jumper, yeah. The point is, stronger women have . . . walked straight passed me, actually.'

She smiled. 'Maybe it is because you liked her.'

'Yeah, past tense.'

'And because I like you.'

'You do?'

'Yes. I think it's your guts, like you said.'

'I knew it. But you'd better not be thinking of using me for my body until Harrison comes crawling back.'

'Of course not. I'd use you until I got an offer from any-one, not just Harrison.'

'Well, all right then.'

'So we should go out, Joseph.'

'On a date?'

'We don't have to call them dates. They could be out-
ings or excursions or . . .'

'You really want to go out with me?'

'I do.' She sat down beside him on the step and moved
in close, taking hold of his hand. He smiled as he saw that
her hand was trembling. She was nervous. He hadn't seen
her like that before.

'But, hang on. What about your dad?'

'He's got my mum. And he's old and . . . it would be
illegal.'

Joe smiled. 'Grace, he's got a gun. He'll kill me and
make it look like an accident.'

'Joe, don't be stupid. He's very reasonable.'

'You're right. He wouldn't do it himself. A guy like
that's got minions. He'll pull in a favour and get someone
else to do it.'

'Don't worry about my dad. He'll just get you to sign
something to say we're getting married in five years.'

'No worries then. What about Tim? He'll hate my guts.
Ironically, the very guts that you love.'

'He'll get over it. Besides, we've got leverage there.
Simone was my friend before she was Tim's girlfriend.'

'Good point. Make sure we use that.' Joe smiled. 'And
what happens if we go to all this trouble, make all these
people mad, and we find out that we don't . . . gel when
we're not . . . all liquored up?'

Grace pulled him closer and smiled, her green eyes growing bigger by the second. 'What happens if we do?' she said and gently kissed him on the mouth.

Joe was in love. And right now it was difficult to remember a time that he hadn't been. It was as though every insignificant detail of his life had led him to this moment. No wonder people did weird things in the name of love, he thought as he unlocked the front door. You could read about it or watch stories about it at the movies, but feeling it yourself was another thing altogether. He'd planned to see Grace the next day, but sunrise couldn't come fast enough. It was all sounding like a Hallmark channel movie.

Joe would have stayed for another movie had he known what awaited his arrival home. In one corner of the house, his mother was hosting a Tupperware party for twenty of her closest friends. While in the lounge room . . . he knew from the moment he clapped eyes on his father that Doctor Tony had confessed. The secret was out. His father wore the expression of a man whose footy team had missed out on a place in the Grand Final by a point. The jig was up and so was Graeme King's blood pressure.

'But why, Anthony? Why?' Mr King said, anguished.

'It just wasn't for me, Dad. I might look at another course at some stage but not right now.'

Joe stayed in the hall, wondering whether he was now listening into his brother's conversations so often that it could be considered a hobby. Then he heard his mother's voice. She must have temporarily escaped her gathering to take up the opportunity to dispense unwanted parental advice. 'At some stage? What other course is there? You got the marks. You've always been so interested.'

'Well, it wasn't what I thought it would be. I don't know what else to tell you. It's not like I have to use all the marks. They don't mean anything.'

Mr King ran his fingers through his thinning hair in frustration. 'What else are you going to do with them? It's such a bloody waste.'

Suddenly there was an outburst from the other end of the house. Joe craned his neck to check the source of the shouting. The Tupperware lady was conducting a quiz.

'That's right. The first Tupperware party was in 1961. Take your pick of the lettuce corer or the orange peeler.'

Joe turned back to eavesdropping on the main event. It was like returning after an ad break.

'How can you know after one semester? You could have at least stuck in there for the year, Anth,' Mr King continued.

'No, I couldn't.'

'Well, you can still go back later, can't you? Maybe a break's all you need, hey, love? You've had a bit of a rough trot.'

'I don't think that's the problem, Mum.'

'But you've always had such discipline. We'd expect this from your brother . . . no follow-through, but you . . .'

'Graeme,' Mrs King said warningly.

Joe was outraged. No follow-through? He began heading into the lounge room to give his father what for, but changed his mind and resumed his position at the listening post.

'Don't bring Joe into this,' Anthony said, his tone growing more hostile. 'It's not about him. And he's smarter than you reckon.'

'Of course he's smart. But there's a difference between being smart and being intelligent,' Mr King said. 'There's no point being smart if you don't have the intelligence to do something with it. You end up wasting your life.'

'And there's no point doing something just because you can. I've always worked hard, tried to make you happy, but now I'm not happy, Dad.'

'I see you didn't drop out of uni before you got to the stage where you learn to blame your parents for everything.'

'Whatever you reckon.'

'Your Uncle Phil and I were never pandered to like that.'

'Uncle Phil's a recovering alcoholic and you're . . .'

'I'm what?'

Joe could hear his heart beating as he stood there, breathing shallow, nervous breaths, not wanting to miss a moment. He'd never heard Anthony talk to his father like this before.

'What do you do every day? A job you've hated for the last twenty years.'

'A job that's given you everything you have,' Mr King yelled.

'I know that. And I appreciate it. We all appreciate it. But do you want that for me?'

'You're not going to love every minute of your job. No one does, Anthony. You need to get real. Sometimes things get difficult and we don't like it. But as an adult, you don't have the luxury of just giving up every time things get a bit tough. Just hang in there a bit longer. We'll get you a tutor if you like.'

'No. I don't want a tutor. And if I'm an adult, like you say, you should respect my decision.'

'But Anthony, you're only eighteen. Your dad and I are just trying to help you make a decision you won't regret later.'

'You're not listening to me, Mum. I'm not going back to medicine. Not next semester or next year. Not ever. It doesn't matter how old I am.'

'I don't think you can categorically say that, Anth,' Mr King said, adopting a simultaneously reasonable and infuriating tone, a trademark of parents the world over.

'Your dad's right, love. What if you wait a while and just –'

'I don't want to wait. I don't want to be a doctor. I don't want to see sick people. I don't want to poke and prod dead people.' Anthony's voice was wavering and Joe could tell he was close to tears.

'Dead people?' Mrs King continued. 'There's a bit more to medicine than –'

'But that's part of it and I don't want to ever see another dead person.' Anthony shouted. 'Ever. It's not for me.'

'Not for you? Well, what is for you? What are you going to do instead?' Mr King asked.

'I'm working at a sports shop at the moment.'

'A sports shop?' Mr King muttered, incredulously. 'This just gets more and more ridiculous.'

'I don't know what I want to do yet. But whatever I end up doing, I hope that you can both be proud of me again one day.' Anthony stormed off to his room.

'Did you know about this, Joe?' Mrs King asked, catching sight of him in the hall.

'Yeah, I did.'

'What? For how long?'

'I don't know, Dad. Does it matter?'

Mr King sat back in his chair. 'No. I don't suppose it does.'

'I know you're both disappointed and everything, but he's thought a lot about this and –'

'Not now, Joe, love,' Mrs King said, heading back to the Tupperware party.

Mr King went all quiet as he always did when he was upset. It was unbearable. Joe retreated to his room with Ed. Anthony had meanwhile put one of his indistinguishable blokey band CDs on very loudly, and made a thumping noise that Joe deduced came from throwing himself on his bed. The unstable home environment, Joe concluded, really made it very difficult for anyone to get a scrap of homework done. So he took a leaf out of his brother's book, and plonked down on his bed, firing up Tetris on his Gameboy. It concerned him slightly that lately he'd started seeing Tetris blocks whenever he closed his eyes. He'd even started to dream about Tetris.

Graeme poked his head around Joe's door. 'Your mother's party's over and I'm making a cuppa if you want to watch a bit of the *Seinfield* marathon.'

Joe was not sure what the protocol was here. He decided to refuse in the interest of brotherly relations, tenuous as they were. 'Actually, Dad, I should . . .' But then he saw the look on his father's face, a look of absolute bewilderment. Mr King was confused and upset and obviously genuinely wanted some company. Joe's company.

'Yeah, that'd be good.'

Joe and his dad laughed as Elaine lost the respect of her co-workers through abysmal dancing and again as Kramer pitched his coffee-table book idea.

'Another cuppa, Joe?'

'Yeah. I'll get it.'

Joe returned with a tray of tea and biscuits. 'You have sugar, don't you, Dad?'

'Yeah. Thanks. What do you think I should do about your brother?'

'Pardon?'

'I don't know what to do. I don't understand it.'

Joe nearly choked on his mint slice in surprise. He couldn't remember a time when his dad had looked so – human, or asked his advice on anything. 'Time.'

'Sorry?'

'I'd just give him a bit of time. He needs to think about things.'

'You can think about things too much though. Sometimes it's better to just get on with it.'

'I know what you mean, but I suppose there are some times you can't, even though you want to.'

'I don't want him to waste his life.'

'He won't. He'll be all right. He'll fall on his feet eventually.'

'Or come to his senses.'

'He might just need to try a few things before he finds – a niche.'

'But trying things, rolling with the punches . . . your brother's not like you. He's always been ambitious.'

It wasn't the first time he'd heard it, but it still stung. 'Yeah, I s'pose so. I'm pretty tired, Dad. I think I'll go to bed.'

'Joe, I didn't mean . . .'

'Forget it.'

'I just meant that you'll be all right. I'm the last person who should be giving career advice. Your brother was right about that. I never quite found the job for me.'

'Yeah.'

'Still, not everyone loves what they do. If you're lucky you do, but most of us . . . we survive.'

Joe was about ready to bail on the pep talk.

'I s'pose you fill your life with other things to love.' Mr King looked Joe right in the eyes and smiled a smile that made Joe wish he would do it more.

'I didn't ask how your night went?'

'It went great,' Joe said, as he got up to go to bed. 'We raised a heap. A couple of grand.'

'Well done. That's great.'

Joe retreated to the kitchen where he found Mrs King making the next day's lunches.

'Mum, I *can* make my own lunch,' he said, exasperated. 'Remember that short course I did last summer?'

'Very funny. I know you can do it but I like doing it for you. Besides it's good to have stuff to do to take your mind off certain things.'

'Anthony will be OK.'

'I hope so.'

'In the meantime, I'm just enjoying the novelty of being the good son.'

'Oh, Joe.'

'Come on, Mum. That's why Dad's so upset about this, because Anthony was his hope. Dad's just been waiting for me to stuff up again. He was almost relieved when I smashed that window the other day, as if he was right again. It's never going to change, no matter what I do.'

'You're wrong, love. He adores you. He's just not . . . one of those gushing people. It doesn't come easily to him. Never has.'

'Yeah.'

'And he's never really known what to do with you.'

'Because I'm the son that flouts the rules?'

'Partly.'

'What the hell's flouting anyway?'

'I think he's scared of you, in a way.'

'What do you mean?'

'You haven't ever really worried about the future and you've always fallen on your feet. You haven't had to plan every second of your life. Dad's like Anthony.'

Maybe that's what Joe's dad had meant earlier that evening. He hadn't meant to insult Joe at all. If anything, his father had been dangerously close to paying him a compliment.

'You're like me, Joe. I never knew what I wanted to do when I was growing up. I went along and fell into a whole lot of different things, which turned out to be the best way for me.'

'I haven't always known that I'd fall on my feet,' Joe said.

'Well, you do a good impression of it, and that's sort of the same thing.'

'I should get into playing poker then. Under-age gambling. Dad would love that.'

'You're all right with me, no matter what you do.'

'Thanks, Mum.'

'I was thinking about what we talked about the other day – about strengths. And I wanted so much to tell you something inspirational, that you'd always remember and be able to attribute to your wise old mum. But I don't know what to say.'

'That's all right. I think I have to work it all out for myself anyway. I'm getting there slowly.'

Mrs King smiled. 'All I could come up with was that I

don't care what you do – clean windows, drive an ambulance or go to space. Whatever. As long as you're happy.'

'Space would be far too claustrophobic. Besides, I'm ideologically opposed to the Space Program, ever since they sent those dogs up.'

'Whatever you do, you're already someone, anyway. You know that, don't you?'

'Yeah,' he muttered.

She took his face in her hands, looking him straight in the eye. 'Don't you?'

'Yes, I do,' he said, smiling at the realisation that he really meant it. 'I know it's all about the journey, but I still wish I had some idea of where I'd end up. Belinda's the high-flying King with her job and life in London, and regardless of what Anthony ends up doing, he's the smart King. What King am I, Mum?'

Mrs King smiled. 'You're the King of . . . Whatever.'

Joe raised his eyebrow. 'Catchy.'

'You're the good guy, Joe. The good guy who calls your dad's mobile to make him feel important. The boy who's done three debs, when most boys wouldn't even do one. And I know about the window. Numchucks, my foot.'

'I'm a pretty crappy good guy, Mum.'

'The best good guys aren't perfect.'

'What about Jesus?'

Mrs King smiled. 'He trashed a temple and hung out with a prostitute.'

'True.'

'You make people feel good. And not because you're a

270

loser and they feel better when they compare themselves to you. You make them laugh and feel important. That's quite a talent. Whatever you do – you're you!' She leant in and kissed him on the forehead.

'Goodnight, Mum.'

Anthony still had his music up loud when Joe went to bed. Ed followed him into his room and settled immediately at the foot of his bed. He was about to thump on the wall when he noticed another sound. He put his ear to the wall and listened for a minute. He heard it again, this time more clearly. The muffled sound of his brother crying. It wasn't just quiet crying, it was sobbing. Loud, inconsolable sobbing.

Joe got as far as his door before he realised that there was nothing he could do. Anthony wouldn't want to talk. And if Joe tried to make him, he'd just end up embarrassing him and making things worse. So Joe did the only thing he could. He called to Ed and headed to his brother's room. He slowly opened Anthony's door, making it appear as if Ed had nosed it open and pushed Ed gently through. Standing at the door he heard Ed jump up on the bed. 'Good boy, Eddie. Come here,' Anthony said.

Ed might have been short on advice, but he was a great listener.

20

'I'll pick you up this arvo, if you like,' Anthony said, as he and Ed dropped Joe off at school.

'I finish at three.'

'OK, three o'clock then.'

'Thanks. By the way, there are some CDs in a Target bag on the desk in my room. Isabelle gave them to me. Said they're yours.'

'Right.'

'So we'll meet here then?'

Anthony nodded.

'See ya, Eddie. Bye, Anth.'

'She dumped me.'

'What?'

'Isabelle. I s'pose she told you?'

'No, she didn't. That's rough.' Joe waved to Lawrence,

Tim and Grace, as they walked through the school gate, obviously surprised by the display of King brotherly relations.

'Yeah. She'd moved on. Sorry, you'd better get going.'

'Yeah, I should. What's on for you today?'

'Not much. I'm not working so I'll probably do some washing or something to keep Mum off my back.' Anthony paused for a moment. 'Is that who I think it is?'

Joe looked behind him. His eyes met Mr Woods'. 'Hey, sir.'

'You'd better kill a few more moments, Joe. You're dangerously close to being on time.' Mr Woods continued on through the school gate.

'Yeah, that's Woods all right. Do you wanna get some brekky?'

'What? Now?'

'Yeah, you heard him. I can't be on time.'

'I think he was joking.'

'We're only watching a video in English, and I could very well miss something important in biol, but I'll catch up.'

'That'd go down really well with Mum and Dad – me derailing your studies.'

Joe laughed. 'That train missed the station long ago. Come on, eggs? Hotcakes? McMuffins?'

'OK then,' Anthony said, looking around like he was driving a getaway car.

Joe waved to Mr Woods who waved back, confusion sweeping across his face.

'Forgot something, sir. I'll be back,' Joe called out the car window.

'Are you sure you won't get into trouble for being late to school?' Anthony asked as they got stuck into their hotcakes.

Joe laughed. 'It's OK. They're not going to strip you of your former school captain privileges. Your name's up on the board in big gold letters. They put it up the other day. The dux board's up, too. It's quite a nice effect seeing your name twice. Lessens the pressure for me.'

'Yeah, I am sorry about that.'

'You've more than made up for it, believe me. Do you think Mum and Dad are coming around a bit though?'

The last few days had been pretty tense at home. Mr and Mrs King were carrying on like they were in a silent film. Mr King only spoke in emergencies, each of his rare sentences dripping with subtext.

'Pass the salt, Joe?' *Because I know I can't rely on your brother to pass it to me.*

'Have you seen the remote?' *Anthony's probably given it the flick, too.*

'How's the school work, Joe?' *How's the bludging, Anthony?*

'Maybe.' Anthony chewed thoughtfully. 'Apart from Mum crying when *Medic Alert* came on the other day.'

'Yeah, apart from that. Dad had that chat to you last night. That looked encouraging.'

'He asked me to move my car.'

'Yes, and then after that. You two were chatting like a couple of girlfriends.'

'He asked for his street directory and gave me some dry-cleaning to take up the street.'

'Progress. Baby steps, Anth. Don't do anything just to try to make him happy, because I don't think we can.'

'Yeah.'

'Hey, it'd be good if Belinda could have a baby out of wedlock. That'd take the heat off us for a while.'

'Yeah, anything that makes life easier for us. But she's never been a team player.'

'I'm probably going to Lawrence's after school if you want to come,' Joe said, getting to his feet. 'I need more butter.'

'Get me some, will you?'

Joe reappeared with extra sachets in hand. 'God, you'd think I'd asked the guy for a lung. It's just butter. So, did you want to come?'

'Where?'

'Chris' this afternoon. He's home on Wednesdays.'

'Nah, I've got other stuff to do. I might be working.'

'But you said you'd pick me up.'

'Oh, yeah, I did. I probably won't be able to. Sorry, I forgot. Do you think Ed's all right in the car? Maybe we should go?'

'He's fine, Anth.'

'I need to get a knife. Wish me luck.'

'Here, use mine.' Joe finally got the courage to ask the question that he'd been skirting around for weeks. 'Why don't you want to see Chris, Anth?'

'I told you, I'm probably working.'

'Not just today. Ever since you got back from New Zealand. Did you have a fight? Because if anyone knows about fighting with the Barrys . . .'

'There wasn't a fight,' Anthony said, a little annoyed. He got his knife and sat back down, saying nothing for a couple of minutes. 'How can there be a fight when I go over there all the time?'

'Because I go over there all the time and you're never there. Chris asked me the other day whether you were still alive . . .'

'That's not funny.'

'It wasn't meant to be. Hey, I don't care one way or the other if you tell me what's going on, but you should know that I know that you're speaking crap. I don't get why you have to pretend you're going to Chris' house. Why you just can't go there?'

'So Mum and Dad didn't start asking questions . . .'

'But your secret's out now. What does it matter?'

Anthony threw his cutlery aside and picked up his remaining hotcake, signalling that their conversation had come to an end.

'OK then. I'll see you,' Joe said, picking up his tray.

'Where are you going?'

'To school. Can you open the car so I can get my schoolbag?'

Anthony followed his brother to the car park. 'I'll drive you.'

'Don't worry about it.'

'You're already late. Come on, let's go.'

'I'd rather walk.'

'You mean you'd rather waste a bit more time?'

'No. I'd rather walk.'

'Whatever,' Anthony said, passing Joe his schoolbag from the boot.

'Exactly. Thank you. Well, this has been fun.'

'What?'

'These last few weeks have been a bit weird. So if you could just call me one of your innovative names so we can go back to normal, that'd be great. Turd-burger – I used to like that. Arsewipe, that was another favourite.'

'What are you going on about, you moron?'

'An oldy, but a goody. That's a start.' Joe patted Ed on the head and began walking away.

'See you then,' Anthony called. 'I'll pick you up.'

'Whatever.'

The temporary theft of his catchphrase ignited some-thing in Anthony that caused him to run after Joe, with Ed in tow. 'Wait, Joe.'

Joe stopped, turning to face his brother. 'What?'

Anthony stared blankly. 'I don't know.'

'Don't bother picking me up this afternoon, because I really don't know what time I'll finish.'

'I'm sorry.'

'For what?'

'For lying about Chris.'

'So you *did* have an argument?'

'Yeah. No, not an argument. It wasn't really anything much. Things have just changed. You know how it is.'

'Things? Like with you and Isabelle?'

'A bit. But not really.' Anthony sat down on a brick fence.

'Anth, I'm not in the habit of pulling teeth. It doesn't matter, OK? Just don't lie to me.'

'That's what it was – or is. I know it shouldn't matter, but it does – to me. I tried to forget about it like Chris, but I couldn't.'

'Forget the accident?'

'Yeah. And Sam.'

'He was the guy who . . . from Canada?' Joe sat down beside Anthony, watching a couple of late school kids race up the street.

'Yeah, one of the ones who died.'

'You knew him?'

'As much as you can know someone after five days. It wasn't as if we were best friends.'

Ed rested his head on Joe's lap. 'Was he from your hostel?'

'The three of us shared a room with some German guy who we never saw. It shouldn't still be a big deal. I felt stupid crying about it, 'cause like Chris said, it wasn't about us.'

'He said that to me, too.'

'I met Sam's mother and his sister. If anyone deserved to be sad – they'd known him forever.'

'I think you get to be sad, Anth. It doesn't matter how well you knew him. It's bloody sad.'

'She was nice – Sam's mum. I tried to give her back his watch.' He pulled up his sleeve and showed Joe the Nike watch he'd been wearing since he'd arrived home.

'That was Sam's?'

'We did a swap. My Blundstones for his watch. I told him he could easily get a new pair, but he was worried he wouldn't have time. They were pretty new anyway. He was rapt in them.'

'She didn't want the watch back?'

'She said I should keep it. And I was so glad. I wasn't even going to tell her about it, because I wanted to keep it for some reason. Do you think that's weird?'

'Nah.'

'Chris thought it wasn't healthy. He said we needed to forget it and move on. But I wanted to remember. Every morning we were there, Sam and I walked to the bakery to get brekky.'

Joe smiled. 'Chris still in bed?'

'Lazy bastard, yeah. Sam was disgusting. He had a pie and sauce each time, washed it down with coke. By the third morning, he'd planned my trip to Canada. He said we had to ski. Some mornings I wake up, convinced I made it all up, and then I see the watch and . . . I'm relieved.'

'Relieved?'

'I don't know. Not relieved that it happened, just glad that I have something to remember him by, because I want to remember Sam every day – a guy I only knew for five days. Now that's weird.'

'Romeo and Juliet only knew each other a few days.

And look how huge that was – not that I'm suggesting that you were, you know . . . in love with this boy.'

Anthony gave Joe the sort of look that TV courtroom judges gave lawyers who are dangerously close to contempt.

Ed stared up at him as if to say 'make your point, counsellor'.

'It doesn't matter whether it was five days or five years. No one can tell you how you should feel. You were on an adventure holiday. It's like a roadtrip movie – you only had each other to rely on, you're there, living in the moment, everything and everyone else is secondary . . . In those five days at some point, you were probably the most important people in each other's lives.'

'Yeah, I s'pose.'

'Do you ever think that when they say in the movies that someone who died wouldn't want everyone else to be miserable, that maybe they would? I would – at least for a little while. Grumps would – forever.'

Anthony smiled. 'Chris wasn't there. He doesn't remember most of it. The way he tells it, we just had a close shave. But I was standing around, watching all of it. Seeing them pull the bodies out of the water.'

'Shit. I didn't know that.'

'How can I sleep when that's all I see when I close my eyes? I try to make myself see other stuff, but it just comes back. We all mucked around together heaps, and the only image I have of Sam is when they pulled him out of the water – seeing my boots on his feet.'

'God, Anth. I don't know what to say.'

'Looking at those boots. It was like . . . I don't know . . .'

'Like it should have been you?'

'Sort of.'

'Not that I mean it really should have been you . . .'

'I know. No, it was more like it could have been me. There was no reason why it wasn't.'

'There was no reason why it was Sam, either.'

'I don't get it, Joe. How come a misery guts like Grumps will live forever and someone like Sam doesn't get to hit twenty?'

'I dunno.'

'What could he have done that was so bad that he deserved to die?'

'I dunno.'

'I just don't get it.'

'You know, the answer's probably nothing. I reckon it might be as simple and as awful as when your time's up, your time's up. There's no real answer, and trying to find one will only drive you mad.'

'So then what do you do?'

'You're asking me? I don't know – use the time you do have, I guess. Life only really holds two certainties: we're born and we die.'

'That's cheery, Joe.'

'Nah, it's just true. It's not meant to be depressing. I reckon all we have to do is try to be better on the way out than we were on the way in.'

'But babies come into the world perfect. They have that whole innocence thing.'

'Oh, yeah, right. Maybe I remembered it wrong. But babies don't do anything good, do they?'

'Apart from demonstrating the miracle of life and helping to fulfil their parents' dreams.'

'True. But adults can do lots more. We can feed ourselves and go to the toilet and change the world.'

'That's what I was trying to do – the last bit. But six years at uni, then another few as an intern. Then more time to specialise. That's no life.'

'Yeah, you're probably right. It's a lot of hard work.'

'Too much hard work,' Anthony agreed.

'What kind of loon would choose to sign on for that life?'

'Exactly. It's crazy.'

'Yeah, crazy. But imagine at the end of it, sometimes those crazy folk are able to give people more time. That'd be a pretty damn good thing, hey?'

'Yeah. But I can't do it.'

'Maybe. Anth, I think you should talk to someone else about this. Don't get me wrong. I'm glad you've talked to me. But you should also talk to someone who knows about this stuff.'

'I know. But therapy? It's just so – American.'

'So is Maccas, and that's good stuff.'

'You make sense, Joe,' Anthony laughed.

'It's just, you're not going to be able to do anything until you feel better about this. And you need to tell Mum and Dad what's going on – when you're ready. They can be all right sometimes. I'll go with you if you want.'

'Yeah. Maybe. We should probably get going.'

They headed back to the car. Joe remembered that day at the airport – the no hug day. He had the feeling again. But he knew now that they weren't huggers, and there wasn't anything wrong with that. It was an urge that he was sure would soon pass, like his sister's obsession with writing on wet concrete. Not that the family didn't appreciate the lasting legacy of her wet concrete days: *The Fonz Rules* printed twelve times had been a great addition to their driveway.

'I'm so sorry that it had to happen, Anthony. It's shithouse,' Joe said patting Anthony's shoulder.

Anthony smiled, wiping a stray tear from his nose. 'It is, isn't it?'

'Joe, where have you been?' Grace asked, surprised by his sudden appearance behind her in the recess tuckshop queue. 'Tim thought you'd been kidnapped.'

'No, I had brekky with Anthony.'

'As you do.'

'He's a bit messed up.'

Grace handed her money over and opened her potato chips. 'Really? Anything serious?'

'Maybe. He's deferred.'

'Who's deferred?' Lawrence asked, kicking a soccer ball across the quadrangle to Brad.

'Anthony,' Joe explained.

'Why?'

'Long story, Laws.'

'Is it about the trip?'

'A bit. He'll be all right though.'

'Yeah. So are you still coming over tonight, Joe? The surround sound is now fully operational.'

'Your dad worked it out?'

'Nah, Chris did. We decided to pretend to him that it just started working. Are you in? Tim's bringing the DVDs.'

'Actually, Grace and I are going out.'

'We are?' Grace said through a mouthful of chips.

'Yes. Life's short and we've wasted enough time. Tonight's the night.' He went to kiss her but she put a hand up to hold him back.

'Joe, I'm still eating.'

He shoved a handful of chips in his mouth and gave her a long, passionate kiss.

'What charming symmetry,' Lawrence laughed.

'I'd better go, but I'll see you in Art,' Grace said to Joe, once they'd finally disengaged. The promise of seeing her would almost make going to class worthwhile. He watched her disappear into the distance.

'Brad, over here,' Joe called, motioning for the ball.

Brad did a huge kick, the ball almost landing on the roof.

Joe looked at him in disbelief. 'How hard is it to do a kick that I can catch? Do I look like Inspector Gadget?'

'Your turn then,' Brad called, moving forward until only about three metres separated the boys.

'Very funny. I'm a good kicker.'

Brad moved back a step. 'One question, Josie: where are the pussycats?'

Tim came out from the senior school building and put his books down. He crept up behind Brad and signalled for Joe to pass him the ball. Joe did a glorious high kick, sending the ball straight into Tim's arms.

Brad seemed quietly impressed. 'All right then. Girls against boys. What do you say, Lawrence, are you in? Come on,' Brad said. 'The three of you against me. Josie and the pussycats.'

Tim grabbed the ball from Brad's arms. 'You'd better watch out when I get a gun, Bradley.'

'Joe,' a breathless voice called, as Joe headed to the library for his free period. 'Joseph King. Freeze this instant.'

Joe turned around to find himself in a familiarly uncomfortable position – face to face with a disgruntled Mr Woods.

'I believe this belongs to you,' Woods said, handing him a blue slip that he recognised all too well.

'Detention? For what?'

'For forgetting whatever it was you forgot this morning. I didn't see you in class. I don't suppose you have a note explaining your mysterious absence?'

'Oh. No, I don't, sorry. Detention's fair enough. OK.'

'OK? You're not going to argue? Come on, Joe, there must be a reason.'

'I was recording a charity Christmas song.'

'Pardon.'

'I really don't have a reason, sir. I was just late.'

'Just late? I've got dinner with friends tonight. I can't tell them that.'

'What can I say, Mr Woods? You're only doing your job. It's reasonable.'

'I can't use that.'

'I was late. Rules are rules. It's fair. Have a good weekend. I'll see you Monday, sir.'

'But I might be willing to negotiate.'

'Nah, Mr Woods. Really, it's all good.'

After school, Joe spotted Anthony in his usual place across the road. He headed towards the car. Ed poked his head out the passenger window, blissfully sniffing the air. Anthony got out of the car and waved. Joe realised that at that moment he was looking at someone who was lost and anxious and lonely. But somehow all right. Anthony was going to be all right and so was Joe. The time in between now and being all right might be destined to be pretty ordinary, but in the end, it would work out.

Anthony smiled as Ed madly pulled on the lead. Joe was proud of the progress he and Anthony had made with Ed. It hadn't happened like he'd imagined. He'd thought they'd be tediously training him for hours a day, feeling every minute of it. But it had been much simpler than that. They'd spent time with him, rewarded him when he'd done the right thing, loved him even when he hadn't, and, without their noticing, he'd started to thrive.

'Mum and Dad are at home. Are you going to be around for a bit?' Anthony asked.

'Yeah, for a bit.'

Joe got in the car. Maybe he would be a paramedic. Or maybe he wouldn't. Anthony probably wouldn't be a doctor. And who knew what Belinda or Joe's friends would end up doing? He hoped that his sister would come home one day. But whatever happened, eventually, like Ed, they would all somehow thrive in their own ways, too.

Also by the author
RAINCHECK ON TIMBUKTU

Lucy has her life all planned out:
- perfect job at 21,
- engaged to ideal man at 26,
- married at 27 and a half,
- building ideal home at 28 (fully equipped with a stereo surround-sound wide screen TV and a comfortable, yet stylish couch)
- birth of perfect daughter at 30.

What does *not* so neatly fit into her organised life is a mother with a bombshell, an ex-best friend with an unfortunate liking for low-life boyfriends, a series of badly dressed, metallic-eyeshadowed teachers and a (very) friendly boy next door.

Kirsten Murphy is smart, clever and very, very funny in this tale of life, love and a longing for Timbuktu.